DESIRING YOUR
Love

Valery Archaga

Cover design by Daniela Triana
Edited by Ashley Olivier
Formatting by Lotus Ediciones, Jessyca Vilca Aparicio

ISBN: 979-8-9999863-0-6

For information, contact:
Valery Archaga
valeryarchagaauthor.com
Printed in the United States of America
First Edition

Dedication

To my mom, sister and every single mother who has ever carried the weight of the world on her shoulders and still found the strength to smile for her children: You are proof that resilience has a heartbeat, that unconditional love can move mountains, and that even when the world told you, *"you can't,"* you whispered back, *"watch me, bitch."*

Playlist

Nothing's Gonna Hurt You Baby - Cigarettes After Sex
I Can Do It With A Broken Heart - Taylor Swift
Homesick - Waves To Earth
Too Sweet - Hozier
Amor de Cine - Humbe
Don't Blame Me - Taylor Swift
River - Bishop Briggs
Do I wanna know? - Arctic Monkey
Brooklyn Baby - Lana Del Rey
CHIHIRO - Billie Eilish
Ride - Lana Del Rey
Empire Now - Hozier
Who Are You - BamBam ft SUELGI
In The Air Tonight - Phil Collins
Make It Right - BTS
L'AMOUR DE MA VIE - Billie Eilish
Eres tú - Matisse ft Reik
Flor Palida - Marc Anthony
Eat Your Young – Hozier

Content Notes

This novel is a work of contemporary romance and contains mature themes.

It includes references to teenage pregnancy, family rejection and abandonment, physical, verbal and emotional abuse in the backstory, the struggles of single motherhood, media intrusion, paparazzi pressure, miscarriage, death, as well as consensual and descriptive sexual content.

While the story ultimately focuses on healing, resilience, and love, some readers may find these themes difficult.

Reader discretion is advised.

Prologue

Phoebe Santiago

Zaragoza, Spain

Some chapters of our lives are better left buried, their pages with shame and regret. But I realize that the truth has a way of demanding to be heard—even the most humiliating truths.

It began in my junior year of high school, when I was seventeen, light brown hair, soft freckles, hazel eyes, cheerleader captain, a total bitch for most of my cheermates and drowning in circumstances beyond my control.

My parents, consumed by their gambling addictions, had invested their last remaining hope in me. "You're our ticket out," my mother would say, her eyes hollow from another night at the casino. "Find yourself a rich boy, Phoebe. It's the only way."

They had scraped together enough money to keep me in that prestigious school, betting everything on the possibility that I might marry into wealth. I was their investment, their final gamble.

I have to sacrifice my dignity and body to meet their demands.

Then there was Alan Galeano, a year younger but in my grade, beautiful, his dark hair, his blue eyes were so captivating in the way that made entire hallways turn to watch him and his brothers pass. His smile could illuminate the darkest corners of any room, and when he asked me to be his girlfriend, I felt something I hadn't experienced in years: genuine happiness. For a moment, I allowed myself to believe that maybe, I could have something pure.

But purity was a luxury I couldn't afford.

When Alan gave me a gold bracelet for our six month anniversary as boyfriend and girlfriend right before we finished our junior year, my mother's hands were on it before I could even show her properly. "This is nice," she said, already calculating its worth. My father's voice followed like a serpent's whisper: "You should ask for more. A boy like that, from a family like his—he can afford it."

I hated myself for every request that followed, watching Alan's eager face as he handed over gifts that would disappear into my parents' debts. He gave everything so willingly, this now seventeen year old boy who saw only love where I harbored secrets.

But Alan wasn't the only one in my life. There was Steven. His auburn hair was always perfectly disheveled, as if he'd just rolled out of bed or out of someone else's. At eighteen, Steven had the dangerous combination of a trust fund, no real consequences for his actions, and the kind of magnetic presence that drew people into his orbit whether they were smart enough to resist or not. He moved through the world like someone who had never met a problem daddy's money couldn't solve, and offered me something my crumbling home never could: shelter. A room where I could sleep peacefully, away from the shouting matches and creditors' calls. Steven knew exactly what I was, what I needed, and what I was willing to give in return. With him, there were no pretenses of love, no guilt—just survival.

I thought I could balance it all, keep these two worlds from colliding. I thought I was clever enough to navigate between the boy who loved me and the man who provided for me.

I was wrong.

The night everything unraveled began like any other celebration. Our football team had won the championship, and Steven was throwing a party at his house. Alan and I had agreed to arrive separately, he had family obligations, it was his sister's birthday. I thought I had time, thought I was safe in Steven's arms, in his jacuzzi, believing Alan wouldn't arrive for hours.

But life has a way of destroying our carefully laid plans.

When Alan appeared in that doorway, his face transforming from confusion to devastation to something colder than I had ever seen, I knew that every choice I had made was about to demand payment. The boy who had loved me so completely, so innocently, was gone. In his place stood someone I didn't recognize, someone whose heart I had just shattered beyond repair.

"Can I join?" he asked, his voice steady despite the storm I could see brewing in his eyes.

What followed was the death of whatever we had been and the birth of something far more complicated. Because three weeks later, staring at two pink lines on a pregnancy test, I realized that some secrets don't stay buried.

They grow.

Chapter 1
Phoebe

"You can't do this to me, Steven. I left Alan for you. I've done everything you've asked. You can't abandon me like this," I pleaded with the fool standing in front of me refusing to accept his paternity.

Here, beside the pool in his backyard, was the last place I wanted to make a scene. But his friends were already snickering nearby, watching from the lounge chairs.

He scoffed. "Don't try to blame me for your stupidity. You wanted money to help your parents, and I gave it to you. Now don't come at me with this game, saying you're pregnant and that it's my kid when everyone here knows you've slept with half the school."

Tears burned my eyes, a sob threatening to burst from my lips. "You're the only one I was with who didn't use protection." His words stung, forcing me to confront the fact that I had been living recklessly. Thanks to my parents.

"So, you admit you've been with everyone, which means anyone could be the father of that thing." He looked me up and down with disgust, his lip curling. "The truth is, I must have been really high when I was with you."

I clenched my fist, and before I could register what was happening, it collided with his cheek, making him stumble. The fire in his eyes chilled me to the bone, and all the blood left my face as he stormed forward. He slapped me so hard that I fell to the ground. Then he yanked up my hair, and I could hear his friends laughing at me.

"What's going on here? Steven! Let go of that girl!" An elderly woman appeared from the sliding door, her eyes narrowed on him in disdain.

"Stay out of this, Grandma!" he snapped, tightening his grip on my hair so hard I was sure my skull would crack. In one swift shove, I was floundering in the pool, sending water everywhere as I fell.

But I didn't know how to swim, and I panicked as my feet couldn't touch the bottom. My nose burned from the water rushing in, and my throat choked.

"Help me! I can't swim!" I screamed repeatedly as I finally resurfaced to hear the laughs of everyone around. It wasn't until my strength began to fade that I felt someone grab me and pull me from the pool. I saw silhouettes surrounding me until my lungs expelled all the water within.

I attempted to sit up, but a hand restrained me—Steven. His glare sent a shudder through me to the bone. "Stay down," he ordered.

I shook my head; I didn't want to stay there another second. I sat up as best I could and accepted the hand the elderly woman offered me.

She scowled at him. "Come here, child. I apologize for my grandson; that is no way to treat a lady," she said, offering me a towel. I didn't accept it though; I wanted nothing from them ever again.

I stared at the ground, cheeks heating. "You're mistaken, ma'am. I should be thanking your grandson. He's given me an interesting new perspective." I managed to stand, still feeling dizzy and shaking. Without another word, I grabbed my small purse from one of the lounge chairs and walked toward the exit.

"Phoebe," Steven called out just before I crossed the threshold of the gate.

I looked at him as if I wished his body would explode into a million pieces right then and there. I waited for him to say something, but he didn't. Then I left that house with a baby who would have no father because I wasn't going to beg for his attention, his money, or his love.

The fact of the matter was, I brought all of this upon myself by being immature and lacking self control and willpower.

My house wasn't far, but I had no idea how long I had been walking. I only knew that my clothes were clinging to my body and that several cars honked at me when they saw my chest outlined through my soaked shirt. I was grateful it was summer, so at least I wasn't cold thanks to the scorching sun that accompanied me on the way.

When I got home, I spotted my father's car park in front of my house, and a newfound fear made my stomach curl with dread.

My father, Leopoldo Santiago, hopefully didn't notice me because, when he wanted to be an asshole would start questioning me, or asking me for money and the last thing I wanted at that moment was questions for which I probably didn't have eloquent answers. But I gathered enough courage and continued walking. As I stepped into the house, my father, a pale skinned man with light brown hair and piercing green eyes, paced restlessly in the living room. His body rocked back and forth, and he gnawed at his fingers, the nervous ticks of an addict unable to find calm.

He looked at me, and I shivered; it was the second time that day someone had looked at me like that. So cold, so calculating. However, coming from my father made it much more dangerous.

"I'll ask you once, and you better tell the truth." He held up the pregnancy test I had carelessly left under my pillow.

I swallowed hard, fumbling for an answer. "Yes, it's mine," I finally forced out. Before I could say anything else, his hand slapped my already sore cheek—the same one Steven had struck before.

"How could you be so foolish?" his voice boomed. "How could you not prevent getting pregnant?" Me getting pregnant and having a child would throw a wrench on their wishes for sure. "Who's the father? Alan Galeano? Steven García?"

"Does it matter? The only thing you care about is having them fill your bank account with money, but bad news for you—that's not going to happen," I fired back, rage seeping through my pores.

"What do you mean by that?" he hissed, stepping closer to me.

I backed away slowly until I fell onto the couch. "The father won't take responsibility. He wants nothing to do with me, and I want nothing to do with him," I said, but he exploded again.

"You're so stupid. You're just like your mother. Both of you have done nothing but ruin my life." He got so close to my face that I could feel his breath. He grabbed me roughly by the neck. "If they won't take responsibility, neither will I—for you or that bastard. I have a debt, and if you don't help me pay it, you will be the payment."

Ice flooded my veins, my heart hammering so hard I was certain he could feel it through his grip. The room seemed to tilt, his words echoing in my head like a death sentence. My hands flew to his wrist instinctively, fingers clawing at his hold.

"You wouldn't dare," I whispered, my voice barely audible, cracking on each word. The taste of copper filled my mouth—I'd bitten my tongue without realizing it.

He tightened his grip on my neck, making it more difficult to breathe. Black spots danced at the edges of my vision as the full weight of his threat crashed over me. My legs felt like water, threatening to give out beneath me. This wasn't an empty threat—I could see it in his eyes, cold and calculating. He meant every word.

"You know I don't play games."

Tears flowed down my cheeks. A sharp pain in my belly caused me to scream, and I instinctively placed my hands over it.

"It hurts," I gasped, my voice barely a whisper as his fingers dug deeper into my throat. "Please, I might lose the baby, and with it, the chance to make a lot of money." The words tasted bitter as they left my lips, but I knew money was the only language he understood. "You can't go to Steven's father—not after what happened at school, not after everyone saw. But the baby... the baby could be worth something."

Those words made him react. He let go abruptly, and I collapsed against the wall, gasping for air. But instead of relief, a sharp, twisting pain shot through my abdomen, doubling me over. "Ow," I whimpered as the cramping intensified, radiating outward like fire.

My hands instinctively flew to my stomach, protecting what might already be lost. Each breath felt like swallowing glass, my throat raw and swollen from his grip. Cold sweat broke out across my forehead despite the chill from my still damp clothes clinging to my skin.

He raised an eyebrow, studying me with the detached interest of someone examining a broken toy. "Don't try to manipulate me," he scoffed, turning away as if my pain was nothing more than an inconvenience.

"I'm serious. Please, help me get to the hospital." My entire body trembled—from the pain shooting through my core, from the terror of what I might be losing, from the anxiety of being trapped with nowhere to turn. My wet hair dripped steadily onto the floor, each drop marking another second that could mean the difference between life and death for the tiny life inside me.

What else could go wrong? The thought spiraled through my mind as another wave of pain hit. I pressed my back against the wall for support, my legs barely holding me upright. Please, God, I prayed silently, don't let my baby pay for my mistakes. Don't let this be how it ends.

I felt my body losing strength on the couch when suddenly, I was lifted and carried to the car. Relief flooded through me, but I just knew the worst was yet to come.

"Thank you," I whispered and closed my eyes, surrendering to the darkness of unconsciousness.

Brightness blinded me when I awoke, making me wince. The unmistakable smell of disinfectant burned my nose as I slowly cracked open my eyes. A hospital room.

"I'm glad you're awake, young lady," said a nurse as she took my temperature.

"What happened to me?" I croaked, my memory foggy.

Her eyes flicked to mine. "You nearly had a miscarriage, but you arrived in time, and we were able to prevent you from losing your baby. You've been unconscious and running a fever for an entire day. Plus, you arrived at the hospital in a very dire state. Do you not remember what happened?"

Everything suddenly came rushing back, and it hurt to recall the way Steven and my father had treated me, even knowing that I was pregnant.

I shook my head in denial.

"Alright, don't stress yourself; it could be harmful to you," she said.

I nodded, and she left the room. The door hadn't even closed completely when my mother entered, and to my surprise—and salvation—my Aunt Salomé was with her.

My mother, Amelia, looked like a woman whose beauty had been carved away by years of bad decisions. Her bleached blonde hair, grown out at the roots, was pulled back in a messy bun. The knockoff designer clothes she wore hung differently than they had before the gambling consumed everything. Her face had hardened into sharp angles that matched the perpetual disappointment in her eyes.

Aunt Salomé was everything my mother had once been. Her warm brown hair framed a face that still held genuine kindness, and her gentle eyes immediately found mine with maternal concern that had been missing from my life for far too long. Where my mother radiated frustration, Aunt Salomé carried herself with quiet, nurturing strength.

Mother stormed over to the hospital bed, her cheap heels clicking angrily. "You idiot! How could you get yourself pregnant?" she snapped.

"Mom, I—" I tried to sit up, but she cut me off.

"No excuses. You're going to marry Mr. Benjamín Uclés. You'll pay off your father's debt and make him believe that this child is his."

The words hit me like a physical blow, each one landing with the force making me sick. My mind reeled, trying to process what she had just said. Marry a stranger? Lie about my baby's father? The room seemed to spin around me, the beeping of the heart monitor growing louder in my ears.

Benjamin Uclés—I knew that name. Everyone did. He was old enough to be my father, maybe older. Rich, yes, but there were rumors about him, whispers that made my skin crawl. And she wanted me to marry him? To let him believe this baby was his?

My stomach churned with more than just physical pain. This wasn't a mother protecting her daughter. This was a desperate gambler making one final bet, using me as the stakes. The realization that I had never been her daughter, only her insurance policy, crashed over me like ice water.

How could she ask this of me? How could she look at me lying in this hospital bed, possibly losing my baby, and see nothing but a solution to her problems? The betrayal cut deeper than any physical wound.

I thought of Steven, of the baby growing inside me, of the future I had imagined—however uncertain it had been. Now she wanted to erase all of that, to turn me into a lie, a fraud, a prisoner in a marriage built on deception.

My hands instinctively moved to my stomach, protective and desperate. Whatever happened, I couldn't let this innocent life become part of her sick plan. But trapped in this bed, weak and alone except for Aunt Salomé's kind eyes, I felt the walls closing in around me.

Was this really my only choice?

"Amelia! Have you lost your mind?" my aunt gasped. Her reaction gave me a flicker of hope—at least someone in this room still had a conscience. "Yes, Phoebe made a mistake by getting pregnant so young, but she is an adult, and you can't force her into anything."

Mother sneered, "Well, it's either that or she aborts the baby. We won't be the laughingstock of the town, having a daughter pregnant and unmarried. Much less will we endure the humiliation from the Garcias."

"How do you know?" I whispered. She pulled my phone from her purse and threw it onto my chest.

"Because your dad told me, and that Steven guy was calling you. When I answered, he asked for you. I told him you were in the hospital, and do you know what he said? He told us to get you an abortion, or else his family would destroy us. That they wanted nothing to do with you or that child. So, your options are limited. You will marry Benjamín, and that's final. We owe the Montecristo Casino three hundred thousand dollars—money we lost trying to win back what we'd already gambled away. The interest keeps growing every day, and they're not the kind of people who accept late payments. Benjamín Uclés owns that casino, and he's agreed to forgive the entire debt in exchange for a young wife. You are the only choice we have."

The woman who had carried me in her womb for nine months now wanted to use me as a bargaining chip to settle their gambling debts. My chest ached from overwhelming disappointment as the full picture became clear—I wasn't their daughter anymore, I was collateral. She left the room, cursing under her breath about ungrateful children and impossible situations.

Aunt Salomé approached my bed and sat beside me. She gave me a hug, the kind only Alan used to give me. He always took care of me and liked me for who I was: the cheerleading captain who loved being the center of attention because she couldn't get it at home. The girl who longed to be loved but fell for the wrong person. I wished there was even the slightest chance that this baby was Alan's, but there wasn't.

"Oh, sweetheart... Have you been living in this kind of hell?" my aunt gently asked. I couldn't answer; I just held onto her tighter, the pain too much to bear.

"Help me, Auntie. Don't let them sell me. Don't let them kill my baby," I pleaded, still holding her tightly. My eyes blurred with tears.

"Of course, I will help you," she promised.

Just then the door swung open, revealing a man in a doctor's coat with blond hair.

"Hello, Phoebe. How are you feeling?" he asked as he reviewed some documents in his hand, sitting in the chair near the desk.

I swallowed. "I feel fine. Better. Thanks," I said quietly.

"Your tests are stable now. We've addressed the mild dehydration you arrived with, but what concerns me the most are the bruises on your face and neck. If you are a victim of abuse, you must not remain silent. You need to report it, as both you and your child could be in danger."

I nodded. But I knew I couldn't do anything. My family would kill me.

He handed me some papers. "This is your discharge paperwork. You haven't had a fever for the past few hours, and if you take these medications, your pregnancy should progress normally. Please try to avoid situations that may put you in danger or cause you stress."

I couldn't say anything; I could only nod in agreement.

My aunt smiled. "Thank you, doctor. And don't worry, help has already arrived."

"I'm very glad to hear that." He turned to me. "You can go to the administration office to settle the bill, and then you'll be free to leave." With that, the doctor exited the room.

"I'll quickly stop by a store I saw next to the hospital," Aunt Salomé said when he was gone. "I'll buy you some clothes and settle the hospital bill. You're coming with me to Madrid, and that's not negotiable. Your mother mentioned she was going somewhere—I don't recall where—but she'll be gone for a while, and your father is at the club with his 'friends.' Let's make the most of this time."

I couldn't help but protest. "I need to go home to gather a few things. I can't depend entirely on your money. I have some savings and items I can sell to contribute to the expenses."

"I make more than enough money to support you, child. Let's not waste time; I'll take care of everything. Wait here for me." She squeezed my hands and smiled at me.

"Thank you," I whispered before breaking down in sobs again.

I didn't understand why life had dealt me this hand. I could only hope that with Salomé, things would be different. She left the room, and I used this time to reflect on what to do with my life. I no longer had to think only about myself; now, there was also a baby to consider.

"Don't worry, it's not your fault that your mother is a fool and that your father doesn't want us," I said to myself, or rather, to the little baby growing inside me. "I won't choose that life for us, no matter how much it costs me. I'll study and give you a dignified, honest future. Something completely different from what I've lived through," I said, caressing my belly, which still felt flat. I stood up and went to the bathroom to clean my face and fix my hair a little.

Several minutes later, my aunt returned. "Are you ready?" she asked, holding my discharge papers and a bag of clothes.

"I'm grateful for all you're doing for me," I said, wiping away my tears.

"You don't have to. It pains me to know that my sister has become a monster. You are not to blame for her ambitions or her gambling addiction. Now, let's go before they return."

We bought tickets to Madrid, and fortunately, we arrived just in time to board a train leaving in a few minutes. As I watched Zaragoza fade into the distance, I wished I could forget everything that had happened in this city. However, I was sure of one thing: eventually, I would have to return and confront everyone who had hurt me.

But I wouldn't come back alone; I would be ready to stand my ground.

Chapter 2
Phoebe

Madrid, Spain
Eight years later.

"Mom, Mom! Wake up, someone's knocking on the door," said my son Noah, his small freckled face inches from mine. His wild red hair stuck up at impossible angles, and his green eyes held that familiar glint of mischief that usually meant trouble. At seven, he had the kind of mature curiosity that made him ask questions I wasn't always ready to answer, combined with just enough little boy energy to keep me constantly on my toes.

I glanced at my phone, seeing it was 7:30 in the morning.

"Calm down, sweetheart. I'm coming," I replied with a yawn.

He left the room, giving me a moment to change my clothes. I had only returned from my hospital shift a few hours earlier.

Thanks to my Aunt Salomé, I was able to graduate and study nursing. During the train ride that brought us here, a woman went into labor, and seeing my aunt assist in bringing a new life into the world made me fall in love with the medical profession.

Becoming a doctor was too expensive, and my aunt was already doing enough by taking care of Noah and me while I focused on my studies. So for now, nursing was my path.

Tragically, two weeks after I began working at the hospital, my aunt was taken from me by a drunk driver just outside the building.

Noah was only three years old, and even though he was small, he asked about Aunt Salomé every single day. It broke my heart. I devoted myself to taking care of him and doing my best at work because that's what I had promised my aunt: to always give my all for Noah and myself.

After having Noah, my body changed, and I loved seeing myself in the mirror. My hips widened, my breasts grew, and my waist widened only slightly, giving me that hourglass illusion. I adored my curvy figure, especially what I could do with it as a woman.

I wore cropped tops that showed my belly button and sleeveless shirts that revealed my arms. I experimented with different hair colors and makeup styles. To many, I was "the chubby one," but it didn't bother me. I had learned that a woman's beauty wasn't determined by her body; it was defined by her confidence and self assurance.

I chose to love and value myself, something I was not able to do back then, so I ignored other people's opinions. Only mine mattered; only how I felt about myself.

"Mom, hurry up!" my son urged. I quickly styled my hair and rushed to the door after putting on a low cut top and jeans.

When I opened it, I was frozen.

"Hello," Steven said, and it was like the world stopped. All the blood left my face, and my legs threatened to give out. God, he looked exactly the same as he did seven years ago. He assessed me from head to toe, not with disdain but with astonishment. "Can I come in?" he asked.

The patter of footsteps echoed behind me before Noah said, "Mom, who is he?" He stood beside me and stared directly at Steven, gaze curiously.

I struggled to find the words. Finally, I said, "An old friend from high school, sweetheart. Don't worry, just go to your room."

I was grateful that Noah was so obedient. Without a word, he left, casting one final glance over his shoulder.

Turning back to Steven, I took a deep breath. "What do you want?" I demanded, locking eyes with the man who was my son's father yet refused to be part of his life. I could only wonder why he was here now.

"He resembles me a lot from when I was little," he said with a smirk.

I crossed my arms. "I won't ask again. What do you want?"

"Relax. Trust me, the last thing I want right now is to be here, but my grandmother is dying, and she's insisting on seeing you."

I couldn't process his words. I recalled his grandmother; I had encountered her a few times at Steven's house. Including the time she defended me from him slapping me and pushing me in the pool. But why would she want to see me on her deathbed?

"How did you find out where I lived?" I said quietly.

He shrugged. "Money solves many problems. I wasn't sure where to search, but your mother suggested you might be in Madrid. I hired a detective, and he found you. Pack your things; we're leaving."

"Are you insane?" I scoffed, unable to believe the nerve of this guy. "You show up at my apartment, tell me you don't want to be here, yet here you are, demanding that I pack up and leave with you? No, thank you. Get out of my house. Seven years, Steven—seven years have passed," I said. "And you haven't helped one bit with raising Noah."

But Steven only stepped inside, sat down on the sofa, and crossed his legs as if he owned the place.

"You should thank your mother. After what happened, my grandmother went abroad for a couple of years and was at home when your mother arrived, threatening to damage my family's reputation after my parents decided not to give her more money. She told her I got you pregnant and left you. She demanded a large sum of money. We didn't give her what she sought, but she's already been reported to the authorities. Any moment now, she'll be arrested."

His story was coherent. I had spent the past few years constantly moving due to my so called mother's relentless pursuit. Every few months, she would track us down with a new scheme—sometimes calling my work to demand money for "her grandson's welfare," other times showing up at Noah's school claiming to be his concerned grandmother and trying to take him for "a visit." The school had called me in a panic that day, explaining how a blonde woman had arrived with fake documents, insisting she had custody rights.

I'd had to change Noah's school three times, move apartments four times, and even change my phone number twice. Each time I thought we'd found peace, she would resurface like a bad penny, always with her hand out, always with threats about what she'd do if I didn't comply. The constant looking over my shoulder, the fear every time someone knocked on our door unexpectedly, the way I'd taught Noah to never talk to strangers who asked about his family —it had all been because of her endless greed and manipulation.

The authorities, she'd said. Finally, someone was taking her seriously as the threat she'd always been.

"I can't just leave. I have a job, an apartment, and my son just started first grade."

His eyes narrowed. "You'll request a transfer at work, and for his school. I'll pay whatever it takes to get you out of here," he said, standing and stepping closer to me. "I'm giving you two days. I have some business to handle in the city. Don't try to run —I'll know. You're coming back with me to Zaragoza, and I don't want to make this difficult for you. I don't want my son to form a negative impression of his father."

My blood ran cold. "He's not your son. Noah is mine, and *only* mine. That's how it's always been, and that's how it will remain," I said angrily, stepping away from him.

"That's irrelevant now. I'll return in two days. Ensure everything is sorted by then." He seized my chin between his fingers, and I flinched. "You know I dislike being disobeyed, and unfortunately for you, you have everything to lose if you decide to oppose me."

"You're still a miserable bastard," I spat. He tightened his grip.

"Proudly, gorgeous. You know the deal—two days." With that, he let go and walked out of my apartment, letting the door slam behind him.

I collapsed onto the couch, hiding my face in my hands. I didn't want to cry, but it felt inevitable. Just when my job was going well and Noah had found a school he loved, everything went to hell.

A small hand rested on my shoulder, prompting me to quickly wipe away my tears. Above all, I had to be strong for my son.

"Do we have to go with him?" Noah asked, worry evident in his voice. So, he had heard everything. My heart sank for him. I worked to maintain my composure, not wanting to transmit my anxiety to him.

"Yes," I said, holding back tears. "I don't like it, but we have to."

"Is he... my dad?" he whispered, his eyes widening. I nodded. I wouldn't say more; I didn't want to influence my son's feelings toward Steven.

"Yes, but that won't change anything, sweetheart. We're moving to another city, but it'll still be just you and me. No one will separate us. We'll find a new school, and we'll be okay. Alright?" I assured him, and he nodded.

Two days passed, and thanks to the head nurse at La Paz Hospital, I was able to secure a transfer to the maternity ward at the General Hospital in Zaragoza.

We researched schools online and found one near the hospital for emergencies. Noah liked how it appeared picturesque in the photos, and he loved the playground and activities. Since my apartment was rented furnished, I didn't have to move much, just our belongings. We had to leave behind some of Noah's toys, so we donated them at the building's entrance.

Just on time, the doorbell rang. Two days on the dot. I wasn't surprised; I already knew who it was. My son opened the door, and our bags were packed, sitting by the bed.

"Do you have everything, Noah?" Steven asked, with little emotion on his face.

Noah turned to proudly show his small backpack with an eager nod.

It was time to go.

"Alright, let's go." I knelt to Noah's level, gently caressing his cheek. "No matter what happens, I will always be by your side, okay?"

He threw his arms around me and hugged me tightly.

"I love you, Mom," he said, kissing my cheek.

My heart pounded, not knowing what would happen once we arrived. Thoughts of my "incubator" flooded my mind; the fear that someone might try to take Noah away from me, along with so many other worries, swirled inside me at that moment.

Looking behind where Steven stood at the door, I noticed two other men in suits.

Steven had grown a bit taller, but his body was the same as before. His face now showed more coldness than ever, and I felt no attraction toward him. What I did feel, however, was the overwhelming urge to kick his ass back into his mother's womb.

I laughed to myself at my own thoughts—unintentionally, out loud.

"What's so funny?" he asked, raising an eyebrow as we walked down the stairs inside my apartment building.

"Nothing, just thinking about life's ironies."

He ignored my comment, and we reached the first floor, where the administrative offices were. Mr. Fausto, the landlord, received my keys, and we headed for the car, which was opened by another man.

Steven turned briefly. "You'll be riding in this car. I'll see you when we arrive. I have an apartment arranged for you."

"You shouldn't have bothered. I already have a place to live, but thanks," I muttered as I got into the car with Noah. The door closed, and we started moving.

I didn't want to accept anything from him. I had never needed him before, and I certainly wouldn't know that we were in Zaragoza.

Soon, the car arrived at the airport, and we boarded the plane that would take us to our destination. Noah's eyes went wide the moment we stepped onto the aircraft, his freckled face pressed against every window we passed. "Mom, look how tiny the cars look!" he whispered in amazement, bouncing on his toes as we found our seats. He peppered the flight attendant with questions about how planes stayed in the air, traced the safety card with his finger like it was treasure, and declared the airplane peanuts "the best snacks ever invented."

Hours later, when the plane touched down in Zaragoza, reality began to sink in. As we walked through the terminal, Noah chattering excitedly about everything he saw, my mind raced with a thousand questions and doubts. What was I doing here? Nearly eight years ago, I had run from this world, from these people, carrying nothing but shame and a baby I was determined to protect. Now I was walking back into it voluntarily, bringing my son —their son—into a life I'd spent years trying to escape.

My hands trembled slightly as I adjusted Noah's backpack on his shoulder. Would they accept him? Would they try to take him from me? The boy skipping beside me had no idea he was about to meet a family he'd never known existed, people who might have more claim to him than I was comfortable with. Every step toward the arrival gate felt like walking toward an uncertain future, one where I was no longer in complete control of our destiny.

When we arrived at the entrance, people were already waiting for us.

"We're going to see my grandmother first," Steven informed us.

I merely nodded; I was the most eager to find out why the old woman wanted to see me.

But looking at the house, I sighed, recalling how I had left it all those years ago. The imposing stone facade still commanded respect, its tall windows gleaming in the afternoon sun like watchful eyes. The manicured gardens hadn't changed—every hedge perfectly trimmed, every flower bed arranged with mathematical precision. It was the kind of house that whispered old money and older secrets, where even the doormat probably cost more than most people's monthly rent. The wrought iron gate I'd once snuck through as a desperate teenager now stood open, welcoming but somehow sinister.

Taking my son's hand, we walked to the entrance. The marble foyer still took my breath away—soaring ceilings, crystal chandelier, and that sweeping staircase that had always made me feel like I was trespassing in a museum.

Once inside, I noticed Steven's mother in the living room, her silver hair pulled back in the same elegant chignon she'd worn for decades. Even in casual clothes, she carried herself with the kind of refined authority that came from generations of breeding and wealth. Her sharp blue eyes assessed everything with the precision of someone accustomed to finding fault.

She was accompanied by a girl I recognized immediately as Allison, an ex friend and former classmate. Allison had grown into her prettiness—blonde hair now professionally styled, designer clothes that fit like they were made for her, and that same calculating smile that had made her popular in high school. She looked like she belonged in this house in a way I never had.

Both women regarded me with disdain. In response, I gave them my brightest smile, which appeared to annoy them even more.

"So, this is the woman you knocked up? Wow, son, I thought you had better taste," Steven's mother sneered, shaking her head in disgust.

"Hello, ma'am. My name is Phoebe, and yes, your son's taste is a bit twisted," I replied, glancing at Allison; no magnifying glass was needed to see that she had undergone multiple cosmetic surgeries. I vividly remembered how flat her chest used to be. "Anyway, let's get to the point," I said, turning to Steven.

He nodded and led me to a door on the second floor, where his father, Steven's dad, was waiting. The study was exactly as I remembered—dark mahogany panels lining the walls, floor to ceiling bookshelves filled with leather bound volumes that looked more decorative than read, and heavy burgundy curtains that filtered the afternoon light into something somber and serious. The massive oak desk dominated the room, its surface polished to a mirror shine and arranged with the kind of precise organization that spoke of a man who controlled every detail of his domain.

Steven's father stood behind that desk like a general surveying his battlefield. Age had only added to his imposing presence—his once dark hair now distinguished silver at the temples, his tall frame still commanding despite the slight stoop that came with his late fifties. He wore a perfectly tailored navy suit even in his own home, the kind of man who probably slept in pressed pajamas. His pale blue eyes, so much like Steven's but colder, assessed me with the clinical detachment of someone evaluating a business transaction.

Everything about him radiated power and control —from the way he held his shoulders to the measured way he breathed. This was a man accustomed to getting what he wanted, when he wanted it, and who had never been told "no" by anyone who mattered.

"Dad," Steven called, and the man looked at me in surprise before turning his gaze to my son. He approached Noah and knelt before him.

"What's your name, little one?" he asked, gently taking Noah's hand.

"Noah. Noah Santiago," my son replied with a smile. Steven's father studied him intently before smiling in return. He then glanced up at me, his expression softening.

"Thank you for taking responsibility and raising my grandson alone. I admire you for that. My mother is resting, but she wishes to meet her great grandson before she goes." His expression clouded with grief at the words.

"Pablo..." the elderly woman's frail voice called from within the other room, barely more than a whisper that seemed to take all her remaining strength.

A profound sadness descended in my chest as I heard that weak, trembling call. I had only met Steven's grandmother a handful of times seven years ago—brief encounters where she had looked at me with the kind of cold assessment reserved for unwelcome guests. She had been a stranger then, someone who existed on the periphery of my chaotic relationship with Steven, more legend than person in my mind that once offered me a hand to help.

The man urged us to go inside and approach the bed. She seemed significantly older than the last time I had seen her, though my memories of her were so limited I could barely make the comparison. What struck me wasn't nostalgia, but the universal tragedy of watching any human being fade away. Her once imposing presence—the little I remembered of it—had been reduced to this fragile form lost in the massive four poster bed.

Her skin was paper thin, stretched over bones that seemed too prominent. The woman who had once commanded this household with stern authority now looked small and vulnerable under heavy quilts, her breathing shallow and labored.

I didn't know her well enough to mourn who she had been, but seeing anyone in this condition—calling out weakly for comfort, clinging to life by such a thin thread—stirred something deeply human in me. It was the kind of sadness that transcends personal connection, the recognition of mortality that makes you hold your loved ones a little tighter.

"Mom, look, your great grandson and his mother are here," Pablo said gently.

The woman slowly opened her eyes, initially looking disoriented. Then, her gaze fixed on me and my son. "You're a beautiful young woman," she murmured.

I stepped forward, resting my hand on her shoulder. As I would do with any of my patients.

"You are much more beautiful than I am," I responded, bringing a smile to her face.

"Thank you. I appreciate your coming to see me. I assure you, after this, you can return to your life, and my grandson won't disturb you."

Steven rolled his eyes. "That's not your—"

"Enough!" Pablo commanded, clearly annoyed.

"Please let me see the boy," the elderly woman requested, holding out a trembling hand.

Pablo gently set Noah on the bed next to her. My son looked uncertain, his green eyes darting between the frail woman and me, clearly unsure what was expected of him in this strange place full of people he'd never met. He sat stiffly on the edge of the bed, his small hands folded in his lap.

"It's okay, sweetheart," I whispered, giving him an encouraging nod.

After a long moment of studying her face, Noah slowly reached out and very gently patted her hand—the kind of careful, tentative touch children use when they're not sure if something might break. "Are you sick?" he asked in his honest, seven year old way.

The old woman's eyes focused on him with effort, and something shifted in her expression. Noah, still cautious but warming slightly to her gentle presence, added softly, "My mommy says when people are sick, we should be extra nice to them."

His innocent words, spoken with the careful politeness I'd taught him for meeting new people, made tears well up in her eyes. It wasn't the instant affection of a grandchild who knew his grandmother, but the sweet, tentative kindness of a good hearted child trying his best in an unfamiliar situation.

"Assist them, Pablo," she whispered.

I shook my head, looking at them in astonishment. Walking to the other side of the bed, I delicately took the elderly woman's hand. "I don't want anything. We've lived a modest and peaceful life. I'm a nurse and will soon begin working at the general hospital. My son and I are content that way."

"Your mother said that you were having money problems..." the woman hesitated. I felt a sense of shame.

Pablo took Noah and Steven out of the room, leaving us by ourselves.

I cleared my throat. "Seven years ago, I didn't leave because of how Steven treated me or the danger Noah faced when I almost lost him. I left because my own parents wanted to use me and my son as bargaining chips for their debts. My aunt Salomé took care of us and helped me build a career that I love."

"That's good, dear. You have no idea how guilty I felt that day you left. If I had known you were pregnant, I would have made Steven take responsibility. I would have forced him to do the right thing by you and the baby, no matter what his parents said or how much they protested. But you disappeared so quickly, and by the time I realized what had really happened, it was too late to find you."

Her frail hand trembled slightly as she spoke, the weight of years of regret evident in her voice. "I failed you both—you and that precious boy. A grandmother should protect her family, not let them scatter to the wind because of pride and stubborn foolishness."

"It wasn't your fault. I believe we all reap what we sow. I had a reckless youth and made the mistake of trusting the wrong person—of loving the wrong person. But when Noah was born, I was truly happy, and I'm determined to give him a life very different from mine. As for my mother..." I took a deep breath before continuing, "I sincerely apologize. Unfortunately, we don't choose our parents, children, or grandchildren, and we certainly can't control the kind of people they become."

"I'm so glad you've turned your life around. Thank you for coming. Now I can leave peacefully, knowing my great grandson has a wonderful mother and isn't suffering or lacking anything," she said, touching my cheek.

I clasped her hands in mine. "Don't worry, I'll continue to protect him from anyone who tries to separate us," I said, thinking of Steven with a wince.

I leaned down and kissed the old woman's forehead. She nodded, gently stroking the back of my hand with her thumb.

When Noah returned to the room, he remained by her side until it was time for lunch. I bid farewell to Mrs. Efigenia, promising to return the following day.

As we finished our meal, Pablo turned to me.

"Phoebe, I hope you don't take offense, but I would like to conduct a DNA test between my son and Noah. This is purely for legal purposes, and don't worry—it won't affect you or my grandson in any way. My mother wants to include the boy in her will, and the lawyer suggested a test in case my son or my wife decides to contest it."

His words rendered me speechless.

A DNA test. The phrase echoed in my mind like an alarm bell. After seven years of running, of building a life where Noah was simply mine, they wanted scientific proof of what we all already knew. But it wasn't really about proof, was it? It was about legitimacy, about making Noah official in their world.

My chest tightened with conflicting emotions. Part of me felt vindicated—finally, acknowledgment that Noah belonged to this family, that he had a right to their name and their legacy. The grandmother's will meant security for my son, a future I could never provide on my own.

But another part of me recoiled. What if the test somehow gave them more claim to Noah than I was comfortable with? What if making him legally theirs meant losing some part of him to me? For seven years, I had been his entire world, his only family. The thought of sharing that, of him having loyalties divided between two lives, terrified me.

And then there was the deeper fear—what if Steven's wife decided to contest anyway? What if this test, meant to protect Noah's inheritance, actually opened the door for them to challenge my custody? What if bringing Noah into their legal sphere meant they could take him away from me entirely?

"You can take the DNA test; I have no issue with that. However, I want a guarantee that no one will ever attempt to take Noah away from me."

"You have my word."

With his promise sealed, I left the house that day. We settled into the place I had rented.

The apartment was lovely, with its clean lines and neutral tones creating a sense of calm I desperately needed. The furniture was elegant but comfortable, nothing too formal or intimidating, and there were thoughtful touches like soft throw pillows and warm lighting that made it feel like a home rather than just a place to stay. Noah ran from room to room, claiming the smaller bedroom as his own and already planning where to put his toys. For the first time in years, I felt we would live peacefully here.

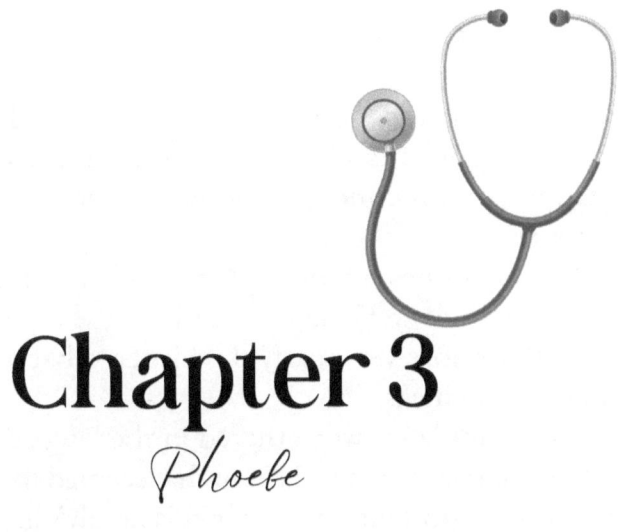

Chapter 3

Phoebe

The next morning, as we headed out to buy groceries, a young woman stepped out of the apartment next to ours, wearing a nurse's uniform. Her name was Aida, and upon seeing Noah, she immediately offered to help. A few days later, I joined the hospital staff and found her working there as well. We were the same age, and she worked in pediatrics and loved children.

Whenever we could, we visited Mrs. Efigenia. Steven's father was kind to us. During one of our visits, he handed me a signed document from Steven in which he promised to stay away from me. That moment brought me immense relief.

The call came on a Tuesday morning while Noah was getting ready for school. Pablo's voice was quiet, strained. "She passed peacefully in her sleep," he said simply.

I found myself staring at the phone long after he hung up, processing the strange emptiness I felt. Mrs. Efigenia—a woman I'd barely known but who had somehow become a bridge between my past and Noah's future—was gone.

The funeral was a small, dignified affair. Noah sat between his grandfather and me, his small hand occasionally reaching for mine when the service grew too solemn. I watched him trying to understand what death meant, his young mind grappling with concepts too big for seven years to fully comprehend.

"Is she in heaven now, Mommy?" he whispered as we watched the casket being lowered.

"I think so, sweetheart," I whispered back, surprised by how much I meant it.

Two days later, we gathered in the lawyer's office—the same mahogany paneled room that seemed to be the setting for every important moment in this family's life. The reading of the will felt surreal, like watching someone else's life unfold.

When the lawyer announced that Mrs. Efigenia had left forty percent of her considerable assets to Noah, to be received when he reached adulthood, the room fell silent. Forty percent. I tried to wrap my mind around what that meant, what kind of future was secured for my son.

"The funds will be managed by a trust," the lawyer continued, "with Mrs. Phoebe Santiago named as the sole executor."

Steven's mother's sharp intake of breath was audible across the room. I felt the weight of every eye on me, the responsibility settling on my shoulders like a lead blanket.

The phone call came five days after Mrs. Efigenia's funeral. An unfamiliar voice, official and detached, asking if I was the daughter of Amelia Castillo.

"We found your contact information in her belongings," the officer explained. "I'm sorry to inform you that your mother was found deceased yesterday morning."

The words hit me like a physical blow, even though I'd spent years expecting this call. My mother—dead in some corner of the city, alone, probably surrounded by the consequences of her own choices.

"Was she... did she suffer?" I asked, though I wasn't sure I wanted the answer.

"It appears to have been an overdose. Likely quick." he replied. I sighed after hanging up.

I spent the next two days wrestling with a decision that felt impossible. Part of me wanted to let the city handle her burial, to wash my hands of the woman who had tried to sell me to pay her debts. But another part of me—the part that remembered being five years old and crawling into her bed during thunderstorms —couldn't let her disappear without acknowledgment.

"You don't have to go," Aida said gently when I told her about the funeral. "No one would blame you."

But I knew I would blame myself later.

The cemetery was gray and cold, matching my mood perfectly. I stood alone beside the simple casket—no flowers, no mourners, just me and the woman who had given me life and then spent years trying to destroy it.

"I don't know why I'm here," I said aloud, my voice carrying across the empty space. "You probably don't deserve this."

The wind picked up, rustling the leaves of a nearby tree.

"But you were still my mother." The words came out broken, heavy with years of pain and disappointment. "You were terrible at it, but you were still my mother."

I thought about Noah, safely at school, unaware that the grandmother who had haunted our lives was finally gone. I thought about the choices she'd made, the desperation that had driven her to such extremes.

"I forgive you," I whispered, surprised by how much I meant it. "Not because you deserve it, but because I need to let this go."

The relief that washed over me was unexpected —like setting down a weight I hadn't realized I'd been carrying for years.

Walking away from that grave, I felt something shift inside me. The chapter of my life that had been defined by running from her, by fear of what she might do next, was finally closed. I only wished I could have found this peace with my father too, before it was too late.

The first visit from Steven's mother came two weeks after the DNA results arrived. I watched from the kitchen window as her sleek black car pulled up to our building, and my stomach knotted with anxiety.

"Noah, your grandmother is here to see you," I called, still struggling with how strange those words sounded.

She arrived with an armload of expensive toys and a smile that didn't quite reach her eyes. "Hello, darling," she said to Noah, her voice taking on an artificially sweet tone I'd never heard before. "Would you like to see what Grandmother brought you?"

Noah, ever polite, thanked her and carefully examined each gift while I watched from the doorway. There was something performative about the whole interaction —like she was playing a role she'd rehearsed but didn't quite believe in.

Over the following months, her visits became a routine. Every Saturday afternoon, precisely at two o'clock, she would arrive with presents and stories about the family Noah had never known. She taught him to play chess, brought him books about their family's history, and slowly began introducing him to what she called "proper behavior."

"Noah should learn to ride horses," she mentioned one afternoon while he was in his room. "All the men in our family have been excellent riders."

"He's seven," I replied carefully.

"It's never too early to start building character," she said, that practiced smile never wavering.

I began to see the pattern—every suggestion, every gift, every lesson was designed to mold Noah into the kind of grandson who would reflect well on the family name. She wasn't getting to know him; she was grooming him.

Months flew by, and in the blink of an eye, my Noah turned eight.

Recently, he had become fixated on finding me a partner. It broke my heart when he discovered that Steven had married Allison. In his small mind, he had imagined reuniting his parents. But now, his new mission was to find me a husband or boyfriend.

"You need someone to take care of you when you're working late," he had announced over breakfast that morning, his serious expression making him look far older than his eight years. "Like how my friend Emilio, his mom, has one boyfriend now."

I'd tried to explain that I was perfectly capable of taking care of myself, but Noah had that determined look that meant he wouldn't be easily swayed. As I gathered my scrubs and prepared for another twelve hour shift at the hospital, I could practically see the wheels turning in his head, already plotting his next matchmaking attempt.

"Aida will be here in an hour to watch you," I reminded him, kissing the top of his red head. "And remember, no more asking the neighbors if they have single sons."

"I make no promises," he replied with a mischievous grin that was pure Steven.

I shook my head, grabbed my keys, and headed out into the evening. Working at the hospital had become my sanctuary—the one place where I was simply Phoebe the nurse, not someone's mother or executor or the woman with the complicated past.

"Yeah, it looks really bad. His girlfriend won't leave his side," said Wendy, a nurse in the break room, bringing my focus away from my thoughts. She flipped her blonde hair over her shoulder, making a face.

"Imagine nearly getting killed by a crazy woman at your own brother's wedding," added Kimberly, scrunching her nose, her blue eyes twinkling with amusement.

"Who are we talking about?" I asked, joining the conversation and looking up from my lunch.

"Alan Galeano had an accident yesterday and is in critical condition," Wendy explained, causing my heart to pound.

I hadn't heard that name in quite a while, and it felt terrible knowing he was in such a condition.

For weeks, Alan's accident was the primary topic of conversation in the hospital. Especially, when in the same hospital was the woman who almost killed him. Rebeca Succolu, the daughter of a former director of the hospital that was involved with human and organ trafficking.

One day, while making rounds on his floor, I noticed his family from a distance. Fortunately, no one recognized me. From a far, I observed a petite young woman with black hair and Asian features stepping out of his room. She was very beautiful and appeared profoundly affected by Alan's condition.

The following day, she was admitted after fainting, and her test results confirmed that she was a few weeks pregnant. Rather than feeling upset, I felt genuinely happy for them.

The next day, during my midday shift, Dr. Martinez approached me with a smile that made my heart skip. "Alan opened his eyes this morning," he said simply.

I dropped my clipboard, my hand flying to my chest as if to keep my heart from bursting right out of it. "Thank God," I whispered, then louder, "Thank God!" Several nurses turned to look as I wiped away tears I didn't realize had started falling. Possibly I was over reacting., but after nearly a month in a coma I felt happy he was about to reunite to the news of a family of his own.

A few hours after that, that same night, his girlfriend was rushed to the emergency room again.

"Phoebe, come with me for an ultrasound. Bring the scanner," urged Dr. Zion, and I quickly followed her instructions.

As we entered the room, I couldn't help but smile at the sight before us. Alan sat beside the hospital bed, his fingers intertwined with his girlfriend's, his thumb tracing gentle circles across her knuckles. When she turned to look at him, his entire face lit up—the same soft, wonder filled expression I remembered from years ago, but now directed at someone who could return it completely.

"Twins," the ultrasound technician announced, pointing to two distinct shapes on the monitor.

Alan's breath caught audibly. His free hand flew to cover his mouth, eyes darting between the screen and his girlfriend's face as if he couldn't decide which miracle to focus on. "Two babies," he whispered, his voice thick with emotion. "We made two perfect babies."

His girlfriend laughed through tears that had started flowing the moment she heard the news. "Are you ready for this?" she asked, squeezing his hand.

"With you?" Alan leaned forward to kiss her forehead, then her nose, then her lips. "I'm ready for anything." He placed his palm gently on her still flat stomach, his expression pure reverence. "Hello, babies. It's your daddy."

The way he looked at her—like she hung the moon and stars just for him—made my chest tighten with a mixture of happiness for him and the sharp pang of what might have been. This was the love Alan had always deserved, the kind that was freely given and joyfully received.

For a moment, I felt envious of her.

He used to look at me like that years ago, and I didn't appreciate it.

And here I was, wishing someone would gaze at me with that same intensity, complicity, and love.

The doctor described the details of the pregnancy and the essential precautions they should take.

As he left the room, I couldn't contain what I had been holding inside.

"I'm really happy you found such a wonderful woman for yourself," I said while cleaning the ultrasound scanner. Feeling too embarrassed to face him, I spoke with my back turned. "Have I changed so much that you don't recognize me, Alan?" I asked after receiving no response.

I turned around, and this time he was staring at me with a serious expression.

"Do you two know each other?" his girlfriend inquired, glancing between us.

Alan nodded appreciatively.

What he said next completely surprised me.

"Yes, princess. This is Phoebe."

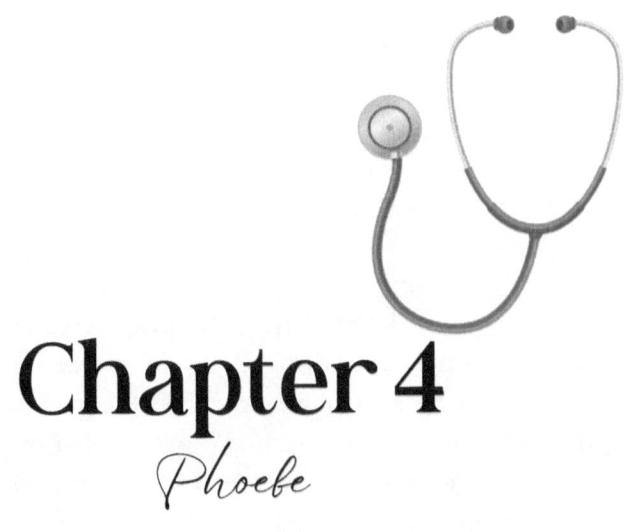

Chapter 4
Phoebe

"Relax, I'm not here to cause any trouble. I just wanted to say how happy I am to see you with your partner," I assured them, placing my hands over my chest with a smile. I had heard about everything they had gone through because of a terrible woman; it was the most talked about gossip in the hospital.

"You really do look different," Alan commented. I smiled at his remark; it was obvious that the thin, blonde girl he had known in school was long gone.

"Yes, life changes us." I paused, my chest tightening. "I'm really sorry, Alan. Please forgive me for taking this moment, but you never allowed me to explain things back then. It will only take a minute —I just need to get this off my chest. It has weighed on me all these years," I said. This might be my only opportunity to do so, and I couldn't pass it up. Alan looked toward his partner, as if seeking her approval.

"It's fine, Phoebe, but you'll need to say it in front of my wife," Alan said, holding his wife's hand. She looked at him with admiration, a gentle smile forming on her lips.

I swallowed. "That's okay with me. I imagine she already knows what happened between us," I said, uncertain about how much she was aware of. "Well, Alan, I…" I hesitated, feeling embarrassed and a little intimidated by the two pairs of eyes watching me so intently.

I wasn't sure if I was doing the right thing by sharing all my story with them, but I needed to. When I looked at them again, Alan's wife had bright, glistening eyes, and Alan himself appeared completely shocked. I quickly clarified things.

I hurried to assure them, "Before you start thinking otherwise, let me confirm it's not your child. My son is Steven's. He abandoned me, and to this day, my son is being raised by me. My Aunt Salomé helped me get back on my feet and now look at me—I'm a certified nurse. My entire life is dedicated to my patients and my son. I never needed Steven, and the only people who visit us from time to time are his parents. The truth is, I used you, and I wasn't honest with you. You are an incredible person, and I'm so happy that life has rewarded you with a wonderful woman and two little ones on the way."

Alan's eyes turned to his wife, the petite, graceful woman with Asian features. She smiled warmly at him in return.

"I'm really glad this reunion happened," Alan said. "Honestly, I didn't realize how much I needed to hear all of this to let go of the resentment I carried against women for so long. Now, I understand both my mistakes and yours. I truly forgive you. I think this gives me closure on a relationship that, in many ways, destroyed me.

"I cared about you, but now that I reflect on it, I don't think it was love, it was more a matter of attraction and affection. As for me, you can find peace.."

I nodded and smiled; it appeared that I wasn't the only one who needed this moment.

"For me as well," I admitted. "I'm sorry for the pain I caused you, and once again, I'm genuinely happy for you. I wish you all the best with your growing family." I turned my attention back to the ultrasound machine.

"Actually, we already have a three year old boy," Alan added, catching me by surprise.

"That's wonderful," I said with a smile. "I need to check on other patients now. It was nice meeting you," I told his wife before turning to him. "And Alan, it was great to see you again. Get well soon, and best wishes for your pregnancy."

I wheeled the ultrasound machine toward the door. Before stepping out, I glanced back at them one last time. They were still gazing at each other like two lovestruck teenagers. I sighed, then closed the door and walked down the hall.

It felt as though a massive weight had been lifted from my shoulders. Alan was the one person to whom I owed an apology for taking advantage of his love.

But truly, I was happy for him. He was with a wonderful woman, had a child, and soon two more would be welcomed into their family.

That night, when I arrived home, I hugged Noah tightly.

"Are you watching the replay?" I asked as I sat down beside him. The television was showing a match between Atlantico Madrid and Barcelona.

He shook his head. "No, it's live. They're playing in another country, and the game has gone into overtime. They're fighting for a spot in the Champions League semi finals," he explained, his eyes glued to the screen.

I watched an Atlantico Madrid player get tackled, his calf taking the hit. He wore the number ten jersey, and his last name was Guzman. My son stood up, concerned as the medics rushed to him, but moments later, the player got up, gritting his teeth against the pain.

And wow, what a gorgeous man! His blue eyes, slightly tanned skin, short beard, chestnut hair, strong legs, and the smile he gave while reassuring everyone that he was fine. After a few seconds and a spray on his calf, he continued playing.

"That's why he's my favorite player. Just watch, he'll score a goal soon," my son said confidently.

I continued watching the match with him, and ten minutes later, the long awaited goal came. And yes, I was completely captivated by the sight of the man taking off his shirt, revealing his toned and sculpted abs.

"When I grow up, I want to be like him," my son said.

I smiled, but internally, I felt a deep conflict. Noah looked up to a stranger as his role model. I made a mental note to check the schedule of upcoming matches and figure out my days off so we could go see his team play live.

For the next few weeks, life followed the same routine: going from the hospital to home and back again, with a grocery run once a week before returning. I was grateful to Aida for always being willing to look after Noah.

My son was mature for his age, and I loved him for his confidence in believing he could take care of himself. But in my eyes, he was still a baby who needed my attention.

I could never forgive myself if anything happened to him while he was alone.

"Looks like it's going to be a quiet morning. There are only two patients on the floor. One had a baby girl, and the other a baby boy. The father of the little girl fainted in the middle of the delivery—" My colleague's story was interrupted when Wendy suddenly stood up after answering the phone.

"Forget what I said about a quiet day. We need to prepare the OR immediately—a code red is incoming," she warned us, her expression stricken with panic.

We immediately sprang to our feet and prepared for the emergency.

"Did they tell you what it is?" I asked as I washed my hands.

"A forty one year old woman, eight months pregnant with twins, has an intrauterine hemorrhage and unstable blood pressure."

Hearing that shook me to my core, bringing back the worst memory I had as a nurse: the only time a patient under my care died, just hours after childbirth, due to a pulmonary embolism.

"Phoebe!" Wendy called out, snapping me out of my thoughts.

We prepared the OR until the patient arrived: an unconscious Asian woman named Jia according to her chart. I tried to keep my mind clear and focus on following the doctors' orders.

My heart pounded in my ears as the cardiac monitor displayed a declining heart rate. The second baby was born: a tiny girl. The pediatrician examined her while the mother's condition worsened. However, once the cardiologist stepped in and took control, things gradually stabilized under his guidance.

Nearly an hour later, the mother and babies were finally out of danger.

"They are so beautiful," Wendy said as she carried the newborns to the neonatal unit. I remained with the mother, making sure she was comfortable in her room.

"Aitor…" Jia whispered softly. I assumed that was her husband's name.

After confirming that everything was stable, I was surprised when she regained consciousness so quickly. Usually, after such a complicated delivery, patients remain drowsy for hours. But she seemed eager to wake up —probably worried about her children.

"My babies?" she asked with anxiety.

"They're fine. Your son was born first, then your daughter. Both are beautiful," I reassured her with a smile. Jia nodded and closed her eyes to rest.

I stepped out to inform the family that she was awake, and I was in for a huge surprise. Standing outside were Susy, Alan's wife, and Aitor, Alan's brother. His eyes were red and full of tears. As soon as I told him the news, he ran into Jia's room without hesitation.

The maternity ward finally began to calm down after that. I was grabbing warm blankets for a patient when I passed by the restroom and heard someone calling for help.

"Help! Somebody help me!" The voice was muffled but desperate.

I rushed to the door and tried the handle—locked. "Hello? What's wrong?"

"Phoebe? Is that you?" It was definitely Susy, and she sounded terrified.

"Susy, what's happening? Are you hurt?"

"She tried to kill me!" Susy's voice was high pitched, and agitated. "Rebecca is here!"

My heart hammered against my ribs. "Susy, I'm calling security right now. Stay away from her, do you hear me?"

I immediately stepped away and called security. They arrived within seconds. When I returned with them, I saw Susy in the arms of an older man, crying and visibly shaken. I stepped inside the restroom—and there was Rebeca, lying face up, blood seeping from her head. Her eyes were open, empty.

I crouched down to check for a pulse. There was nothing. Rebeca was forever gone. I went outside and saw Dr. Martinez.

"We have to call it in," I said quietly to Dr. Martinez. "We need the police."

From that moment on, Susy became my friend. A new friend I didn't know I needed, and one she needed as well. I had no contact with Alan; everything was between us, and he didn't seem to mind.

Eventually, Susy came for her four month prenatal checkup and personally handed me an invitation to her wedding and rehearsal dinner, scheduled for three weeks later.

"Aren't you afraid of the bad luck thing? Having an ex at the wedding?" I joked, raising an eyebrow as I looked at the invitation.

She waved me off. "I don't believe in that nonsense. Besides, you're our friend. What if you meet your Prince Charming at the party? My grandfather invited plenty of his friends," she teased with a playful grin.

"I love how excited you are about matchmaking, but the moment I mention that I'm a single mom, he'll run for the hills. I'm not in the mood for disappointments, so I'll just stay loyal to my little Noah; he's the only man worth my time. Though eventually, he'll replace me with another woman too," I chuckled.

She laughed. "Oh, don't pout. You're beautiful, young—you shouldn't shut your heart off forever."

I understood her point, but the idea still scared me.

For a single mother like me, letting someone new into my life wasn't just about my own emotional stability; it also meant bringing a stranger into my son's world.

And what if things didn't work out? We'd both have to deal with the heartbreak.

Noah yearned for more from his father, and I felt awful for not being able to provide him with a family that includes a mother and a father who love one another and love him unconditionally.

"You're right; I need to start working on myself to prepare for the event."

Her lips curled into a knowing smile. "Many would love to lose themselves in those beautiful curves. You're sure to have suitors lining up—I'm confident of it," she teased.

I shook my head, and we said our farewells.

The rehearsal and wedding invitation from Susy and Alan lingered in my mind all day. I intended to go, but if I wanted to present myself properly in high society, I needed to put in a bit more effort into my appearance.

As usual, I came home exhausted. I was in the process of taking off my shoes when my son rushed over, tablet in hand.

"Mom! Look! Omar is about to launch a new fitness routine!" he said excitedly, showing me the promotional video.

"Looks like we'll be starting it in a few days," I replied, and he beamed.

With my friend's wedding celebrations only three weeks away, the difference may not be drastic, but some changes should be noticeable.

Sure enough, on launch day, my son was already holding my credit card, waiting for my approval. From day one, I followed the workouts and took note of all the advice—meal portions, water intake, and various tips he shared. But there were many moments when I completely lost track of what he was saying, mesmerized by his smile or the way his arm muscles flexed. That man left me weak in the knees, and sweating my ass off.

The day before the wedding arrived, and as luck would have it, Aida had a shift during the rehearsal dinner. I wasn't about to leave my son alone, so after work, I stopped by the mall to find something more appropriate for the occasion for him.

I chose to wear a pink loose dress. Noah ended up in a black suit, which I thought looked handsome on him.

The venue was positively beautiful, with soft fairy lights and white flores, hanging from the ceiling of the massive tent. I couldn't imagine having a special moment like this anywhere else, and I was so happy for them when I saw everything after our taxi pulled up.

"Noah, please be mindful and don't speak unless spoken to," I reminded him as we exited the car.

"Yes, Mom," he responded.

I raised an eyebrow. That "Yes, Mom" could signal trouble. He was well behaved, yet he was incredibly outspoken.

By the time we entered the garden, the servers were already bringing out the food. The space was transformed into something magical—strings of warm white lights draped between ancient oak trees, elegant round tables dressed in cream linens, and vibrant arrangements of roses and peonies creating splashes of color against the lush greenery. The setting sun cast everything in a golden glow that made the whole scene look like something from a fairy tale.

Servers in crisp white uniforms moved gracefully between tables, carrying silver platters laden with culinary artistry. I caught glimpses of herb crusted lamb with rosemary sprigs, perfectly grilled salmon topped with delicate citrus garnish, and colorful Mediterranean vegetables arranged like small paintings on each plate. The aroma of garlic, fresh herbs, and roasted meats filled the evening air, making my mouth water despite my nervousness.

Susy and Alan greeted us warmly, looking absolutely flawless. Susy was radiant in a flowing emerald green dress that complemented her dark hair, which was swept up in an elegant chignon with delicate pearl pins catching the light. Alan looked distinguished in a perfectly tailored navy suit with a crisp white shirt and silver tie, his face glowing with the kind of happiness that only comes from marrying your best friend.

They led us to our table, chattering excitedly about the ceremony and thanking us for being there. I was half listening, taking in the beautiful details of their reception and watching servers pour wine from bottles that probably cost more than my monthly rent, when my eyes landed on a familiar figure already seated at our assigned table.

Omar Guzman.

My heart nearly leaped out of my chest.

Alan introduced us to his family before he and Susy left to mingle. A tense silence settled over the table. And, of course, despite my earlier request, Noah was the first to break the silence.

"Sorry we're late. My mom had a lot of work at the hospital," he said as the waiter set a plate down in front of him.

"Do you work at the hospital?" asked a gorgeous mid aged woman with black hair and blue eyes.

I nodded, recognizing Mrs. Jimena, Alan's grandmother, who had previously seen me at work.

"Yes, she's a nurse in the obstetrics department. She assisted in delivering Aitor's babies and has been helping monitor Susy's pregnancy," she affirmed.

All eyes were suddenly fixed on me. It had been a long time since I had felt so scrutinized.

"No way!" my son suddenly exclaimed, as if he had just realized who was sitting next to me.

I acted as if I didn't know who it was.

"What is it, sweetheart?" I asked, sensing warmth creeping into my cheeks.

"It's Omar Guzman, my favorite soccer player—the one you watch while exercising!"

I turned, feeling embarrassed, and met his gaze.

"It is a pleasure to meet you," he said with a wry smile, amusement twinkling in his eyes.

That gaze. That grin. That tone.

Something within me, something that had been neglected for far too long, melted.

It felt as if a fire I believed had long been extinguished was now ignited.

Chapter 5

Omar

One year ago

They say money can't buy happiness, but I used to believe it could at least buy authenticity. I was wrong about that, just as I was wrong about so many things.

I had everything the world told me I should want: wealth that stretched beyond reason, fame that opened every door, a body that had never known real sickness, and a future mapped out in golden promises. At twenty seven, I was the heir to an empire, a star in professional football, and the kind of man that mothers pointed out to their daughters at charity galas.

I was also completely alone.

Not in the way that people usually mean when they talk about loneliness. My calendar was perpetually full, my phone constantly buzzing with invitations, my social media flooded with comments from people claiming to love me. But love—real love—had become the one thing my fortune couldn't purchase, no matter how desperately I tried.

You see, when you have everything, everyone wants something from you. They see the designer clothes and think about the connections you could provide. They notice the expensive watch and calculate how much their association with you might be worth. They hear your last name and their eyes light up with possibility —not affection, but opportunity.

I had become a collector's item in human form, valuable for what I represented rather than who I actually was beneath the surface. The women who pursued me weren't interested in my thoughts, my fears, my dreams beyond the football field. They wanted Omar the brand, Omar the stepping stone, Omar the ticket to a better life.

And I was so tired of it all.

By the time I met Marina, I had already weathered countless relationships that followed the same devastating pattern: initial attraction, carefully orchestrated romance, the gradual revelation that I was merely a means to an end, and finally, the crushing disappointment when they moved on to bigger, better opportunities. Each time, I told myself the next one would be different. Each time, I was wrong.

Marina was supposed to be my salvation from this endless cycle. She was the coach's daughter—someone who understood the world of professional sports, someone who had her own connections and didn't need mine. When she insisted we keep our relationship secret, claiming her father would disapprove of the distraction, I actually felt grateful. Finally, I thought, someone who wanted to protect what we had rather than exploit it.

For five months, I lived in that beautiful delusion. Five months of believing that her cautious affection was genuine concern, that her reluctance to be seen with me publicly stemmed from respect for my career rather than shame about our connection. Five months of hope that maybe, I had found someone who saw me as more than a trophy to be won.

I should have known better. The signs were all there —the same calculated sweetness I'd experienced before, the strategic timing of her affection, the way she always seemed to know exactly what to say to keep me invested but never quite satisfied. I had become an expert at recognizing these patterns, yet somehow I had convinced myself that this time was different.

The night everything unraveled was supposed to be a celebration of my sister's latest fashion triumph. I had been looking forward to finally introducing Marina to my family, even if just as a friend. I had been planning to tell her about the apartment I'd bought, imagining a future where we wouldn't have to hide, where we could build something real together.

Instead, I found myself standing in the shadows of my sister's success, watching the woman I thought I loved wrapped in the arms of another man—not just any man, but my sister's ex boyfriend, the son of someone who was like family to us and my teammate.

The passionate way she kissed him, the comfortable way she melted into his embrace, told me everything I needed to know about where her true feelings lay.

At that moment, I realized that Marina hadn't been protecting our relationship from her father's disapproval. She had been protecting her real relationship from my interference. I wasn't her boyfriend; I was her safety net. Not the man she desired, but the backup plan she kept warm while pursuing what she actually wanted.

The worst part wasn't the betrayal itself—I had grown almost accustomed to that particular flavor of pain. The worst part was recognizing that no amount of success, wealth, or fame could protect me from being reduced to a utility in someone else's life. I could buy anything except the one thing I craved most: to be valued for who I was rather than what I could provide.

That night, watching Marina with someone else, I made a decision that would change the trajectory of my life forever. I decided I was done being anyone's second choice, done being the consolation prize, done pretending that conditional affection was better than honest solitude.

"Omar, don't be discouraged. That girl was only after your popularity and fortune. You know I'm not one to judge without knowing someone first, but I don't need to meet her. Just seeing what she was capable of reveals her intentions," my mother, Patricia Galeano, said, caressing my cheek while taking the glass of rum from my hand.

The living room of my parents house was dimly lit by a single lamp, casting long shadows across the worn leather sofa where we sat. The coffee table held an open bottle of rum and our empty glasses, while family photos watched from the mantelpiece above the cold fireplace. The heavy curtains were drawn tight against the night, creating a cocoon of warmth and privacy where my mother's gentle words could work their quiet magic.

"I really thought she was the one, mom," I said with a hiccup, the alcohol already taking control of my words and body. Seeing my sister's ex-boyfriend and "friend" together with the woman who was going to be my fiancée was a hard blow for me.

"Let me tell you something, Omar, good things take time to arrive, because what comes easily, easily leaves. The woman who's meant for you will be unique, someone with whom you'll feel a connection far beyond intimacy. She'll be difficult to win over, because good things come at a cost, my son. And I'm not talking about expensive gifts or fancy restaurants. You men are quite foolish, conquering women with material things, activating their ambitious side, when you should be more modest; the extravagances can come later." My mother said taking a sit set to my father

"Listen to her. I won her over by just inviting her to dinner by the beach, talking about things women like—music, movies, travels. OW!" my father, Roger Guzman exclaimed when my mother elbowed his ribs.

Roger Guzman still had the build of an athlete with broad shoulders and strong hands that once commanded the field. Though his playing days were behind him, he carried himself with the quiet confidence of someone who'd known glory. Gray now touched his temples, and his knees complained on cold mornings, but when he talked about football, his eyes sparked with the same competitive fire that had made him formidable on the pitch.

"You didn't tell any lies," Mother retorted, crossing her arms and pouting.

He raised an eyebrow at her and scoffed. "So, what did I do wrong?"

"You came to interrupt the serious conversation I was having with my son." She waved an accusatory finger at him. "We don't often have him here at home, and you're always talking about football and everything with him. Now that I can have a conversation to help him avoid these bad moments, you come and interrupt it."

And although I felt emotionally down, the show these two put on made me laugh.

"I appreciate both of you. If your intention was to lift my spirits, you've succeeded." I stood up and, stumbling, made it to my room. I threw myself face down on the bed, and without energy for anything else, I fell asleep.

The next morning, I was awakened by the incessant sound of my phone. I groggily sat up and saw several missed calls from both my grandparents and my agent. My heart raced, assuming the worst. Then I remembered I was at my parents' house and nothing bad had happened.

Relieved, I took a quick shower and went downstairs to see my father looking a bit upset on the phone. My phone rang in my hand, and again it was my agent, Alexis. Okay, so maybe we weren't out of the woods yet.

"What do you want so early, Alexis?" I said, rolling my eyes as I answered the call.

"For you to travel to Madrid now. You've already attended your social event, seen your family. Now it's back to reality, champion." I knew his call wasn't productive, but my grandparents' calls were.

"Yes, Alexis, thanks to you I already have a flight in a few hours, right?" I sighed.

"That's right, and it's better for you to stay away from that girl you told me about. I just saw the exclusives that came out, and one of them talks about her and Álvaro." Alexis explained.

"Don't talk to me about those two, and I'm telling you now, find a way to keep what I'm going to do to that idiot inside the locker rooms."

"Omar, don't you dare—" I hung up.

Alexis was often exasperating, especially when reminding me of things I already knew. I approached my father to ask why he looked worried, walking back and forth.

"What's happening?" I said, sitting on the couch. My head hurt from drinking so much, but I could bear it.

"Your sister disappeared last night," he said bleakly, and I jumped to my feet.

"How? What about her security?" I exclaimed, taking out my phone to call Lucio, her bodyguard.

He waved me off. "We've already located her. She's fine, and I hope she'll be arriving soon. That young lady has a lot of explaining to do." His face twisted with worry.

"She certainly does. She can't be playing with her safety like that. Just because she is heartbroken." The truth is that Aitana always enjoyed a lot of freedom. She was responsible and independent, she may have made decisions that weren't the right ones. But she was a badass, and I admired her as her little brother.

Hours later, my sister appeared entering the front door, and if it weren't for my mother's help, I would have given her a lecture. It was super evident that she had spent the night with someone.

"I can't believe you two were going to argue with Aitana, who is thirty years old. She's no longer a child who needs you to defend her." My mother scolded us when Aitana went back to her room. Leaving us in the middle of the hallway.

Frustrated, I ran my hands through my hair. "I agree, but what I don't want is for Aitana to get hurt. Men these days can be very cruel. She'll always be the youngest of us all. I wanted to pull her ears before I left."

"Are you leaving?" Mother asked, and I nodded in affirmation.

"Yes, Alexis is already hounding me to return to Madrid. I think for now I'll focus on my career and the projects I've left somewhat pending. I have quite a few advertising campaigns." I shrugged.

"That's fine, my child, focus on yourself and don't forget what I told you yesterday. Don't rush into making decisions, prioritize yourself above all." She caressed my cheek.

"I will, but I'm worried about my sister. Yesterday, seeing Álvaro with Marina could have made her do things impulsively."

She touched my shoulder and shook her head. "I don't think what she did was out of spite. Just look at how her eyes lit up when she talked about the man. Your sister has been emotionally detached from people since she was little. She cried over Álvaro, not because he cheated on her—she had already forgiven him for several infidelities. She cried out of anger for having wasted two years of her life trying to feel good with him. We must let her explore her feelings, make her decisions, and if she happens to make mistakes, we'll be here to lift her up, help her, encourage her, and support her."

"You really do give good motivational speeches, princess," said my father, appearing at the door. He hugged Mother from behind and hid his face in her neck.

Mom rolled her eyes. "As the men of the house, I agree that you feel the duty to protect her, but you must let her fly or swim freely," she pointed out, looking between me and Father.

"She's right. Well, Mr. and Mrs. Guzman, duty calls, and so does Alexis," I said, showing them my phone ringing once again; my babysitter was being a real pain in the balls.

"Take care, son, I hope that you don't break Álvaro's face," my father said, narrowing his eyes as he pulled away from Mom. "Yes, Alexis already called me."

I snorted. "Bootlicker. Wait until I get there and tell him to accept all the campaigns they've offered us," I said, and they nodded. With that, I left my parents' house with my security and headed towards the airport for my flight back to Madrid.

After arriving, I went straight to my apartment. The key turned with its familiar resistance, and I stepped into my own space, a stark contrast to my parents' warmth filled home. Where their house smelled of coffee and canela, mine carried the faint scent of gym equipment rubber and the eucalyptus diffuser I'd forgotten to refill weeks ago.

Without a doubt, the silence was deafening. My apartment was minimalist to the point of being almost monastic, a single gray couch faced the window overlooking the city, my workout equipment neatly arranged in the corner where a dining table should go. The walls were bare except for a single framed photograph: not of family or friends, but an abstract black and white print I'd bought because it reminded me of static, of peaceful emptiness.

So I put on my usual music, something calm, and began a workout routine. I was a big fan of Hozier's songs, his voice filled the sparse room through my bluetooth speaker, melancholic melodies bouncing off the bare walls. My mother didn't like them because they were too "depressing."

I have the theory that the music we like represents us a lot. Especially our mood; the music you listen to depends a lot on how you feel. As I moved through my planks and push ups on the cold floor, Hozier's raw lyrics about solitude and introspection felt more honest than the cheerful salsa my mother played while cooking, or my father's nostalgic match commentary recordings that he sometimes played in the background like white noise.

The city lights began to flicker outside, my floor to ceiling window, turning my apartment into a fishbowl of solitude, Hozier's voice the only thing keeping it from feeling completely hollow.

I finished taking a shower and doing some cleaning when my phone rang. Glancing at the screen, I didn't feel anything I used to when seeing that name, Marina. I answered the call but didn't say anything.

"Omar, Omi. Forgive me for what happened yesterday, but my father told me that..."

I left the call on speaker and continued putting things in order. I didn't believe anything she told me, so after giving her the opportunity to speak and explain, it was my turn to talk.

"If I wasn't your first choice, don't call me to be your second, because that won't happen. I hope you find what you've been looking for, that thing I couldn't offer you." Without waiting for her answer, I ended the call.

Then I looked out the window at the lights on Serrano Street and took a deep breath. There was no triumph in ending things with her, no satisfaction in delivering those words. Just... relief. Clean, simple relief, like finally setting down a weight you'd carried so long you'd forgotten it wasn't part of you.

Several minutes later, the doorbell rang. I thought it was Alexis, but when I opened the door, my friends came in, uninvited as always.

Diego sprawled across my couch with the casual authority of someone who'd claimed that spot a hundred times before. He was built like a midfielder, compact and sturdy, with restless energy even when sitting still. His dark eyes scanned my face with the practiced assessment of someone who'd known me since youth academy days, reading my mood like he'd read opposing teams' formations.

"Did you get engaged?" Diego asked, sitting on the couch, and I shook my head. His question was deliberately absurd, his way of testing how bad things really were.

"I brought poison..." teased Amílcar, taking the soda bottle out of the bag he carried. Amílcar was the youngest on the team and always made us laugh with his peculiarities. At twenty two, he still had that rookie eagerness, his bleached tips badly grown out, wearing designer sneakers that cost more than most people's rent. His humor was his armor deflecting any serious moment with perfectly timed ridiculousness. He held the cola bottle like it was contraband, his boyish grin infectious despite my mood.

"Stop messing around, Amílcar, can't you see the guy needs something stronger?" chided Gonzalo, taking a seat next to Diego. Gonzalo was our unofficial captain off the field, the one who organized dinners, remembered birthdays, and somehow always knew when someone needed checking on. His premature gray temples gave him an air of wisdom beyond his twenty nine years. He carried himself with the quiet confidence of a defender, solid and dependable, the kind of friend who showed up without being asked.

Amílcar frowned. "Sorry, but tomorrow they need us to have fresh legs at training."

"What would I do without my ladies?" I joked, and they smiled.

I leaned back in my chair, shaking my head with a grin. "You know, when I first met you guys, I thought this whole team thing would be just like my previous team—everyone for themselves. But you're all ridiculous in the best way."

Diego put his hand to his chest, raising an eyebrow. "Don't say such things because... it's tempting," he said, offering me a seductive wink.

We all burst out laughing. I wiped my eyes, still chuckling. "Seriously though, I'm glad we became friends. My previous teammates were always so competitive with each other —never really trusted anyone. Here, it's different."

"Different how?" Amílcar asked, raising his eyebrow.

"I don't know... maybe it's because we're all far from home, or maybe it's just you guys, but it feels like we actually have each other's backs. Like, really have them." I grew more serious for a moment. "When I had that rough patch for three months with my knee injury, you didn't just ask how I was doing—you actually listened and were there for me."

"Of course, hermano," Amílcar said, meaning it. "We're in this together."

Diego nodded. "Besides, who else is going to appreciate your terrible taste in music?"

"My music taste is excellent!" I protested, launching into a defense that had them laughing again.

I stayed chatting with those who had invited themselves to my apartment, grateful for these friendships that had grown deeper than I'd expected.

Eventually, women would come into our lives to set us straight, but for now, we'd be the most sought after bachelors in Madrid.

Chapter 6

Omar

I t had been such an exhausting year, full of work —between training sessions, matches, interviews, new projects, and problems that continued to arise in the family, life was becoming increasingly complicated.

"I never thought this would sell like hotcakes," remarked Alexis upon seeing the statistics of the fitness course in which I participated along with some sponsoring brands.

I glared at him. "Yes, I distinctly remember you telling me that a person like me shouldn't sell my image so mediocrely. You can't even lift a forty five pound weight, while we work every day to strengthen our bodies, and it takes sacrifice and discipline to achieve having a good physique. So I'm going to ask you to never again denigrate this work unless you wish to stop being my agent."

Alexis's mouth fell open slightly, his confident posture deflating as he blinked at me in shock. For a moment, he seemed genuinely speechless—something I'd never witnessed before. His usual quick retorts were nowhere to be found.

"I... Omar, I didn't realize..." he stammered, then caught himself, his face flushing slightly. He cleared his throat and raised his hands in surrender. "Yes, relax. It won't happen again." His voice was quieter than usual, almost uncertain.

I nodded, watching as he shifted uncomfortably in his chair, clearly still processing my outburst.

"I'll, uh…" he paused, running a hand through his hair —another nervous gesture I'd rarely seen from him. "I'll go see if you have any more commitments so you can go to Zaragoza and enjoy your vacation," he added, his tone notably more respectful than before.

The season had ended, and although Reyal Madrid had beaten us by six points, we had finished in second place in the EA Sports league table in Spain. It had been a very good and close competition. Now I had taken a break from the team's summer activities, wanting to spend time with my family.

My phone rang announcing a text message. I glanced at it casually, expecting another sponsorship inquiry or team update, but my heart skipped when I saw the sender's name. Lucio—my sister Aitana's bodyguard.

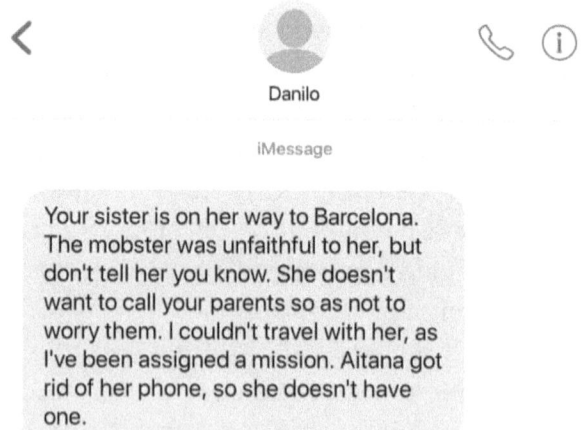

Danilo

iMessage

Your sister is on her way to Barcelona. The mobster was unfaithful to her, but don't tell her you know. She doesn't want to call your parents so as not to worry them. I couldn't travel with her, as I've been assigned a mission. Aitana got rid of her phone, so she doesn't have one.

I clenched my fist because precisely what I didn't want to happen was happening. My sister had given herself completely to a man who didn't take long to hurt her.

Just as I stood up, Alexis approached me with his tablet in hand.

"Omar, I've checked your schedule," he said, scrolling through the screen. "You have no commitments for the next few days. You're completely free to go to Zaragoza."

I turned to face him, my jaw set with determination. "Alexis, I need you to do something for me urgently."

"Of course, what do you need?"

"Get me a device with my sister's line—and I want a new phone number too. Can you handle that today?"

Alexis raised an eyebrow, clearly puzzled by the unusual request. "A new line? Omar, what's going on? This seems sudden."

"Just do it, please. It's important."

"Alright, but may I ask why the secrecy? The new number, I mean."

I crossed my arms, my expression growing serious. "Let's just say we'll see how brave my sister really is. If she wants to face her problems or run away from them."

Alexis studied my face for a moment, then nodded slowly. "I can have both ready within a couple of hours. Should I ask any questions, or...?"

"No questions. Just get it done."

"Understood," he said, already pulling out his own phone. "I'll make the calls now."

Two hours later, I had what I needed. I said goodbye to him and set to work going to Barcelona in search of my sister.

I would be tender at first, trying to sympathize with what she's feeling, because I knew what it was like to have your heart broken, or at least to get excited about someone and then have it end up being nothing.

I stopped by a store, buying everything needed to cheer her up. I remembered that when Marina visited me and was on her period, she would ask for sweet things, and that would make her happy. I sighed while taking a package of six small cakes. People kept looking at me; it was already quite late, so there weren't many people in the place.

Locally, people already knew that my family was from here, and they treated us like any human being, but always more than one would approach to ask for a photo.

I soon arrived at the building where she lived. The modern glass tower stretched fifteen stories into the Madrid skyline, its sleek facade reflecting the city lights below. Aitana had chosen the penthouse, of course—she'd always been drawn to heights, claiming they helped her think clearly. The building's entrance was understated but expensive, with polished marble floors and subtle lighting that spoke of wealth without shouting it.

A doorman in a crisp uniform nodded respectfully as I approached. "Buenas noches, Señor Omar. Miss Aitana is expecting you?"

"No, it's a surprise," I replied. He nodded in response. The lobby was quiet at this hour, save for the soft hum of climate control and the distant sound of traffic filtering through the thick glass windows. A few residents passed by, well dressed professionals and older wealthy couples who lived in this exclusive part of the Salamanca district.

The elevator was mirrored and silent, rising smoothly past floors of other wealthy inhabitants. I caught glimpses through the lobby's floor to ceiling windows of the tree lined street below, where expensive cars were parked beneath designer streetlamps. This was the Madrid of old money and new success, where privacy was purchased along with the real estate.

As the elevator climbed toward the penthouse, I wondered if Aitana felt as isolated up here as the building suggested, or if the height gave her the control she'd always craved.

I knocked on the door, and when she opened it, I was struck by how fragile she looked. Aitana's usually pristine appearance was completely undone. Her pale blue eyes were rimmed with red and brimming with fresh tears that had already traced silver paths down her flushed cheeks. Her face was puffy and blotchy, the kind of swelling that comes from hours of crying.

She was wearing an oversized gray sweater that hung loosely on her small frame, the sleeves pushed up carelessly to her elbows. Her dark hair, normally styled to perfection, was pulled back in a messy bun with strands escaping to frame her face. She wasn't wearing any makeup, which was unusual for her—even at home, Aitana typically maintained some level of put together appearance. But now she looked raw and vulnerable, like a much younger version of herself.

Her lips trembled slightly as she tried to form words, but nothing came out. The sight of my normally composed sister in such a state hit me harder than I'd expected.

I dropped the bags on the floor without a second thought and pulled her into my arms, feeling how small she seemed as her shoulders shook against my chest.

"There, there, little one. You don't look like my older sister," I said, caressing her back.

"H-how did you know?" she said, hiccupping, wiping her tears, and blowing her nose on my delicate black t-shirt.

I grimaced. "Aitana, don't be disgusting! This will dry later, and people will think it's something else." She looked at me without understanding, and after a few seconds, she seemed to understand my message. She laughed, which was what I wanted to achieve with my comment.

"Has this happened to you before?" she asked, and I just shrugged my shoulders as I entered her apartment.

The penthouse was quintessentially Aitana—every detail meticulously chosen and perfectly arranged. Floor to ceiling windows dominated the main living area, offering a breathtaking panoramic view of Madrid's glittering skyline. The space was open concept with soaring ceilings, decorated in neutral tones of cream, soft gray, and white that somehow managed to feel both luxurious and sterile.

A massive sectional sofa in dove-gray velvet faced the windows, flanked by glass coffee tables that held carefully curated art books and a single white orchid. The kitchen was a masterpiece of modern design—glossy white cabinets, marble countertops, and high end appliances that looked like they'd rarely been used. Everything had its place, from the designer bar stools lined up perfectly at the kitchen island to the abstract paintings hung at precise intervals along the walls.

But tonight, cracks showed in the perfection. Tissues were scattered across the coffee table, a half empty wine glass sat abandoned on the kitchen counter, and throw pillows were askew on the pristine sofa. Even in her breakdown, though, the apartment maintained its magazine worthy appearance, this was a space designed to impress, not necessarily to comfort.

The scent of expensive candles lingered in the air, mixed with something that might have been her perfume or the faint staleness of tears and sleepless nights.

"No, but I remind you that my physical needs have made me use some garments to clean myself, and on black clothing, white and shiny stains remain," I said, feeling my chest wet from my sister's nasal fluids.

"How disgusting, Omar, but how nice it is to see you again, little brother," she chuckled, offering a paper towel, and I cleaned myself.

Alright, now it was time to get down to business. "You'll decide how we kill him, but I'm cutting off his balls, that's for sure. No one has the right to humiliate you like that; I don't care if he's memory impaired. Lucio called me, said he didn't want to bother my parents because you surely wouldn't want to see them and explain what happened. He also told me about your phone, so I brought you one. I didn't know if you wanted a new line or your number, so I requested SIM cards with both options," I said, taking the phone out of the bag.

I put the two cards in front of her, and she took the one with her number. I smiled because it meant she wasn't going to let the idiot win, or at least that's what I wanted to believe.

"That's my sister. Don't let yourself be intimidated by him. I also brought some things to watch movies and some things that women like."

She made a very funny and cute pout when she started taking things out of the bags.

"Do you want me to get a sugar overdose with all this?" she joked, and I shook my head. Just then, the doorbell of the apartment rang. Aitana's smile immediately vanished, her face going pale as her eyes darted toward the door. She froze mid-movement, the package of cakes still in her hands.

"Relax, it must be the third thing I prepared for us," I said, knowing it was the pizzas I had ordered before getting out of the car. I paid and put the boxes on the kitchen counter.

She opened the first box to reveal a classic Margherita —golden, bubbling mozzarella stretched across a perfectly charred crust, with fresh basil leaves scattered on top and a rich tomato sauce that filled the air with the scent of oregano and garlic. The second box held her childhood favorite: a simple ham and cheese pizza, the kind we used to share as kids when our parents would let us stay up late watching movies.

Aitana stared at the familiar sight for a moment, then picked up a slice of the ham and cheese. As she took her first bite, the cheese stretched in long, gooey strings, and I watched her close her eyes as if savoring not just the taste but the memory. When she opened them again, fresh tears had welled up.

"You remembered," she whispered, her voice thick with emotion. The pizza was still warm, steam rising from where she'd bitten into it, but it seemed like she was tasting something far more significant than melted cheese and dough—she was tasting home, childhood, and the comfort of someone who truly knew her.

"The woman who wins your heart will get a treasure with legs," she said with her mouth full.

My instinct was to take advantage of the compliment, but instead, I decided to change the subject.

"Want to watch something? We could put on *The Princess Diaries* or *Enchanted*—I know those are still your favorites."

"Are you sure you're not gay?" she asked when I mentioned the names of her favorite children's movies. We both burst out laughing.

"Very sure, but I should remind you that I grew up with you and know your tastes. Go and put on any movie you want. With real characters; we already live too much in a fantasy." My sensitive side had passed. Now would come the cruel reality. "The truth hurts, sister. Embrace it, believe it, love it."

She scowled. "Don't treat me like your coach treats you."

"I'm sorry, but it is what it is. I've already given you love and affection, so now come the scoldings." I raised an eyebrow at her.

She made a puppy dog face. "Let's watch the movie, then you can scold me all you want."

In the end, she didn't even finish watching the movie; I was grateful that she fell asleep quickly. I went to get a blanket, covered her, and prepared to take the bag I was carrying. I went to her room, took a shower, and went to sleep in her bed with a smile on my face.

There's no doubt that I was a cruel brother, letting her sleep on the couch instead of her comfortable bed. But too bad.

As every day, my biological clock woke me up at five in the morning, regardless of what time I had gone to sleep. I wasn't going to waste being in this city, so I took out some sportswear and went out to train as I did every day.

After a few hours and an extensive tour of the city, I returned to the apartment, where my sister seemed to have just woken up.

"We have to hurry if we want to arrive on time to Alan's and Susy's rehearsal dinner." She nodded and went directly to her room.

"Omar!" she exclaimed after seeing the bed undone.

"Sorry not sorry" I said, taking a towel out of the hallway closet. She shook her head and closed the door.

Upon arriving at the event, I looked at my sister and could feel how uncomfortable she felt, being surrounded by so many people in love and eyes on her. Until she exploded, telling those present at the table with us, who were my grandparents and my parents, about her failed relationship with the mobster and that she didn't want any mentions of him.

I could feel my father's intense gaze on me. I knew he would ask questions when he had the opportunity. The speeches began from the adults, giving advice on how to have a successful marriage and how to take care of their family.

When the toasts ended, they began to serve the food. Until my eyes caught the presence of two newly arrived figures. The most exquisite woman I have ever seen in my life, along with a child who was clinging to her hand.

My body shivered seeing the angelic face of the woman, the color of her reddish hair, and her body... they were a complete work of art.

"Pinch me," I said to my sister in wonder.

"What?"

I didn't turn to look at her because I didn't want to take my eyes off that beautiful woman. "I need you to pinch me so I can know if the beauty my eyes are seeing is real."

Our eyes met for a few seconds, and the woman appeared surprised to see me. She lowered her gaze to the little one, whom I was already intrigued to know if he was her brother, nephew, cousin, or son.

Alan introduced us, and I smiled at the woman named Phoebe and her son, Noah. Both sat right to my left side. I couldn't take my eyes off her face, which was slightly flushed, at the same time that she was biting her lip, and I was developing an indescribable desire to devour her mouth.

The attraction and tension I felt in various parts of my body was so strong that if it weren't because the little one was present, I would have thrown myself at her. The child seemed to notice my presence and put his mother on the spot by saying that she followed my fitness plan and that he was a big fan of the team.

My family began with the interrogation. My grandmother mentioned that she was a nurse, and I felt much more admiration for the lady literally by my side. Until my father, as always, launched the uncomfortable questions.

"Are you married?" he asked, earning an elbow from my mother.

"Dad," I said seriously. I didn't know if his intentions were to make her uncomfortable. Phoebe, looked a bit embarrassed, and seconds later it became very evident seeing her flushed cheeks.

Her son spoke up, "My mother is not married, sir, doesn't have a boyfriend, and hasn't had one for a long time. She only has me. She says I'm the only man in her life, but I've also seen her crying when she's watching a happy couple in a movie." He frowned.

"Noah," she exclaimed, reprimanding the little one, and I smiled.

"Let him be; he's doing a good job defending his mother from a very uncomfortable question. Roger, if she's married, is it important?" my mother asked incredulously.

"Well, he did me a favor by asking it, because I received an answer in my favor," I said, taking a sip from my glass without taking my eyes off the beautiful woman before me.

Phoebe cleared her throat, taking the glass of water in her hand and bringing it to her lips, averting her gaze from mine.

"Now let the girl and her boy eat in peace. You are very pretty, dear, that's all, and I think they already want to pair you with this single grandson of mine." my grandmother said.

Phoebe opened her eyes wide, choking on her water. My heart lurched as she started coughing violently, her face turning red. I shot up from my chair, my hands shaking as I reached for her, not knowing if I should pat her back.

"Easy, sweetheart. Raise your arms and try to breathe deeply," I said, standing up to help her. She did what I asked, and little by little she calmed down. "Grandma, you'll kill her before she accepts going on a first date with me," I scolded, earning Phoebe's attention.

After a small intervention by Susy, my entire attention was towards Phoebe and the child who knew more about me than I did myself. There was no doubt that this pair would drive me crazy, and I was willing to lose myself in their madness.

Chapter 7

Omar

I've never enjoyed a family gathering like I did this evening. That game of glances I had with Phoebe, made my heart race.

That shyness, innocence, and even desire in her gaze did nothing but captivate me. It was as if with just one look she completely stole my existence. Yes, here I was again, intense about a woman, but what she made me feel was different.

It was like a werewolf story when they found their destined mate—their moon, with whom they will spend the rest of their lives. In my case, it was a delicious and exquisite pink treat, just like her dress.

She said goodbye to everyone at the table, and I felt restless. I wasn't the saint of the family, but neither was I a womanizer, and I wanted to talk to her without so many eyes on us, so as not to make her uncomfortable, especially her son.

Phoebe and her son began walking toward the exit.

"Well, don't just stand there," my mother hissed, shooting me a pointed look. "Go after her before you regret not asking her out."

"I'm going," I said, already pushing back from the table.

There was no need for her to say it; I had the intention of doing it anyway.

"Did you come in your car?" I asked when I caught up to them.

"We don't have a car; we came here by taxi," said the little boy, earning a scolding look from his mother.

"Alan will ask one of the guards to take us home. Thank you for asking, but we don't want to bother," she said, avoiding looking at me.

"No way, I'll take you."

Phoebe's eyes shot up to mine, surprised at my proposal.

"Yes! Mom, please, let him take us," pleaded her son.

She seemed to debate her answer. "Alright, I should go back to tell Alan," she said finally.

I quickly took out my phone and looked for my cousin's number. It rang three times until he answered.

"I'll take Phoebe and her son home," I announced, and without waiting for his response, I ended the call. "Ready, shall we go?" I said.

Noah let go of his mother's grip when he saw that I offered him my hand. The warmth of his small hand, accompanied by his smile, melted my heart.

"Really, we don't want to cause any trouble. We know you're a very busy and public person. I don't want the press to see us together and have everything be misinterpreted," Phoebe said anxiously, and although she was right in what she was saying, I couldn't care less.

"If that happens, do you have to explain to anyone?" I asked, and both she and her son shook their heads. "Well, neither do I," I replied with a smile.

"Let's go, Mom. Remember I have to get to training early tomorrow," said Noah, catching his mother's attention.

She had no choice but to follow us to the car. I asked for her address and synchronized it in the car's GPS.

Noah was the one talking to me throughout the journey, his excitement barely contained. "Omar, I looked you up on my tablet! You scored twenty three goals this season—that's incredible!"

I glanced at him in the rearview mirror, surprised by his knowledge. "You've been doing your homework."

"Yes, and in the Champions League, you scored eight goals! My best friend Emilio said that's almost impossible, but I told him you're the best player ever."

"Emilio sounds like a smart kid. Does he play soccer too?"

"Yeah! He's my teammate. We practice together all the time. I scored six goals this season," Noah said proudly, then his face fell slightly. "But that's not very good compared to you."

"Six goals is excellent for someone your age. Keep working hard and who knows how many you'll score next season."

Noah beamed. "Really? Carlos and I want to be professional players like you someday. We practice penalty kicks every day after regular training."

"That's dedication. What position do you like most?"

"Midfielder, like you! I want to make assists and score goals. Coach says I have good vision on the field, whatever that means."

I smiled. "It means you see opportunities that other players miss. That's a gift."

"Do you think... do you think I could be as good as you someday?" Noah asked, his voice filled with hope and admiration.

The question hit me harder than I expected. Here was this kid, looking up to me with such pure enthusiasm, not knowing the complicated connection we shared.

"With the right training and dedication, you could be even better," I said honestly.

"My grandfather signed me up for this really good soccer school," Noah continued, his excitement building again.

"He takes me when Mom can't, which is most of the time because she works so much."

"Your grandfather sounds supportive."

Noah's expression grew more subdued. "Yeah, he's great. Way better than Steven. I have a dad, but he doesn't love me or my mom. At least that's what it seems like."

The casual way he said it, like it was just another fact about his life, made my chest tighten with an emotion I couldn't quite name.

"Son, don't you think you've talked enough?" Phoebe asked, looking at Noah with intense eyes, her cheeks flushing red with visible embarrassment.

"Yes, I'm sorry," he said, lowering his head and keeping complete silence.

"I could take you to training tomorrow," I offered, parking the car at the entrance of the apartment building was typical of Zaragoza's residential neighborhoods—a sturdy five story structure built from the region's characteristic reddish-brown brick and stone. The narrow balconies featured simple wrought iron railings, some adorned with small potted geraniums that added splashes of color against the earthy facade.

"Yes!" Noah said.

"No!" Phoebe said at the same time, her voice louder than his. She turned to me. "Thank you for bringing us home. This is enough trouble already. I also take this opportunity to thank you, as my son has been following your career for years and sees you as a role model. Again, thank you for bringing us."

I hurried to get out of the car and open the door on her side so they could both get out.

"Thank you very much, Omar. Meeting you fulfilled one of my dreams," gushed Noah, and he approached me to give me a hug that caught me off guard.

"Can I go up with you?" I asked, and again one said yes and the other no.

"It's better to say goodbye here," Phoebe said, punching in the entry code as her cheeks remained red. "Go ahead, son." She gestured him forward.

Noah began to walk into the building while smiling and waving his hand in farewell.

"Good night," she said goodbye, but I couldn't let her escape like that.

I tried to take her hand, and we both instantly pulled our hands away as a slight static energy separated us.

"It seems that even our bodies can't resist the energy that connects us," I teased, and she blushed harder. She crossed her arms over her chest, making her neckline much more visible. My eyes were instinctively invited to that place.

"Why are you doing this, or better said, why are you talking to me like this?" she asked, covering her chest with the coat. "I don't understand why go to so much trouble for me."

"Being honest, from the moment I saw you, I knew you're the woman I want to spend the rest of my life with." I couldn't believe those words came out of my lips, but those were the ones that were born within me.

She took two steps back, completely stunned.

"Me? The woman of your life?" She approached this time, placing the back of her hand on my forehead. "You don't have a fever. How many drinks did you have before we arrived?" she asked.

"Only two glasses of champagne. I don't like cigarettes, and I don't do any drugs, so I'm 100 percent aware of what I'm saying," I assured her, closing the distance between us. I lowered my gaze, and she raised hers.

Her brows furrowed. "No, this can't be. I must be asleep and dreaming. People like you don't notice people like me."

"People like me? Am I a Martian from another planet?" I laughed, and she smiled.

"You know very well what I mean. Look at me," she said, lowering her gaze to her body.

"I am, and you can't imagine how much I like what I see." I caressed her chin with the back of my finger. Her cheeks flushed again. Through her eyes, I could see the sea of emotions she was going through in her mind.

"This is what you say to all the women you'd like to take to bed, right?" she asked, moving away, clearly putting a wall between us in her mind.

"No, I've never said these words before," I tried to defend, but she shook her head.

"Do you expect me to believe you? Let's see, a famous footballer as handsome as you, noticing a woman with a very curvy body like mine, with a son, and who doesn't belong to your same social class. I'm sorry, but it seems impossible to believe. Not even in books do these things happen, because almost no one writes romances like this," she said, and again I shortened the distance with her.

"You think I'm handsome, sweetheart?" I asked, this time caressing her arm with my fingertips.

"Is that all you heard?" she scoffed, and I shook my head.

"I heard everything perfectly, and let me tell you that from the moment my gaze fell on you, it was something without explanation," I said, and she raised an eyebrow, unable to believe my words. "Okay, if you don't believe me, I can prove it. Accept being my companion tomorrow at Alan and Susy's wedding."

She didn't respond immediately, instead taking her time to answer.

"I'm not up for these things, Omar. I appreciate your interest in me, but this can't be," she said and quickly entered the building, leaving a feeling of abandonment inside me. This was only the first attempt of many; that woman would soon leave the market because she would be only for me.

I left and went to my apartment since it was very close by. After going inside, I took a shower, put on some sweatpants, walked to my bed, took my phone, and dialed.

"Cousin, what time is this?" Alan asked in a groggy voice.

"Are you already sleeping?"

"No, I'm eating dragon soup. If I'm answering you, it's because I'm not asleep."

"Ha, ha, very funny. I want to ask you a favor."

"What kind of favor requires calling at this ungodly hour?"

"I need to know everything you can tell me about Phoebe. The girl from today—Noah's mother."

There was a long pause on the other end. "Omar, listen to me carefully. That woman has suffered more than you can imagine. If you're only interested in having sex with her, look in another direction. She doesn't need another man treating her like garbage."

"It's not like that, Alan. I'm serious about—"

"Are you? Because she's been through hell. Kicked out of her house pregnant at eighteen, worked multiple jobs to survive, dealt with her crazy mother stalking her for years. She's built a life for herself and that kid with nothing but determination."

"I understand that, but—"

"Do you? Because she doesn't trust easily, and for good reason. Every man in her life has let her down. Except for me, but that's for another conversation."

Before I could respond, I heard rustling and then a different voice came on the line—sharp and threatening.

"Listen here, you overpaid pretty boy," Susy's voice cut through the phone like a knife. "If you hurt my friend, I swear I'm going to break your knees and you won't be able to play ever again. Don't mess with a pregnant woman's friend. We don't have patience for games."

"Susy, give me back the phone," I heard Alan protesting in the background.

"I'm serious, Omar. Phoebe has been through enough. She's finally stable, finally happy. If you're just looking for entertainment, find someone else."

"I'm not—"

"Good. Because if you break her heart, you'll have to deal with me. And trust me, I know where all the pressure points are in those fancy legs of yours."

"Susy, come down, princess" Alan's voice came through again, apparently having wrestled the phone back. "Now let us sleep. Seriously, Omar, think carefully about what you want here."

The call extended for a few more minutes as Alan filled in more details—how Phoebe had struggled in school, how she'd been manipulated by her parents, how hard she'd worked to create a safe life for Noah. But I already had many details I needed to put my conquest plan into action.

Though after hearing all of this, I wasn't sure "conquest" was the right word anymore. Because first, I had to help her *heal*.

The next morning, I got up as I normally did, but this time I would do something very bold. I knew the name of the soccer school Noah attended. I would make a surprise visit, hoping to see Noah and his mother.

I arrived much earlier than the students and their families began to arrive, finding myself in Director Paul's cramped office overlooking the practice fields. The room was a shrine to youth football—walls covered with team photos spanning decades, shelves lined with trophies of various sizes, and certificates proclaiming the academy's success in developing young talent. Through the large window behind his desk, I could see the pristine green fields where morning dew still glistened under the early sunlight.

Director Paul was a man in his fifties with graying hair and the weathered look of someone who had spent most of his life outdoors. His eyes held the sharp intelligence of someone who had seen thousands of hopeful young players come through his doors. He wore a simple tracksuit with the academy's logo, practical and unpretentious.

"Thank you very much for this favor, Director Paul," I said, adjusting my casual clothes—jeans and a simple polo shirt, trying to look approachable rather than like the celebrity footballer I was known to be.

"I'm the one who should be grateful," he replied, leaning back in his worn leather chair. "Having Omar Guzman visit our academy is an honor. The boys will be absolutely thrilled." He gestured toward the window where the empty fields awaited the day's activities. "Though I must admit, I'm curious about your sudden interest in our little academy. We're hardly the most prestigious school in the city."

I could hear the distant sound of car doors beginning to slam in the parking lot—the first families arriving for morning training sessions.

"So you're after the mother of one of the boys?" he asked with a wry smile, and I nodded.

"What can I say, director? You can't control the heart, and it was love at first sight," I crooned, and he laughed at me.

"What are their names?" he asked.

"He's called Noah, and his mother is Phoebe." The color drained from Director Paul's face, and he blinked several times as if trying to make sure he'd heard correctly. He slowly placed both hands flat on his desk, staring at me with a mixture of shock and something that looked almost like concern.

He whistled. "Well, good luck with that. Mrs. Santiago has a strong character; she already knows how to handle comments and even indecent proposals from other parents who come with their children." He glanced over my shoulder. "Look, there they come now. They're always one of the first to arrive."

I turned my gaze toward the same place he was looking. Phoebe approached with her hair tied in a ponytail, wearing sweatpants and a rock band top.

"Omar!" shouted Noah when he saw me. His mom just looked at me with a raised eyebrow.

"I offered to teach today's class, so for today, I will be your coach," I informed them.

She crossed her arms, turned, and walked to the bleachers. My eyes were glued to her back, her waist, her sculptural hips, and her bottom. God, how I wanted to touch it!

More people began to arrive, and in less than half an hour, cameras and journalists were all over me. I cursed under my breath because that wasn't my intention in coming here. But eventually the class ended, and everyone began to ask for my photograph and autograph.

For a brief moment, I looked up and could see how Phoebe and Noah were crossing the entrance gate. Damn, I couldn't miss them!

"I'm sorry, I promise to come back another time to sign your soccer balls and take pictures. Right now, I need to leave." It hurt me a little to see the disappointed faces of the children, but I needed to go after my sweetheart and get her to accept going with me to the wedding.

I sprinted out, looking for them in both directions until I spotted them and ran over.

"I can't believe you did this," Phoebe said with disbelief.

I offered her a grin. "I would do anything for you to accept my invitation."

After a moment of deliberating, she said, "Alright, I will go with you."

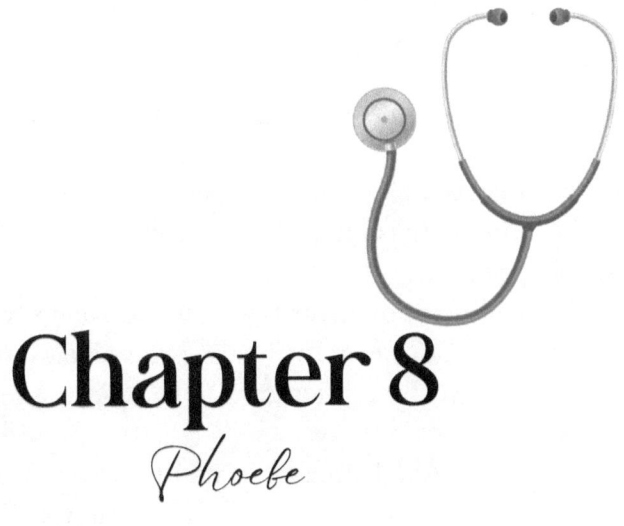

Chapter 8

Phoebe

My legs trembled just remembering what happened at the party. The embarrassment I felt from Mr. Guzman's question was beyond explanation. Add to that the player's hands on my back, his way of telling me to calm down using the word "Sweetheart" was like a fireball hitting my body. My entire body burned, but not in the same way as my cheeks.

As if that wasn't embarrassing enough, having a very willful son answering for me was the cherry on top of it all. I appreciated the intervention of Mrs. Guzman and Mrs. Jimena; however, being between my son and Omar Guzman didn't make the situation any easier.

When we said goodbye again, I didn't expect that man to be capable of following us and offering to take us to the apartment. I was afraid because, being a public figure, speculation would most likely arise, and that's the last thing I need at this point in my life.

All of this seemed like it was taken from a dream, a novel. During the journey, several topics came up that personally hurt me a lot. Omar, whatever way you look at it, was a stranger to us, and although sexy and deliciously appealing, he didn't need to have all the information about our lives.

Upon arriving at the building, I didn't know exactly how to feel; the truth is I needed a moment to breathe given what was happening.

My son went up after saying goodbye with a hug, which did nothing but tug at my heart. I was always moved by how easily my son could interact with people, something I didn't have.

Although I had already thanked the man for bringing us, I felt the need to know why he was so interested in me and if what he told his grandmother about asking me on a date was true. After a light conversation where my tongue expressed more than it should, everything became very uncomfortable.

"Okay, if you don't believe me, I can prove it. Accept being my companion tomorrow at Alan and Susy's wedding."

I didn't respond instantly; perhaps other women wouldn't hesitate to give an affirmative response, but I couldn't. The truth is that I didn't want all of this to get out of control, so for everyone's sake, I replied.

"I'm not up for these things, Omar. I appreciate your attention and your interest in me, but this can't be." Without giving him the opportunity to insist, I entered the building, and upon closing the apartment door, I leaned against it.

The truth is that if this was a dream, I didn't want to be awakened. How could a man like the great Omar Guzman Galeano be interested in me?

Sighing like a schoolgirl, I smiled and looked at the ceiling.

"You like Omar," Noah said, startling me and bringing me back to reality.

I hurried to correct him, "Don't say such things; you know it can't be possible."

"I don't think so, but the way you're smiling gives me that impression," he said with his arms crossed, his gaze inquisitive.

"None of that. Go brush your teeth; it's already too late for a bath. Remember we have to get up early for your training," I reminded him, eager to change the subject.

"Fine." He already knew how to do these things without my help.

So, I went to my room, took off my shoes, and walked to the mirror, where I looked at myself for a moment. I'd always been very confident about my body; I didn't mind others' opinions, but what Omar said left me analyzing my response.

I had belittled myself by saying that people like me couldn't fall in love with people like him. I needed to show a little more self-love; the value of people is what we carry inside, that is, what we are. Not because of how my life had been or for seeing myself alone with a child, much less using the context of my body for that.

The self-scolding lasted a few minutes until I went to take a bath to relax and rest, without success, because the proposal and the intense gaze of that imposing man didn't leave my dreams.

The next morning, I struggled to wake up after my restless night.

"Mom, it's time. We'll be late," said Noah, nudging my body.

Peeling open my eyes, I saw light coming through the window and rushed to get up and go with him to his practice. I took the sportswear I liked to wear; while he trained, I liked to take a walk around the field.

I wasn't the most loved among the mothers because they thought I did it to incite their husbands to sin; however, it was to exercise without losing sight of Noah.

We arrived almost at the same time; Noah liked to help the coach place the cones on the field, so he was always the first to arrive. Upon entering, from a distance, I could see the man who had tormented me all night. My son didn't hesitate to go to him, surprising the coach.

I couldn't believe what this man was capable of doing to see us again. The truth is that, although it bothered me, I had to admit it was a nice gesture. I smiled as I turned my back, after he confessed that he would give today's training.

This time I didn't want to do what I always did; I didn't want to attract anyone's attention or get the usual uncomfortable comments. As the training progressed, more and more people with reporter faces could be seen taking photos towards the field, especially where Omar was.

My chest tightened with each new arrival. I shifted restlessly on the bleachers, crossing and uncrossing my arms, unable to find a comfortable position. The familiar panic began creeping up my throat—that suffocating feeling of being watched, judged, dissected. I pulled my baseball cap lower, trying to hide behind the brim as cameras clicked incessantly around us.

My palms grew sweaty as I noticed other parents stealing glances in my direction, their whispered conversations punctuated by not-so-subtle head nods toward me. The weight of their curiosity felt crushing. I found myself holding my breath, my shoulders hunched defensively as if I could physically shield myself from their speculation.

When I saw Noah's face fall, watching how the other children and adults stole Omar's attention, completely forgetting about the boy who had been so excited just moments before, something protective and desperate rose in my chest. The sight of my son's disappointment, combined with the growing circus around us, made my decision easy.

I couldn't let Noah become collateral damage in whatever media frenzy was brewing. With trembling hands, I pointed toward the exit, my heart hammering against my ribs as I prepared to do what I always did—run before things got worse.

Noah turned to look at Omar, but he wasn't looking at us, so I had no choice but to take his bag and leave with him.

"Don't be sad; you know everyone got excited to see him and wants his autograph and photo," I assured Noah, noticing his head down in defeat as we walked.

"I know, but I don't know if I'll be able to see him again and have the opportunity to ask for his advice on how to make a good left-footed shot like the ones he makes," Noah whined, frowning as he looked at me.

I smiled, but seconds later a shiver ran down my back when I heard Omar call us.

I couldn't believe what was happening, and I let him know. He asked me again if I could go with him to the wedding, and this time I couldn't refuse. He had taken the time to come to that place, for us and to please my Noah.

"Alright, I'll go with you," I finally gave in, and the first thing he did was take my hand and press his lips to my cheek. My cheeks blushed red in response.

He grinned. "Thank you, sweetheart. I'll pick you up half an hour before the wedding."

I nodded my head in affirmation, seeing him wink at Noah and bump his fist before he said goodbye to us. As he walked away, I turned to my son.

"The good thing is that if you don't like him, he likes you. So someone will have to give in." I brought my hand to his head and messed up his reddish hair. He hated when I did that.

"I think we need to call your Aunt Aida. This is an emergency." He nodded, took my hand, and pulled me until we reached our apartment building. I sent a text message to Aida, asking if she was inside, that I urgently needed her, and it wasn't even five minutes before someone was knocking at my door. The advantage of her being my next door neighbor.

"What happened? Did Noah get hurt during training?" The woman entered like lightning directly to see Noah, who was laughing at her, seeing how she checked his knees and ankles.

"I don't need help; it's my mom," he said, pointing his finger at me.

"Oh, what happened?" she asked, scrutinizing my face. She pursed her lips. "You have good color. You're not pale or anything."

Noah laughed. "Omar Guzman invited my mom to be his companion for the wedding she's going to today."

Aida opened and closed her mouth in shock. "Omar Guzman? The player from the colchoneros? Ah! Wait, is it serious?" she asked, and both Noah and I nodded. "How did you meet him?"

"It's a story I'll gladly tell you, but for now, I need your advice to choose the best option for dress, hairstyle, and makeup. Because my brain is not braining right now and only you can help," I said, and with a smile, she nodded her head in affirmation. Aida worked in a beauty salon during her free time from university to pay for medical school.

She clapped her hands together. "First of all, I imagine you with brown hair, a couple of waves in your hair, and a black dress."

My eyes widened. "Black? It's a wedding."

"Yes, which I imagine is at night, and at the same time, it's the wedding of your ex. You need to close cycles and possibly start new ones. We don't know where the dress will end up—"

I stopped her by gently placing my hand over her mouth. She burst out laughing.

"Alright, work your magic," I said with a smile.

"First, let's look for the dress in your closet. The one I gave you that you've never worn."

I couldn't help but stare at her, mouth agape; that dress had a huge back neckline that scared me a lot, as it showed almost down to the lower back. It was a maxi dress made of satin fabric, fitted to the body.

"I can't wear this," I protested, showing the dress after grabbing it from the rack.

Noah came and examined it. "I don't see anything wrong with it."

Aida beamed. "See? Your son approves. Now, let's go find what we need to change your hair color and my tools in my apartment."

We went to the store where they sell all the necessary beauty implements. We bought food on the way, and Aida began to work her magic on me.

After almost four hours of preparation, makeup, and dressing, I looked without being able to recognize the woman in front of me and reflected in the mirror. Aida had cut my bangs so they fell to the height of my eyebrows, then dyed my hair a chestnut brown that looked very pretty. My long hair was loose, at my request, and would help me cover a bit of what the dress didn't cover.

"You look beautiful," Noah gushed, and I smiled. I wanted to shower him with kisses for the compliment, but Aida stood between the two of us.

"No kisses and whining. Go, the man must already be waiting for you," she urged, handing me a small purse where only my phone, a lipstick, and my ID would fit.

I turned to Noah. "Behave yourself and don't give Aida too much work."

"More than you've given me? I don't think so, go calm. Enjoy it a lot. Behave very badly," she said, slapping my behind.

"Aida!" I exclaimed.

"I'm just preparing the ground," she said innocently, holding her hands up.

Noah smirked. "Have a good time. And another thing, I wouldn't mind having Omar as a stepfather," he hurriedly said before running off to his room.

I rolled my eyes. "Listen to him. He knows what he wants and needs." I shook my head; these two would drive me crazy. I left the apartment with much fear. My hands were sweating, my stomach was contracted, and I was even trembling at times, just like a Chihuahua dog.

I reached the entrance of the building, and there he was with his back turned, wearing a suit that perfectly embraced his pronounced muscles. He turned with a smile before his mouth fell open, and he stood frozen, staring at me.

I took a couple of steps, and the man was still stunned. "Is something wrong?" I asked, and he began to cough, hitting his chest.

"You've left me breathless, sweetheart. What beauty of a woman I have in front of me. I love your hair," he complimented, walking around me and biting his lips when he looked at my back. "Let's go, because I don't want to commit something utterly mad with you here and now." He took my hand and opened the door of his sports car for me. Then he got in and set off.

During the journey, neither of us said anything. But just before we arrived, he sought my hand and brought it to his lips, without taking his gaze from mine. My cheeks burned; I should have told him a thousand things, but the truth was that I didn't want to. His words awakened something in me, and I liked that sensation.

"I think I'm in love," he said before getting out of the car.

My heart accelerated, and as much as I wanted to tell him not to get excited over a few nice words, I couldn't; these emotions were something I couldn't control.

He opened the door for me, and I said nothing. Upon exiting, we walked without letting go of each other's hands until we reached where the guests were already starting to sit. It seemed we were almost late to arrive.

There were many people; we greeted Omar's parents, who were in front of us.

"You look beautiful, Phoebe. I like the change! The brown looks beautiful on you," gushed Mrs. Patricia.

I flushed. "Thank you very much, ma'am."

"Call me Patricia," she said, offering me a wink.

Her husband smiled politely at me and turned his full attention back to his wife and the other guests. "You're already part of the family," he said, and I couldn't help but laugh at his comment.

"One date doesn't mean we're already a family, Mr. Guzman," I deflected, but he shook his head.

"What you don't know is that when a Galeano loves, they do it from the first moment, with intensity, with devotion, with passion, and forever. If you want such an intense love, here's mine because you've had it since yesterday at your disposal," Omar said in my ear, and I couldn't help but let out a moan at the revolution I felt inside.

This man was going to kill me with his words. He sought my hand once more and pressed a kiss to my skin.

The wedding march began to sound, and the ceremony began. The wedding was very beautiful and emotional. The vows that Alan read to Susy touched my heart to the point of tears. There was no doubt that their love was intense, pure, and sincere.

A handkerchief wiped my tears without me noticing.

Omar murmured, "Don't cry, precious. I swear that when we get married, it will be even more beautiful."

"I think so much training under the sun is already melting your brain. No one has agreed to marry you." I snorted.

"No, but I'm sure someone will soon, and I'll make that someone very happy."

I rolled my eyes. If sweetness had a name and surname, it was Omar Guzman.

The reception began soon after, and I didn't deny myself the opportunity to have a couple of drinks and dance with Omar, who did it very well.

Like two teenagers, we went to the most secluded part of the place, and Omar gave me a kiss. That wine-flavored kiss finished awakening my body, which was previously asleep; now I felt the need for his caresses to deepen.

I needed to get out of there, or else I could do something crazy. Upon returning to the bar, I took three shots of tequila, one after another, trying to put out this fire that Omar had ignited.

Until my brain began to feel hazy, and I felt slightly dizzy.

"Do you want us to leave?" Omar asked me. "You shouldn't have taken that so quickly."

"Yes, I don't want to embarrass Alan and Susy."

He nodded and helped me get to the car. I felt very embarrassed for not saying goodbye to almost anyone, but I didn't want to create more rumors than they would possibly talk about.

"Do you want me to take you to your home?" he suggested.

I shook my head. "No, Noah shouldn't see me like this."

"How about we go to my apartment? It's a couple of blocks from yours." I was too dazed to really listen to what he said, so I just nodded.

The journey to his apartment was not much different from the previous one, aside from how Omar had his hand on my thigh. The tips of his fingers made circular movements, sending chills through my body.

We soon arrived at his building, and thanks to having the windows open, the air helped me gain a bit of sobriety.

We went up to his apartment, and upon closing the door, he took me by the waist and began to kiss me again. This time it wasn't a kiss of recognition; this was to activate every drop of endorphins in our bodies.

Until he moved away.

"Come, I'm going to give you some water and some clothes to rest in."

"I thought that..." I trailed off, my heart and body racing with the need for more.

He gave me a wry look. "And you're not wrong, sweetheart, but you're drunk, and I don't want to take advantage of you."

"What if I tell you I'm not so drunk anymore?" I offered, but he shook his head.

"I'll believe it when your eyes return to their orbit and their normal color. I'll prepare you a coffee in the meantime, and we can talk a bit about ourselves. How does that sound?" he said, walking to his kitchen, which was immaculately clean, and turning on the coffee maker.

We sat on his couch as it brewed, and he asked me to tell him what had happened with Alan and why our relationship didn't work. It hurt a lot to relive that stage of my life, but if he wanted to take me to his bed or have something serious with me, it didn't matter to tell him.

I narrated everything, and tears came from my eyes at times, but I had already opened Pandora's box and couldn't release my secrets halfway.

"And that's how I ended up alone with my Noah. It cost me a lot to clean from my mind and body all the wounds of the past. Some are now just scars that cannot be seen, but some still hurt."

He placed a coffee mug in my hands, and I took a sip, basking in how it warmed my hands.

"Come here," he said after I finished half of the drink, patting his legs. I didn't refuse and sat on his legs after placing the mug on the table beside him. "No, sweetheart. Put one leg on each side."

I looked at him with fear, but that energy and dominance I liked. I did it, and his hands went to my bare back, which he caressed.

"That's your past, your history, your process; that will never change, but we will take the good out of all that. This beautiful woman who is on my legs, the beautiful warrior who made the decision to be a mother at such an early age. To assume alone the responsibility not only for her life but also for another being. You deserve all my respect, admiration, and—"

There was so much emotion I felt from his words that I had to hide my emotion in his lips, cutting his sentence off with a kiss. We separated and looked into each other's eyes.

"Are you not drunk anymore?" he asked, and I shook my head. "Are you sure?" he asked again, and in response, taking advantage of the position we were in, I gathered my dress and lifted it over my head, leaving my breasts in his view, as I didn't have a bra.

"Is this sure enough for you?" I said, feeling how his mouth went down to one of my nipples.

His strong hands palmed my behind and then squeezed it, causing me to release a loud moan. "If you knew how good it feels to be able to touch your body…"

"This must be one of your fetishes. Do you do it often?" I said without thinking.

"No, but it's inevitable to think of a thousand ways to appreciate this delight. The way I'm going to eat all of this, especially your sweet mouth when you turn to look at me asking for more," he said, approaching my ear.

Hearing him say such things only accelerated my heart and wet parts of my body that hadn't had the deserved or necessary attention. A second later, I felt his tongue running down my neck.

"Today I'm going to eat this sweet treat, suck and bite, and I'm not letting go until I reach its juicy filling."

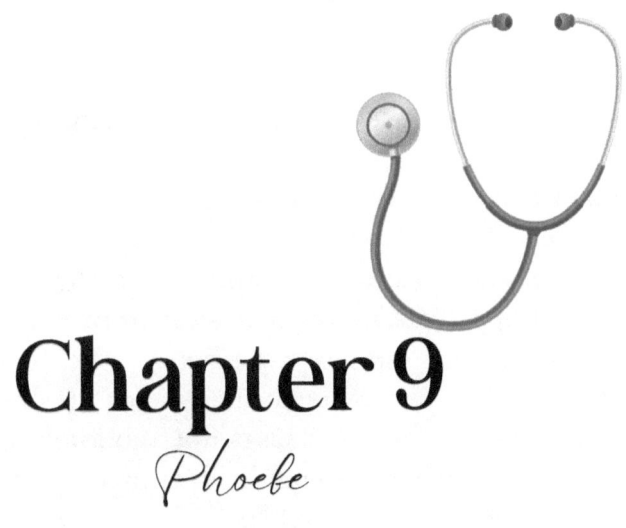

Chapter 9
Phoebe

"Ahh!" I moaned, not from pain but from pleasure when the sweet-talking man squeezed my nipple with his lips.

"Yes, sweetheart, don't suppress your desire. I want to hear you scream in all possible frequencies," he crooned, then did the same to the other side. Omar stood up with me around his waist without much effort, and my eyes never left his for a second. "What will be the perfect place to eat a dessert like this?" he mused, looking toward the bedroom door or the kitchen.

"I enjoy my desserts in my bed watching a movie," I said, clenching my teeth as I felt the tip of his fingers pressing my center.

He smiled and walked to his bedroom to delicately place my body on the bed with black sheets. Then he separated from me and began to unbutton his jacket slowly, never removing his sensual eyes from my body. The jacket ended up in a corner of the room.

"Alexa, play music to seduce a sweet treat," he commanded.

"I'm sorry, I didn't get that," the device replied. I couldn't help but laugh out loud.

"Alexa, play a seductive song," he said, and this time she followed the order and played a song that just listening to it made every hair on my body stand on end.

He seemed satisfied with the selection of the smart device, and with a smile and to the rhythm of "River" by Bishop Briggs, he began to sway from side to side.

"An erotic dance, sweetheart?" he teased without stopping, now removing the buttons of his shirt, where little by little his pectorals and his defined abdomen could be seen.

I bit my lower lip as I gradually appreciated the body that I would enjoy and that would enjoy mine. I hoped not to regret it in the morning, but as Aida said, I would enjoy all of this to the maximum.

"It's not every day that a sexy soccer player like you dances for me," I said, placing my elbows on the bed to be able to appreciate more of the show.

He removed his shirt, which ended up behind me, and then lunged at me like a hungry wolf. "I'll be the only one to do it, because all of this," he said, passing the back of his hand from my cheek, my neck, my breast, my abdomen, and my behind, where he squeezed hard, "is only for me, and I'm not willing to share."

"Show me what I've been missing in these nine years," I gasped, and I mentally kicked myself when I realized that, because of the alcohol still in my body, I had spoken too much.

He separated and looked at me as if something had appeared on my face. "You haven't had sex in nine years?!" he exclaimed.

My cheeks were burning at that. That information shouldn't have come out of my mouth.

"Yes... since the incident with Noah's father, I haven't been with any man, neither in a relationship nor in a sexual encounter," I admitted, avoiding his piercing gaze.

"And I awakened that desire to ride the bicycle again?" he joked.

I nodded my head in affirmation, and he took my face between his hands, squeezing my cheeks.

"Well, sweetheart, it will be an honor for me to teach you again how to make the art of love," he said, then devoured my lips with the same intensity as he was doing on the couch. His mouth went down from my lips to my neck.

"Yes, please make it worth it," I said when his lips reached my breasts, and I thanked that, at Aida's insistence, I was waxed. So when he put his hand within my underwear, I felt nothing but pleasure.

"You're so wet, baby, and I want to taste," he groaned, pulling back to remove my panties. "How beautiful," he whispered, then I felt the heat and moisture of his tongue on me. That was like a current that shook my entire body.

His licks began to be faster, and his hands squeezed my thighs firmly. I bit my lips, but I could no longer hold back my moans. I began to moan louder as the heat and pressure in my belly began to be increasingly intense. Until I melted on his tongue, which didn't stop moving, causing strong spasms in my body.

I tried to close my legs, trapping his face, and it was at that moment that he moved away. He stood up and began to unbutton his pants. I tried to catch my breath, but seeing the thing hanging between his legs made my breathing stop altogether.

I had never seen anything like it in my life, possibly because the guys I had been with still needed growth since we were very young, but for all the sugar in the world, this was way too big.

"Is something wrong?" he asked, raising an eyebrow.

I nervously shook my head. I wanted to say many things, but I bit my tongue so that nothing would come out of it.

He smirked. "Relax, I'll take my time not to hurt you," he said, and without further ado, he settled between my legs.

He took my face and kissed me slowly, and I startled slightly when I felt his thick glans between my vaginal lips. Then he plundered my mouth with his tongue, wanting to distract me from noticing how he pushed a little inward and felt how my body was opening for him. He continued advancing slowly; my insides were trying to take the necessary diameter to accommodate all his thickness. I knew it would hurt, but I was enjoying it.

"More," I gasped when the desperation of having him completely inside me was winning.

His phallus retreated only to be able to push with much more force; I could feel butterflies fluttering in my stomach. Then he did it again, and I let out a cry of pain that made me close my eyes tightly.

He remained motionless, and I could feel how the inside of my pussy squeezed his member tightly. I felt so full.

"I think I just took your virginity again," he said, and by instinct, I tightened my interior, making him close his eyes and hiss.

The burning and heat I felt was indescribable, but it was driving me crazy; I wanted him to move. He came out of me and thrusted again, making me moan as I felt him going deeper and deeper.

"Give me everything you have," I begged, as I could feel that he wasn't completely inside me yet.

"Are you sure?" he asked, doubtful that I couldn't bear it. I nodded, opening my legs to give him more access to me. "Better get on your knees, sweetheart." He separated from me so I could turn around.

He spanked my behind hard, but it was far from causing pain because it was my interior that was the recipient of that excitement. His hands separated my buttocks, and I almost screamed when I felt his tongue playing with my center again. This time his tongue explored absolutely everything in its path, and I shuddered as I felt him concentrate his attention on that forbidden place. I dug my nails into the bed, squeezing the sheets. Was it possible to feel so much with so little?

"There's no doubt that you're exquisite, sweetheart. Now relax for your wolf, Little Red Riding Hood, be a good girl and let yourself go," he said, positioning himself between my legs and beginning to enter slowly but with more depth.

I could feel my interior stretching to receive him, squeezing tightly. The thrusts went from slow to faster and deeper. His strong hands squeezed and slapped my behind hard. At this point, I was screaming like crazy, enjoying all this that was new to me. I had never felt so much in a sexual act; Omar was teaching me another way of seeing sex.

"Omar!" I shouted when he brought me to press my back against his chest, squeezing my breasts hard. My buttocks hit his pelvis, making a very morbid and exciting sound.

"Yes, baby, that's my name," he crooned, moving with more force.

I clenched my teeth when one of his hands moved to stimulate my clitoris; my entire center was wet with my juices, and that made his penetrations much more accurate, and his fingers had enough lubrication to do whatever they wanted.

"Please, Omar," I mewled, feeling a strong orgasm burning everything in its path inside me. "Aaah!" I screamed; my sight blurred, the pleasure too much.

He held me tightly in his arms while letting out a grunt that came out of his soul.

I let my body fall on the bed, but Omar seemed not to want to give me rest.

"Don't fall asleep; you need at least one orgasm for each lost year, sweetheart. You already have two, so seven are missing, and I want more of that juicy filling," he said, looking directly at my spirit because my body came back to life wanting to feel more.

Omar seemed insatiable, because after releasing inside me, he continued thrusting without rest.

My heart was beating fast, as it wasn't just a simple mechanical act of entering and exiting until he was satisfied. He made sure that I felt the most infinite pleasure by implementing different positions, caresses, kisses, grips, and even words to make me vibrate.

I eventually lost count of how many orgasms we had achieved together. I was only aware that Omar was penetrating me in a sublime way and that he was taking his time doing it.

A smile never left his face; he also seemed to feel something different during our union. I wanted to believe that this moment was important, and he wanted to make it special for both of us.

I had never felt so worshipped, important, desired, and like a complete amazon, while at the same time, it felt incredible to hear a man like him snort in such a bestial way.

We both fell on the bed, which was a complete mess, just like us, but we didn't care much. I settled on his chest, and listening to his pounding heart, I fell asleep, but not before hearing him say:

"Rest, my love."

That "my love" made me suddenly open my eyes. I raised my face to look at him, but he already had his eyes closed.

My attention went to the window, which was already beginning to show a soft blue. I urgently needed to know about Noah and go to the bathroom, so I waited a moment longer for Omar to be deeply asleep.

Slowly, I managed to get out of the bed, and upon standing up, I could feel pain all over my body, especially in my hips, and a burning sensation in my crotch. I got to the bathroom, and not wanting to make too much noise to not wake him up, I took a bath towel, moistened it with water from the sink, and began to clean my body.

"Shit!" I exclaimed and covered my mouth. We hadn't taken precautions, but I made a mental note to take the pill when I reached the hospital.

Once clean, I left the bathroom and remembered that I had left my dress in the living room. I looked toward the back of the bathroom where Omar's clothes could be seen. I went there and took a t-shirt, a hoodie, and sweatpants. My hair was a mess, so I also took a cap.

I changed to leave the bathroom, finding Omar lying face-down. His naked back was something very embarrassing to see, as I saw the marks my nails had left. I wanted to think that he wouldn't look for me again and that he would forget what happened. At the end of the day, I imagined that's all he wanted anyway: sex.

With that thought, I left the room. I looked for my purse and found it on a small table beside the entrance. I took out my phone and saw that it was minutes to six in the morning. I had several calls and messages from Aida. The last call was from fifteen minutes ago; her last message was five minutes ago and was a link to a gossip page that just seeing the small image froze my entire body; everything was worse when I opened it and read the headline.

"The Colchoneros forward seems to have a family and a relationship with a mysterious and curvy woman."

There was a photo of when he'd accompanied us home the night of the rehearsal, one of us laughing with him outside the training, and a kiss of us yesterday at the party.

The sensation of how I felt in the past came back to take power over me, overwhelming my body to the point of making my hands shake. I needed to get out of here before someone saw me.

Being so early in the morning, I didn't meet anyone when I left the building, walking quickly and with anxiety to my apartment. Upon opening the door with my emergency key, I let myself fall on the couch and covered my face with my hands.

"Phoebe?" Aida asked, coming out of my room. She ran when she saw the state I was in. "What happened?"

I lowered my hands from my face to look at her with a raised eyebrow and emphasize for her to look at my clothes.

She paused. "I understand, everything happened, but why are you like this? Did he hurt you?" she said, and I shook my head.

"No, it was all so beautiful and special that it seems hard to believe."

"So, what was the problem? Was it what I just sent you?" she clarified.

I nodded my head in affirmation.

She pursed her lips. "I don't think it's a problem; the guy is just making a statement, and that's it. Besides, it was he who insisted with you."

A part of me calmed down; Aida was right, but I still felt fear, and that terror became reality. My phone rang, and it was an unknown number. Aida insisted that I take the call because it could be from the hospital.

"Is it true that you have a relationship with Omar Guzman?" said a voice on the other end of the phone.

All the blood left my face. "It's none of your business." I hung up the phone, and that only increased my fear.

"Who was it?" Aida asked, taking my hands in hers.

"Steven."

Chapter 10

Omar

Phoebe had captivated me a day before my cousin's wedding, but her new image changed, mainly the new hair color and that dress; both wreaked havoc on my chest and groin. The beauty that this woman exuded had no limits; I couldn't believe how she was capable of mixing innocence and sensuality at the same time. She didn't know it, but she had me at her feet.

Last night was the best I've had in my life. My plan was to return to her apartment after the party, but when I took her to my place, I dedicated myself entirely to enjoying my time with my sweetheart.

The softness of her skin, her full lips, her moans, the malleability of her breasts, her bottom bouncing against my pelvis with each thrust I gave her in certain positions… it all created an insatiable appetite for her.

I loved her all night long, almost until seeing the dawn.

I remember very well having gone to bed embracing her body, but I woke up alone on the bed and heard loud knocks on the door of my apartment.

I quickly got up to the bathroom, took a light shower, looked for boxers and sweatpants. I went to the door, since the person kept knocking with great insistence.

"What were you doing in that children's training field?" asked Alexis when I answered.

"My future son is training there," I said, awaiting his reaction.

"What?!" he shouted.

"Exactly what I said. Do you believe in love at first sight, Alexis? Because I'm in love, and to be honest, I think I've found the right one. She has an eight-year-old son, and that's why I was there. If I want to win over the hen, I have to win over the chick first."

"Are you aware of the impact this will have on your career?" he inquired, and the truth was that he was already annoying me.

"My personal life has never affected my performance as a professional. Let me handle my affairs, and you handle yours," I snapped in response.

"You know I've never meddled in your personal life, but have you thought about whether your relationship with that woman could bring problems to her?" he said, handing over the newspaper and his tablet.

I could see the headlines in many of the papers, and I flinched.

"I can assure you that she's not having a good time. There are reporters outside her building, and they haven't let her leave for work."

When those words left Alexis's mouth, I returned to my room to put on more clothes. I wanted to take my lucky cap, since I didn't have a chance to fix my hair, but it wasn't in its place. I ended up grabbing any other one and without wasting time, left the apartment, ignoring Alexis's words.

He had no choice but to get into the passenger seat. "Are you sure this woman is the right one?" he said, making a derogatory gesture.

"Yes, why do you ask?" I said, gripping the steering wheel tightly.

"I don't know, it's very strange that out of so many women, you want to get involved with one like her." I hoped he wasn't daring to go into that territory, because I would throw him from the moving car. "Don't think it's about her body; I'm saying it because of her son. There are so many women who don't have any kind of commitment, who could perfectly be your ideal girl."

"She is the right one, I know that. I forbid you from making any kind of comment about her."

He nodded; fortunately, I was parking the car a few meters from the building entrance. Reporters were everywhere, and upon seeing me, they didn't hesitate to approach, taking photos and throwing their questions.

I shouted at them, "I ask you to leave here; you are disturbing the peace of those who live inside this building. If your presence here is due to the latest rumors, I would like to clarify that I met Miss Santiago a few weeks ago, and I am trying to win her heart. I accept no more questions at the moment."

I continued walking through the corridors of the apartment building. The reporters began to leave, with fewer and fewer remaining.

Seeing all this, I began the journey to Phoebe's apartment to tell her that everything would be alright; however, I didn't expect to find a guy grabbing her by the arm while shaking her violently.

I couldn't resist the urge to kill him. I approached and landed a strong blow to his face, sending him flying to the ground.

"Dare to touch her or my son, and you'll be left without hands!" I snarled.

"Who do you think you are by saying 'my son'? Noah is my son," he fired back, and it was then I recognized him. The guy stood up and straightened his jacket.

"Steven, a man like you doesn't deserve to be called a father. You've never worried about or been interested in your son," I snapped.

"That doesn't change the fact that he carries my blood and my genes. I won't allow you to be near him, and you..." He spun to face Phoebe. "You already know what you must do. I wouldn't mind fighting and challenging your parental rights if necessary. This punch will cost you dearly."

She gaped at him. "You signed away your parental rights; you can't take Noah from me."

"Your rights can be revoked if a judge deems it appropriate for Noah. You're a single mother who leaves him alone or with your neighbor just to go roll around with this guy, an aggressive man who was capable of hitting me in front of Noah."

I turned my head toward the apartment door where Noah was watching everything fearfully.

Steven continued, "Is that the best example for Noah? Outside, it's full of reporters ready to attack you and Noah, all because of your bad decisions. I can give him a home; I'm married and have stability in my life, while you... were, are, and will always be a mess."

Phoebe threw up her hands. "I'm a mess thanks to you! You made me this way from the day I told you about my pregnancy. Don't forget what you did to me that day; there's still a medical and phone record, and several witnesses who can testify how your intention in throwing me into the pool was to kill me and my child. You knew I couldn't swim, and if it weren't for your grandmother, I would most likely have ended my life in that pool that day!"

A blinding flash went off inches from our faces. Instinctively, I yanked Phoebe's hand and pulled her through the entrance of her apartment building, slamming the door behind us.

"Stay inside; I'll solve this," I commanded, my voice harder than I intended. The last thing I needed was for her to get caught up in whatever media circus was brewing outside.

Through the glass door, I could see Alexis already in action, his large frame blocking the photographer who had somehow infiltrated the building's security. The man's camera was being confiscated with the kind of professional efficiency that made it clear this wasn't Alexis's first rodeo with overeager paparazzi.

"You deserved that punch. Did it hurt that a man like me could give them the life they deserve?" I challenged.

Steven sneered. "Phoebe is my woman."

I couldn't control myself and landed another punch, this time to his abdomen and without witnesses around us. I grabbed him by the collar of his shirt to look him in the eyes.

"From the day you did everything she just said, she ceased to be your woman. Having a child together doesn't give you rights over her. She's not your woman; now she belongs to herself and when she uses my last name it will be my woman, and this time, she has someone who puts all his power at her disposal to destroy you. She's no longer alone; stay the fuck away from her and Noah." I released his shirt and left him there in the middle of the hallway alone.

I opened the apartment door, went inside, and Phoebe was on the couch, a glass of water in her hand, and with her other hand wiping her tears.

Noah rushed over to hug me. "Thank you for defending my mom," he said, trembling, and then let me go so he could run to his mother and hug her.

"Aida, could you take Noah to your apartment for a moment? I need to talk to Omar." The seriousness with which those words came out of Phoebe's mouth was very discouraging. Aida looked at me, and I nodded.

"Noah, come," she said, and he obeyed.

I went to sit beside Phoebe as they left. I tried to put my hand on hers, but she stood up, walking toward the kitchen.

"It's better that you don't come back here and that we don't see each other again," she said, and it was like a dart straight to my chest.

"What do you mean?" I asked, and she turned to look at me.

"Omar, I appreciate your attention and... the night we spent together, but it's better if we go back to our lives."

"You can't say it so coldly. Didn't you feel anything for me yesterday while we were making love?" I demanded, my voice trembling.

"No one can fall in love in two days; I remind you that's how long we've known each other. I can't afford to lose custody of my child over a fuck with you. Steven is very capable of doing what he said. I can't take that risk or live with the fear of losing Noah over something insignificant."

Wow, I had never treated a woman badly or said these words to a woman in my life, but now I felt in full bloom how painful it feels.

"I understand you, but let me tell you something. We may have only known each other for two days, but they have been more than enough for me to realize what I want and feel for you. I'm in love with you, Phoebe."

She laughed bitterly. "Don't you understand that I don't love you back? And that I don't want you in my life?" she said.

I approached her and took her hands. "Look me in the eyes and tell me that these last two days have meant nothing to you," I challenged.

Her gaze averted to the floor. Until she looked at me with her eyes full of tears.

"Please, I don't want them to take Noah away from me for something that possibly won't last. You will eventually get bored of me, and Noah and I will suffer the most," she said, and I brought her to my chest, hugged her, and gave a kiss on her forehead.

"I understand your fear; let me help you," I pleaded, caressing her head.

"Don't insist, Omar. I don't want us to hurt each other. We're in time to stop what's happening."

I smiled. Subtly, and without realizing it, she was accepting that she was beginning to feel something for me.

"But why don't you understand that the only thing I want is your love?" I said, and she pulled back.

"You're crazy. How can you love someone in only two days?"

"Do you believe in love at first sight?" I said, trying to make her understand.

"It doesn't matter if I believe in love in general, Omar. What I believe and what I'm clear about is that I won't sacrifice my son, who is my greatest treasure, for something that has no guarantees of being forever. I need to be alone; I'm going to ask you to leave."

I refused. "Phoebe, it's just that—"

"Leave!" she exclaimed, exasperated, running her hands through her hair. The door opened, and Noah ran to my side.

"You're being very mean to Omar; he just wants to help," Noah whined.

I couldn't stay there insisting; she needed her moment to think and analyze things. What happened with Steven, the incident with the media, and my official confession was a lot to take in.

"No, don't disrespect your mother. She feels overwhelmed, and it's normal after what happened. I'm going to leave so I don't make things worse. Take good care of her," I said, walking to the exit without turning to look at Phoebe.

Noah followed my steps, and reaching the door, he stopped me.

"Could you give me your phone number?" he asked, extending his phone toward me.

I nodded, punching the number in and handing the device back. Then I lowered myself to his height. "If you need anything or if Steven bothers you again, don't hesitate to call or send a message."

"Will you leave without reconciling with my mother?" he asked, and I sighed.

"You're too young to understand many things; I can only tell you that it's valid for her to feel the way she does. She's afraid of losing you, and I'm not going to battle against that. Your mother would do anything to not be separated from you," I said.

"Okay, but you have to promise that you won't date any other woman."

Chapter 11

Phoebe

"Mom! Mom! We're in the news," said Noah, interrupting my one-hour nap before going to work.

"I know, honey," I mumbled, feeling him climb onto the bed.

"Does that mean Omar will be my dad?" he asked hopefully, causing me to completely come out of my lethargy.

"No, Noah, Omar is a stranger to us."

He pouted. "But you spent the whole night with him."

All the blood rushed from my face. Oh boy. What was I going to do with this child?

"That doesn't mean anything, Noah," I tried to defend.

"That's what they call it now," he commented, rolling his eyes.

"Whatever your head is plotting, it's impossible," I said, stroking his hair.

"But..." he trailed off as I caressed his cheek and patted my shoulder, inviting him to lie down.

"I know very well what you were thinking, but he only invited me out. It doesn't mean it's for life. What if he just wanted me so he wouldn't go to the wedding alone and then never call me again?" I asked, and he shook his head.

"No, Omar looks at you in a very strange way. I don't know, it's like seeing Puss in Boots in the Shrek movie. It's obvious he wants something with you, and you'll see that I'm right," he said, sitting up and quickly standing. "I have faith in Omar; you know I have a sixth sense with people, and this one is a very good one," he said, leaving my room.

I shook my head, looking at the ceiling. "It seems you've also fallen in love with my son," I said out loud.

"And then you say it's nothing," said Noah from the door, then his footsteps were heard running to his room. He loved to listen behind doors; I wasn't surprised that he knew what happened last night.

Last night, Omar took me like a ragdoll, and I had the pain to prove it. To the point where I could still feel his grip on my hips, and I couldn't sit without feeling pain in my behind or between my legs; however, I felt more alive than ever.

Before the nap, I had taken a bath, so when I got up, I just fixed my uniform and my hair. The apartment door opened with more force than usual, revealing Aida struggling with grocery bags, her face flushed and her movements sharp with frustration.

"I don't think you want to go outside," Aida said breathlessly, dropping the bags with a loud thud and immediately turning to lock the door behind her—not just the regular lock, but the deadbolt too. Her hands were shaking slightly as she fumbled with the chain lock.

Her usually perfectly styled hair was disheveled, strands escaping from her ponytail, and there was a wild look in her eyes that I'd never seen before. She kept glancing toward the windows as if expecting someone to appear there, her whole body radiating nervous energy.

I furrowed my brows in confusion. "Why?"

"There are a bunch of cameramen and reporters downstairs," she explained, and I went to look through the peephole.

"Oh my god, but I have to go to work!" I exclaimed, trying to breathe.

"Well, go calmly. I'll stay to take care of this louse," she said, messing up my son's hair. I approached and stole a spoonful of cereal from where he was eating at the table.

"Mom," he whined, looking at me with a raised eyebrow.

I blew him a kiss and left the apartment. I could see the people before opening the door. I breathed deeply and tried not to lose my calm. I opened the door and began walking to one side, ignoring the presence of the crowd.

"There she is!" exclaimed one, and without giving me space or time for anything, I already had many people around me with their camera flashes on me.

"How long have you known Omar Guzman? Is the child Omar's son? Did Omar abandon you? How old is the child?" Questions fired off back-to-back, taking me off guard.

"The child is my son and has nothing to do with Omar Guzman," said a voice behind me: Steven. He took my hand and almost pushed me out from among the reporters. We entered the building again, and being alone with him in the hallway, it began.

"See what you caused?" he exclaimed.

"It's not your problem what happens here, Steven. I remind you that you're a married man and have no rights over either of us. It's time that you give your wife the right to be the mother of your children and that you forget about us," I said, and he smiled.

He stepped closer, making me back up against the wall, placing his hand above my shoulder. "How about we give Noah a sibling instead?" he hissed, moving the collar of my shirt.

With my hands, I covered myself immediately because I had some bite marks made by Omar. I pushed him away forcefully, and he moved away from me, and I began to climb the stairs.

"So, at the first opportunity, you got into Omar's bed?" he challenged, and I tried to ignore him. "I don't know why I'm surprised. You've always been easy; you don't even reach the level of a prostitute because at least prostitutes charge, and you do it for free."

I turned to give him a slap; Steven's words no longer affected me at all. "Get out of here, Steven," I seethed, walking back to the apartment.

"What? Does the truth hurt?" he taunted, and I didn't want to keep listening to him, so I opened the door of my apartment, and he tried to grab my arm forcefully but ended up with a right hook that he received from Omar. Who I wasn't planning to see again.

All the happiness and calm with which I lay down this morning went to hell in a moment. My nerves shot to the limit.

The argument, threats, exchange of blows, and among other things that came out of Steven's mouth, and that in one way or another made me come to my senses. In the end, I had everything, and that included having to let Omar go, without being able to have him. My son was the most important thing, and I wasn't willing to lose him for my nascent relationship with Omar.

I had to confront Omar and... many of the things I said to him hurt me more than him, but it was the most sensible thing to do in a situation like this.

What I least imagined was that my son would again listen to everything through the door.

Noah had never raised his voice to me, but this time he did.

"He just wants to help," screamed Noah before running out after Omar.

Aida frowned at me, crossing her arms. "I agree with Noah; if you let that man go, it will be the worst mistake of your life."

Chapter 12
Phoebe

Noah came back into the apartment and after giving me a dirty look, went straight to his room.

"Did you see how he looked at me?" I asked Aida, aghast.

She shrugged. "If I were him, I would look at you the same way."

I gave her a raised eyebrow, prompting her to elaborate.

"The villain of his story came again to ruin what for the first time could be a real relationship for you. Regardless of whether it's a possible happily ever after or a happily until never. You know that for a long time Noah has idolized Omar or the idea of having a father, and he saw an opportunity to finally have what he has wanted so much."

"You know it wasn't my fault that I couldn't give him a family or a father as he wanted," I said, feeling my nose and eyes beginning to burn with tears.

Aida approached me and caressed my back. "I know, but at this moment, you must think about what you want to do for the good of your child. That bastard ex won't be the first or the last to be selfish just because you're the mother of his child and he doesn't want to see you with anyone. Like him, there are many, and from my point of view, Steven assaulted you first in front of Noah by grabbing you that way by the arm that..."

She helped me take off my sweater, and together we looked at Steven's fingers marked on my arm. Aida immediately took out her phone and took several photos.

"See? Omar hit him to defend you, and against that, there are several people who can testify, and the building cameras, too," she pointed out.

I sniffled. "I don't want to lose Noah; Steven has something I don't have: money and power. Remember what he does for a living."

She took my hands in hers. "All the more reason to accept Omar's help," she said, and I shook my head.

"No, I've only known him for two days. Don't ask me to put all my trust in a stranger."

"Does that mean that if Omar insists and you go on dates, would you give him a chance?" Noah asked with joy, opening the door of his room.

"I don't know, Noah. Don't push the situation," I chided, and again he slammed the door shut.

Aida gave me a comforting look. "Both of you need time to think. You need to let go of your fears. Steven won't do anything; you've been an amazing mother to Noah all these years. People can't judge you for your past or for your immaturity years ago. Don't forget that you have me and..."

I gave her a sharp look that made her stop talking. "Aren't you late for your shift?" I asked, and she shook her head.

"No, today my shift is from five to five in the morning. You should call because you're already half an hour late. I advise you to ask for two days until all this calms down."

I nodded; immediately, I took out my phone and called my boss. She understood the situation a bit and told me that I should still be aware that if there were many patients, I would have to show up. But for now, I was off the hook.

That same morning Omar had made a statement clarifying the rumors and asking that they leave us alone. My stomach turned when he said he had an interest in winning my heart, but he had to go step by step.

It took three days before we could leave the apartment without being expected or pursued by the local press.

Our life was returning to normal, of course, apart from the fact that Omar didn't stop writing in the mornings to wish a good day for Noah and me, repeating the same procedure at night.

"Phoebe!" called a young man just as I was returning from my night shift at the hospital.

"Yes?" I said, and he extended a box to me.

"I have two deliveries for you."

I looked at the logo of where it came from, and my legs trembled.

"This box and this envelope. Could you sign here, please?" he continued, handing me both things. I held the two items with one hand and signed with the other.

"Thank you very much," I said when he turned around and walked to the other side. The envelope had been placed under the box, so I imagined it was something that came together.

I soon arrived at the apartment, and Noah seemed to be waiting for me at the door.

"What is that, Mom?" he asked as soon as he saw me and the packages.

"Well, it seems someone has sent us something from Madrid and an envelope that I haven't seen. Let me in, and we'll see what it's about."

"Is it from Balbisiana bakery?" he asked before even seeing the logo on the box, our favorite bakery.

"It seems so." I placed the box on the table and took the manila envelope that was underneath. I smiled, thinking it would be a letter from whoever sent the box, but I was rooted to the floor when the first thing I read was, "Lawsuit for parental rights and personal care."

I continued reading and confirmed that it was Steven wanting to revoke the document he signed some time ago. As the seconds ticked by, it became harder and harder to breathe.

"Mom?" Noah asked worriedly when I staggered, holding firmly onto the kitchen counter.

"Call Aida," I choked out, trying to contain my tears.

He took out his phone and dialed the number. He tried several times, then I remembered that Aida was on duty and was going to assist in a six-hour operation. I was having a panic attack. So I went to my room and entered my closet; the darkness helped me calm my anxiety. I sat in that place, trying to inhale and exhale.

I heard Noah's agitated voice, but I couldn't distinguish what he was saying. He approached and hugged me from behind.

"Help is coming," he said, and I continued with my breathing so that he wouldn't feel me so out of control. I felt like a terrible mother for allowing my son to see me this way.

"Thank you. I don't know what I would do without you by my side," I sobbed, this time unable to contain my crying.

"Me neither. I will never leave you, Mom," he promised, kissing my head.

I hugged his slender body, and we stayed like that for a while without saying anything. But a knock on the door made us separate; Noah ran to open it; however, what I heard was a male voice.

"Where is she?"

My eyes widened upon hearing Omar's voice.

"She's in the closet."

"Would you like to eat with me, dear?" a woman asked, and I identified her as being Omar's mother.

"Thank you, Mom," I heard Omar say as he reached where I was sitting.

I raised my gaze, and our eyes connected. An overwhelming need to hug him came over me, and he seemed to realize it. He quickly approached me and embraced me.

I couldn't speak; I just cried in his arms. His caresses helped me gradually calm my nerves.

He helped me stand and walk to the kitchen, holding me by his side. He served me some water, and I didn't hesitate to drink it all. Again, he hugged me and gave kisses on the crown of my head.

"Why is this happening to me?" I sniffled, clutching my hands to his back. For a moment, a thought came to my head and made me furious. "It's your fault!" I cried, pulling away from him. I hit his chest again and again, pushed him, and he seemed unwilling to let me go.

"Blame me all you want, but I'm not going to let that idiot take Noah away from you," he said.

I laughed bitterly. "How will you do that?" I took the paper that was on the table beside me, holding it in his face. "This is already a fact."

"It's not a fact. How easily you're letting yourself be consumed by fear. This is just a summons, not something that already establishes that Steven has custody. I'm going to help you; my Aunt Luz is one of the best lawyers and can help you if you want. I can only offer you one thing," he said.

I looked at him in surprise as he got down on his right knee, took my hand, and said words I never imagined hearing:

"Marry me."

Chapter 13

Omar

"I think you should forget about that woman. It's clear that this could become a huge problem for you, for her, and even for her son," said Alexis when we got to the car after leaving Phoebe's apartment.

I shrugged him off. "All the more reason I'm not going to leave her now that I've caused this problem and she's deeply embedded in me."

"Wasn't it the other way around?" he said, covering his mouth.

"Very funny. Do you want to lose your job?" I snarked, starting the car.

"No... Should I remind you that you have a contract with me signed for two more years?"

"Which can be canceled whenever I want," I pointed out.

"Alright, don't get angry, but if this situation gets out of hand, you'll have to learn not to get hooked with just any woman."

I was about to wring my hand around his neck, but a message sounded on my phone.

Noah

iMessage

My mother thinks you're good, but she doesn't know you.

Thanks for the information, champ. I'll take it into account.

Delivered

It was clear that this meant an opportunity for me. I smiled as I read the message over and over. The sound of a car horn behind me brought me out of my thoughts.

"Earth to Omar, the traffic light is green," teased Alexis, and I immediately put the car in motion. "There's no doubt that woman has completely stolen your sanity."

I nodded in agreement. I wasn't going to contradict him, as he spoke the truth. Getting Phoebe out of my mind would be very difficult.

"Did you come because I had something pending or just because of the news?" I asked seriously.

"You have some commercials to record, and you also have an invitation to the club partners' dinner," he commented, and yes, I remembered that dinner.

"Alright, let's go now. That way, they can leave Phoebe and Noah alone for a bit."

Alexis didn't hesitate to take the phone out of his pocket and began to call to coordinate the entire trip.

Three days passed between recordings and the partners' dinner. During all that time, I didn't lose contact with Phoebe or Noah. Thanks to him, I knew that her favorite bakery was also the same one I preferred.

That morning, before heading to the airport, I stopped by to buy a box with several of her favorite desserts, so they would be fresh. I boarded the jet with the desserts in hand. My parents had been present at the partners' dinner, so we were coming back to Zaragoza together.

"Son, don't you think this is too much?" my father asked, earning an elbow from my mother.

"Of course not. Rather, I think he should have bought another box," she said, smiling happily.

"Some people are just cut from the same cloth."

"I love you, but I'm grateful that my son is thoughtful thanks to me. Because you, my beloved husband, should ask yourself when was the last time that you bought me something like this," my mom added.

"Oooh," I said and raised my hand to my mother, who high-fived me.

Father sighed. "You are so ungrateful, princess. Two days ago, I bought you flowers to decorate your studio."

"It doesn't count because you had to call me and ask which ones I liked."

Seeing my father's disconcerted face was inevitably funny.

"I appreciate having gotten the thoughtfulness from your side, princess," I said, causing Mr. Roger Guzman to growl angrily, crossing his arms. While my mother and I laughed about it.

We soon arrived in Zaragoza, and the first thing I did was go to Phoebe's building. I looked at the time, and according to what Noah told me, she was about to arrive. I didn't know if she was angry, so my plan was just to leave the box outside her door, but the young courier was delivering some envelopes to the mailboxes.

For 50 euros and a photograph, I asked him to do me the favor of delivering it to her personally. I gave him her information, and he said yes; that he was waiting to give her something from his truck anyway. With that, I thanked him and left the building.

"Son, are you coming to the house to eat?" asked my mother, who was with me since my father was upset with our constant jokes during the trip.

"Yes, just let me find something in my apartment, and then we'll go so you can win over Mr. Roger," I replied, and she shook her head.

"I'm almost sure that I won't even need to cook. Your father should be preparing some roast or some recipe from his mother right now."

"How are you so sure?" I asked with a raised eyebrow.

"Need I remind you that I've been married to your father for thirty-one years? I know him very well; it was at his request to go alone. Let's go because I want to see what he'll be doing."

I returned to the car with my mother, and at that moment, my phone rang. I saw it was Noah, so I quickly answered; I was dying to know what impression Phoebe had had upon receiving the box.

"Champ, how are you? Did your mother like the gift?" I asked, and a sob from him disconcerted me. My brows creased in concern. "Noah?"

"They've sent my mom a paper that says something about what Steven said about my custody. She's having a panic attack. I called Aida, but she didn't answer. I didn't know who else to call. You might be able to come help her," he cried.

I tried to calm him, and my heart accelerated. I gripped the steering wheel tightly and seconds later put it in motion.

"Oh, no. Poor creature," my mother commented.

"Could you call Aunt Luz and explain her situation?" I suggested.

My mother immediately did so, and I explained a bit about the situation.

My aunt answered, "The case must be studied in depth, mainly because the healthiest option for the child must be sought. I'll take the case if she so desires."

"Does it help if I marry her?" I asked.

She paused, then said, "Yes and no."

It was heard that someone else was calling her, as I didn't want to keep holding her up. We said goodbye after scheduling a meeting with her. Minutes later, we arrived at the apartment, and my mother followed me.

The door took a while to open. My mother, upon seeing Noah's face, offered to take him to eat to distract him from this bad time.

I approached Phoebe, who was sitting on the floor in the middle of her closet, and hugged her. I knew she was going to blame me for what was happening, and that moment came, but I wasn't going to let her feel alone because she wasn't. Not anymore. I helped her up and we walked to the kitchen to get her something to drink, before talking about my proposal.

Due to what was discussed with my Aunt Luz, I knew there was a possibility, and although I was very aware that this was very precipitous, I had nothing to lose by getting down on one knee and asking her to marry me.

"Omar...I..." she stammered, unable to find the words.

I looked her straight in the eyes, waiting for the answer, but what happened was that she leaned in to kiss me, a kiss that didn't take long to awaken our desire for each other.

I stood up, and urgently, we both began to remove our clothes. I pulled down her pants along with the fine fabric covering her skin. I made her sit on the countertop, opened her legs to have a prodigious and exquisite view of her folds, and as if it were a delicacy, I was invited to devour her sensitive areas, with my tongue stealing gasps, moans, and more.

"Come..." she gasped, pulling my hair to move me away from the source from which I was drinking. I stood up and sought her lips while removing the fly of my pants. "Do it slowly, it still hurts," she said, and that's what I did.

I positioned my member at her center and entered little by little. Her body was like fire in my hands. Each kiss, each caress, each touch burned me more and more.

Kissing her breasts, squeezing her legs and buttocks had become the best of my pleasures. I didn't want to let her go, so at first, my thrusts and movements were slow, but very accurate and pleasurable.

I began to thrust inside her body with much more force and speed. Phoebe clung desperately to me, digging her nails into my back.

"Yes!" she began to scream when the ecstasy of pleasure overwhelmed her. We both reached our orgasm together. I pressed my forehead to hers and gave her a kiss on the nose.

"Is this a yes to my proposal?" I asked hopefully.

She pulled away and got down from the countertop without help, her face sad. "I'm sorry, Omar, but I can't accept your proposal; I can't marry you."

Chapter 14
Phoebe

The impression of seeing him on one knee was strong. A part of me just wanted to throw myself at him and cover him with kisses, but my other sensible part wanted to refuse his request immediately. To my misfortune, his lips invited me to kiss him, and the rest was complete madness. His caresses, his kisses, and his way of controlling the situation made me forget everything around us.

We didn't care about being in the middle of the kitchen, that someone might enter without warning and find us having sex.

Omar awakened this hunger for him that I couldn't control. My heart pounded strongly every time he approached me. His arms were like a place where everything around me quieted down and I felt safe. For someone I had met only a few days ago, he had a lot of power over my body.

I enjoyed the way he made me feel desired, like a goddess for being able to have such a man between my legs thrusting fiercely, his eyes looking at me in a hypnotizing way, and the strength with which his hands squeezed my legs.

The spasms and the voracious fire of passion ran through my body, causing me to close my eyes tightly at the same time as I felt Omar pulsating inside me. All the clouds in my head dissipated the moment he took for granted that my answer would be a yes.

"I'm sorry, Omar, but I can't accept your proposal; I can't marry you," I said, and he immediately adjusted his clothes.

His expression was forlorn, even as he tried to keep his face neutral. "It's okay, I understand. My Aunt Luz is willing to take the case if you wish. I'll send you her number by phone. I'll go see where Noah and my mother are."

I grabbed his arm before he left. "I'm sorry, but try to understand," I pleaded, seeing his face full of disappointment.

"I do, just as I understand that, although you don't know it, you also feel that this is not just sex. I won't impose on your life; I understand your fear. I put myself in your shoes. I can understand that you feel bad about all this, but it's not fair that you stop living just to please others."

He took my face in his hands, and my cheeks flushed.

"You are an extraordinary woman and mother. You have managed to do many things for yourself and for Noah's future. You also deserve to be happy, to be loved and cared for. That's what I want. I understand that you don't accept me now, but be very clear that I will be here *desiring your love.*"

He gave me a kiss on my lips and then another on my forehead where he stayed for a few seconds. I felt it, and truly, it was at that moment when I realized that I had hurt him.

"Omar, I truly..." He put a finger on my lips to stop me.

"You don't have to explain anything, sweetheart. I understand perfectly. I'll go see where they are and come back to drop off Noah."

He pulled away and, like the last time, left without saying a word, leaving me alone in the middle of the kitchen. When he opened the door, Noah appeared with a bag of his favorite fast food that was a few streets from here.

"Thank you very much, Mrs. Omar's mom," said Noah to the lady who was handing him a soda.

"It was nothing, dear. Behave well with your mother. Don't give her headaches," she said, following her son to the exit. "See you later, Phoebe."

I nodded and with a wave of my hand, I said goodbye. I felt embarrassed, not because of what Omar and I had just done, but because of the outcome of it all.

"Come, Mom. Let's eat," said Noah, placing the food near the countertop where everything had happened. I took it in my hands and brought it to the table. I proceeded to clean the countertop and then sat next to my son to eat our hamburgers.

After eating, I stayed in the living room with Noah watching a movie and eating the desserts we had received. I wanted to throw them away since I thought they were from Steven, but Noah clarified that they were a gift from Omar.

My son eventually fell asleep with his head resting on my leg. I caressed his hair and thought about Omar's words.

Omar's proposal didn't leave my mind. Was it possible to rebuild my life without society labeling me as a bad mother? The question overwhelmed me, especially because if I did, I would do it with the most public person I knew, and my whole life could come to light. Noah wouldn't be the only one affected if giving Omar a chance went wrong.

A forceful knock on the front door startled me. Now, I was afraid to know who it could be. Especially if Steven had returned.

"Open up, it's me. You have me with my heart in my throat," called Aida.

Noah sat up, rubbing his eyes, and I stood to go open the door before she knocked the door down.

"What's wrong?" she asked upon seeing my face.

I walked to the table where the paper was and showed it to her.

Her eyes opened wide, and then she threw the paper somewhere in the living room. "Damn, wretched man!" she cursed, and with my finger on her lips, I silenced her.

"That wasn't all, but we'll talk about it later," I told her, and she nodded.

"And this?" asked Aida, picking up a box that I hadn't noticed was on the table next to Noah's room. "It says it's for Noah."

"For me?" asked Noah, jumping off the couch and coming directly to Aida, who was holding the box in her hand. "Can I open it?"

I nodded with a bit of fear. Noah walked to the living room and settled on one of the couches with Aida and me by his side. He opened the box, and his eyes shone upon seeing what was inside. Our surname and number ten could be seen.

"Look, you have a note," commented Aida, taking out a small piece of paper from the side of the box.

"I'm dying to see this number and surname running through the fields of the best stadiums worldwide; I trust that you will achieve it very soon." *Omar G. Current number ten.*

Noah's tears were my breaking point. Omar was a man that even in my dreams I couldn't have imagined; he loved my Noah very much, and I had only made him feel bad.

"Omar is the best," he said, drying his tears while taking out the jersey. He ran to his room. "I'll call him to thank him and try it on," he added before closing the door.

Aida turned to me. "Now that he's distracted, tell me what's going on."

I took a deep breath, letting it out slowly. "Omar came, asked me to marry him, we had sex, and I told him no."

Aida's eyes went completely wide, her mouth falling open in shock. She grabbed the back of the nearest chair to steady herself, then immediately started pacing frantically around the small living room.

"Wait, wait, wait!" she practically shrieked, throwing her hands up in the air. "In that order, or did you tell him no before? Or did he ask you after the delicious deed?"

She spun around to face me, her hair now completely wild from running her hands through it. "Because Phoebe, those are three very different scenarios!" Her voice rose with each word, and she started gesticulating wildly, nearly knocking over a lamp.

"You cannot just drop that bomb on me like it's nothing! A marriage proposal! Sex! A rejection! Pick a lane and explain!" She was practically hyperventilating now, fanning herself with her hands while staring at me like I'd just told her I was moving to Mars.

"Sit down before you pass out," I said, watching her pace back and forth like a caged animal.

"Sit down? Girl, I need a drink, not a chair! Please answer me."

"In that order."

"Oh, no. Poor man. I can imagine it. That's why men later become icebergs, heartless, and then we complain about them, but it's because their hearts have been broken. Men like Omar don't appear overnight. You shouldn't waste the opportunity that life is giving you."

"I know, and I'm super aware of that. The thing is that I must not only think about myself but also about my son and what is best for him."

"And what makes you think that Omar is not good for Noah? Don't you see how attentive he is with him? Look, I understand you, but at least you should give him the opportunity to be friends or something so that you can get to know each other better before taking steps like these. Not to be the bearer of bad news, but if Omar were supermarket merchandise, he is a limited-time offer. He won't always be there, and when you decide, it could be too late."

I nodded; Aida was always cruel with the truth. That's what I loved about her, that she made me hear the truth and not what I wanted to hear. "You're right, but after what happened, I don't even know how to face him."

She pursed her lips. "Well, he will continue to insist if his feelings are sincere. Just don't make him wait too long because he will get tired, and the one who will end up badly will be you."

I nodded and walked to my room to go to the bathroom, and it was at that moment that I realized...

"Again!" I shouted. Aida quickly appeared in my room.

"What happened? Did that idiot call you or write to you again?" I immediately shook my head. "Then what?" she asked.

"It's the second time I've been with Omar without protection."

Aida crossed her arms and shook her head. "You are indeed irresponsible, woman. It would have been enough for you to ask me for it the first time, and I would have gotten it for you. It's been almost a week since you were with him the first time; if there are consequences from that night, taking it now will be of no use."

Chapter 15

Omar

"You've been very serious since we left Phoebe and Noah's apartment. Did something happen? You're too quiet for my taste," my mother commented, noticing how I was bottling everything inside.

"I asked Phoebe to marry me," I said without taking my eyes off the road.

"And she said no, I imagine."

I nodded, clenching my jaw as my mind raged.

"It's logical, Omar. That girl's life has been very complicated, and when she was achieving balance, you appear, and everything turns upside down for her again. Why don't you take some time to get to know each other, go out to dinner, have an ice cream with Noah?"

"I don't know, I understand that your act is noble, but it may be more complicated for her to assimilate; the people closest to her have been the ones who have hurt her. So her level of trust in people is very low. I saw her sad eyes when you left the apartment. Maybe she doesn't feel deserving of you or doesn't want you to get involved so that neither of you has problems," my mother said, and of course, I was clear on those points. It just didn't stop being disappointing.

It was the second time I had asked someone to be my wife, and although one told me yes, in the end, it turned out to be something completely different from what it was supposed to be.

Phoebe was very different, and no matter how much she wanted to push me away, she didn't know that what provoked me the most was the desire to protect her and Noah, to love her, and for her to no longer fear feeling alone, because I would be by her side.

"I don't understand why love has to be so complicated," my mother continued.

"It is, but with Phoebe, I won't stop until she accepts me."

"Omar, don't be offended by my question. Phoebe is very beautiful, and I'm not asking this purely because of her physique, but in general, what did you like about her?"

I smiled softly. "Everything about her. A few months ago, you told me that when love comes into my life, I would know how to distinguish it because it doesn't feel the same as a simple physical attraction. It's something intense that completely takes away your sanity, that you can't do anything without thinking about what she's doing, if she woke up well, if she's already eaten, a person to whom when you open your eyes in the morning, the first thing you want is to say good morning and wish her a good night.

"Noah won my heart, and his life story is not one of the reasons why I want to win them over. My conquest is not only to win Phoebe's love but also Noah's. I want both of them to be part of my life. I won't rest until they can have something they have always lacked: the love of a family," I concluded as I parked the car in front of my parents' house. I turned to glance at my mother, who was looking at me with tears in her eyes.

"I feel very proud of you, son. That you are aware of all that, but what makes me prouder is your beautiful heart. You are definitely what she needs; however, to protect yourself, go slowly. Rushing can only cause both of you to get hurt and even Noah to be affected."

I nodded and got out of the car to open her door and subsequently help her get out of the car. The aroma of food made us look at each other and burst out laughing.

My mother laughed. "I told you; I know Roger Guzman very well. He's so predictable too. I love him."

The door opened, revealing my father with an apron. "You know it's the only thing I can do without needing help from anyone. Let's eat," he said, taking her hand.

We spent a pleasant afternoon, but I had to leave the lovebirds alone because there came a moment when they disappeared, and when I looked for them to say goodbye, I could distinguish laughter coming from the bedroom. So, I left the house on my way to my apartment. When I turned on the car, my phone rang with a video call from Noah.

"Noah," I greeted, and I could see how the camera showed his reflection in the mirror.

He was wearing the uniform that I had forgotten I'd left on the first table I found because what mattered most to me at that moment was getting to Phoebe.

"Thank you very much for the uniform, Omar. It's the best gift I've ever received. Don't tell my mom so she doesn't get sad."

I smiled at him. "I'm very glad you liked my gift."

"Like? I love it. I'll wear it for all my training sessions," he said, and his little face was shining with happiness.

"Excellent, champ, you'll be the sensation in it. It looks very good on you. Your mother wasn't upset?"

"No, Aida is here, and I don't know what they're talking about."

"Champ, I think for the time being, I'm going to stop insisting with your mother."

"You don't want my mom to be your girlfriend anymore?" he asked; I could see the concern on his face, and I shook my head.

"No, it's just that we've started in disorder. Your mother needs to process a bit of what's happening with Steven, and I don't want to overwhelm her more. I'll always be in contact with you, but I'll stop being so insistent with her. If you hear anything, don't hesitate to let me know."

He nodded his head. "I understand, you'll give her the cold shoulder for a few days to see if she's interested in you."

"Correct, champ. Can I count on you?"

He affirmed that I could, we said goodbye, and the video call disconnected.

After that call, two weeks passed.

I didn't write to Phoebe during all that time, but through Noah, I knew that she asked about me and that he told her I always wrote to ask how they were. So indirectly, she knew that I was always aware of them.

Phoebe accepted the help of my Aunt Luz, and from what she told me, they had a lot of evidence and two witnesses who were willing to help, which made me very happy for them. On the other hand, I'd been almost secluded in my apartment or in my parents' house. The need to go look for them was very strong and intense, but I couldn't give in.

That's why when my phone rang with a call during my workout routine, it made me jump with joy to see Phoebe's name on the screen.

"Hello, sweetheart," I greeted, trying to keep calm. "To what do I owe the honor of your call?" I asked, and she remained silent for a moment.

"Hello, Omar. I was calling to see if you would like to come to dinner tomorrow."

"Yes, of course. I'll be there. Any special reason?"

She paused. "Yes, well... No, but we do have to talk about something very important.

"Is everything okay? You sound somewhat nervous," I said to tease a little.

"No, everything is fine. It's just that you haven't done anything wrong, quite the contrary, and you're not to blame for anything that's happening with Steven. It would possibly happen regardless of who showed interest in me."

I smiled like an idiot while looking at myself in the gym mirror and wiping the sweat from my face with a rag.

"I'm very glad you realized that. Is it alright if we actually have dinner today? My father's birthday is tomorrow, and we'll be gathering to celebrate." It wasn't a lie just to accelerate seeing each other. My father was truly having his birthday, and we had to be present. "If you can't make it today, it's perfectly fine; you can join us tomorrow."

"I don't think I can handle the way you all celebrate. It's fine if you can come today." I liked that; she was taking the initiative.

"That's fine with me. What time can I arrive?"

"It doesn't matter, but after six is good."

"I'll see you at six, sweetheart. Have a nice day, take care, and say hi to Noah for me," I said, and from her part, I only received a simple, "Goodbye."

For the rest of the day, I was with my mother, being her driver, while she arranged every detail for tomorrow's party. Around four, I managed to find some free time. I stopped by my apartment to take a shower and change my clothes. When I finished, I had enough time to pass by a bakery and buy something for dessert.

Upon arriving, I rang the doorbell, and the one who opened the door was Noah.

"Omar!" he shouted as he approached me to give me a hug.

"Hello, champ, how have you been?" I asked, messing up his hair.

"I don't know; I'm a little worried," he admitted in a low voice, looking around to make sure his mother or someone else couldn't hear.

"Why?" I asked with curiosity.

"I don't know. My mom's been acting very strange," he said, making my curiosity turn into concern.

"What's happening to your mother?"

Noah shrugged his shoulders. "For a few days, she's been weird. I'm talking to her, and she doesn't pay attention to me, and the last time, she locked herself in the room to cry after coming from her shift at the connection. I don't know what's wrong with her."

I frowned. "Let me see if I can find out what it is. She told me we needed to talk about something important. Don't worry; let's hope it's nothing serious."

He nodded and invited me in. I sat in the living room waiting for Phoebe to appear. The apartment doorbell rang, and Aida appeared at the door.

"Hello?" she asked, surprised to see me there.

I raised my hand in greeting, and she did the same but looked toward Noah.

"Your mother?" she said.

Noah pointed to the bedroom door just as Phoebe opened it, and as much as she tried to cover her dark circles with makeup, they were still noticeable. That only made me feel much more concerned.

"Noah, I have tickets for us to go see a basketball game. Do you want to go?" Aida offered.

Noah nodded eagerly and ran to his room to change his clothes, putting on a red, black, and white shirt of the Zaragoza Basketball team.

"Thank you; I don't know what I would do without you," said Phoebe to Aida.

"Relax. You know I'm here to help you. Who knows? Today might be my lucky day, and I'll find the right one. Noah seems to be a magnet for good men." She winked.

"Aida!" Phoebe reprimanded, coming to the kitchen.

"I won't say anything more, just keep in mind that we'll be back after nine at night." Phoebe was about to speak, but Noah said goodbye, saving Aida's life.

"Are you okay, sweetheart?" I asked, breaking the silence that had fallen after they left.

She sighed. "Yes, it's just that a few days ago, we lost a patient, and it was very difficult for everyone. She was two weeks away from giving birth, but it seems that a fight with the mistress or ex of the husband made her lose her life. She received three bullet impacts, and as much as they tried to rescue her and her son, it wasn't successful."

Her voice broke; on instinct, I approached her and surrounded her with my arms. For a moment, I thought she was going to reject me since I did it while she was cutting some tomatoes.

My hands touched her abdomen; she stopped what she was doing and turned, hiding her face in my chest.

"I'm sorry for behaving like this, but these last years, it's been Noah and me against the world. I can't live without him, but these days, I also realized that I can't live without you either." Her words squeezed my heart; her confession came accompanied by tears, which made this enormous moment very special.

I kissed her head and caressed her back while letting her squeeze me.

"I understood that from day one. My intention is not to cause problems; my intention is to put the world that I possess under your feet. I perfectly understand your fears, insecurities, and concerns. I'm sorry if having come into your life has caused you problems, but since I met you, I want all of you."

She sniffled. "When I hear you talk this way, it's hard for me to believe that someone like you would fall in love with someone like me. I don't say it just because of my physical appearance; I say it because I also have a son, a responsibility that doesn't concern you."

"What can I tell you? I admit I fell in love with the combo," I teased, but I was also being serious.

That made her pull back, and I lost myself in her eyes which, although red and moist, were looking at me with a strong glow; for the first time, she was looking at me differently.

I took her face in my hands and didn't miss the opportunity to kiss her lips. It was a soft and warm kiss with a taste of salt. Upon separating, she smiled, and I think I did the same. Her hand caressed my chin, and I leaned like a puppy at her touch.

"Is your proposal to get married still standing?" Her words made my knees go weak.

"It is, but I think we should start at the beginning, get to know each other. Not just physically and what our insides feel like every time we are this way," I mused, passing my hand through the valley of her breasts. "I love knowing that the one who took the initiative now was you," I said, which made her press her lips and raise her eyebrow.

She pushed me a little away from her. "That's exactly what I was going to tell you."

"So? What was the important thing you were going to tell me?"

"Isn't confessing what I feel important?" she asked, turning her body to continue with the tomatoes.

"It is, but I don't know why, by the way you're trembling, I feel there might be something else you want to tell me."

I saw her swallow, her throat bobbing with emotion. "Yes, the truth is that there is something else I should tell you."

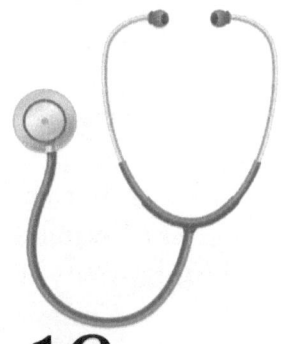

Chapter 16

Phoebe

READ WITH DISCRETION (Miscarriage and death)

Aida's words hit me like a slap.

"Oh, no," I gasp, sitting on the bed.

"Oh, yes. I understand that you completely forgot the first time, but what about this one? You must be crazy about the man to have your mind clouded to that extent."

I had no excuse because that was the truth; being with Omar was like forgetting all my problems and everything in general.

She added, "First of all, you need to calm down. Second, you need to think about what you feel for the man. He has been clear with his intentions. The person who has the problem accepting is you."

"But what if I end up being pregnant? What am I going to do?" I asked as a shiver ran through my body.

"I can almost assure you, I have no proof, but I'm sure. I imagine that night wasn't just once. A man with his stamina isn't a one shot deal, and in his family, they come in twos or threes, and the little ones even walk," she said, and it wasn't until she burst out laughing that I emerged from the echo her words made in my brain. "Your face is worthy of a photograph," she said, imitating my expression.

"This is serious, Aida," I whined, running my hands down my face.

"I know, but until you have confirmation, don't drown in a glass of water. Check your calendar. It's possible there's nothing to worry about.."

"Mom! Come see how the uniform looks on me," Noah called from his room.

I went to the bathroom to wash my face. Then I attended Noah's call; Aida had dinner with us, and it wasn't until the night that I could do what Aida told me.

I knew this part very well, but I still had to face what happened. I was no longer that careless, wild, and unconcerned girl who didn't care about many things due to her immaturity.

I opened the application on my phone, and when I saw on the calendar when Alan and Susy's wedding was, I could see that it was my second most fertile day of my cycle, so the possibilities of ending up pregnant were enormous.

I went to bed trying to sleep and didn't think about it for a moment; tomorrow I would ask the doctor what I could do in this case. I was also thinking about the summons and that I didn't have any trusted lawyer, so the option Omar gave me of his Aunt Luz was my only option.

The next morning, I called the law firm of lawyer Luz Amador de Galeano to schedule a meeting with her where I had to completely expose my relationship with Steven and all the connection we have had over all these years.

Mrs. Luz told me that Steven's lawyers were not including the complete information about the fortune left by his grandmother, that we have a lot in our favor.

Afterwards, I went to see if I could get an appointment at the outpatient clinic on my floor.

Dr. Jiménez was the one who attended to me, and it felt somewhat strange to pose the situation. After a couple of questions, she looked at me in surprise.

"Seriously, you haven't been with anyone since before your son Noah?" she asked again with skepticism.

"Yes, it wasn't until a week ago that I knew what the matter was again, and until yesterday."

"With the same sexual partner?" she pressed.

My cheeks burned, but I knew these were uncomfortable questions that were normally asked. I nodded, and she smiled while typing on her computer.

"Going a little out of our patient-doctor relationship. And speaking to you as your friend and boss, being honest, I feel good envy for you. You lost your nine-year sanctity with such a man. I imagine he's as good as he looks."

The scandal that formed a few days ago was known to everyone in the hospital, and I must say that there were mostly women who congratulated me for having eaten that cake, because that's what everyone assumed, and I wasn't going to waste time denying the truth; I just let them talk what they wanted, neither denying nor confirming anything.

Dr. Jiménez continued, "Going back to our patient-doctor relationship, I can recommend that you take the pill. If it's for protection from yesterday. In the case that something has already been fertilized in your uterus, it won't affect you at all if you take it."

She took the little box from her desk and put it in front of me.

"And can't I take a blood test or something?" I asked, and she shook her head.

"A blood pregnancy test at one week is not reliable; you must wait at least two weeks or up to three in some cases for the hormone to become present, as in pharmacy tests."

I exhaled heavily as I leaned back against the chair.

"I could send you an order to do it if that gives you a bit of peace of mind," she offered, and I nodded.

Twenty minutes later, and I already had the result in my hands, since after taking the sample, I stayed watching Julieta process my test, resulting in a negative. I took the box and looked at it in front of me.

"I think it would be selfish of me not to take it. My situation with Omar is uncertain, then the problems with Steven. Let it be what God wants for his favorite warrior." I said to myself, and took the pill with water. Then I went to conclude my work and started making rounds among the new mothers.

The meeting with the lawyer was very good; telling her that Steven's grandmother was leaving a fortune to Noah would serve to give weight to his interest in obtaining his custody, apart from everything else, the photos that Aida took of my arm and the parental rights that he had already signed. His disinterest in the child since he was in my womb, the threat of abortion I had the day I almost drowned in the pool. I also had to talk to Steven's father; for some time, he had distanced himself and hadn't called Noah, and that silence on his part gave me a bad feeling.

I took the opportunity to ask about Omar's proposal; I asked the lawyer about whether getting married could help my case. She said yes and no at the same time.

Yes, because I could claim that I also have a marriage and can give stability to Noah. And no, because if there is no evidence that can prove a relationship between Omar and me for a minimum of six months, it would not be taken as something stable. It could get me in trouble since the marriage would be after the lawsuit was filed.

She was the one who knew how the other party could use certain tricks against me. So, she told me that this possibility could not help me.

Something that didn't go unnoticed in the last two days was the fact that Omar didn't call me or send the usual good morning or good night messages.

I knew he had left my house very upset, but I didn't think he would stop insisting after my refusal. It wasn't until the fifth day that I asked Noah about it.

"Noah?" I prompted him while we were having dinner.

He glanced up from his food. "Yes?"

"Has Omar called you or sent you a message?"

He smiled, bringing the spoon to his mouth. "Yes, every day. Do you want to see?"

He proceeded to show me the messages; in all of them, Omar emphasized that he should take care of me and not make me angry.

"Why are you smiling?" he asked.

Without realizing what I was doing, I pressed my lips. "Nothing, I just like to know that even though things with me didn't work out, he didn't stop talking to you."

"And when we talk, he always asks about you."

My eyes widened. "Really?"

He nodded. My heart beat hard, and I even felt like crying knowing that I behaved so badly with him and hadn't even sent him a message to apologize or to greet him.

The following days went by unhurriedly but with a lot of fatigue.

At night, I debated whether to write to Omar or not. It was a battle every day, especially when I couldn't get out of my head the last time I saw him.

I needed to know about him, and that's why I was always asking my son if he knew anything or looking for his name on social networks to see if there was a new publication from him. There were always new photos or videos of some play or about some advertising.

That's how my life was reduced to almost two weeks. Until the notification appeared on my phone that I hadn't updated my cycle for three days. It was like a punch to my gut.

I had left the topic the day I took the pill, and that only made my little calm go down the drain.

I was getting ready to go out to drop Noah off at school and then to my day shift. That day I was almost dragging Noah down the street; I needed to get to the hospital and get out of this doubt that had my nerves at a thousand miles per hour.

"I'll see you in the afternoon, honey," I said, giving him a kiss on the head as I did every day, and then I took the taxi to the hospital. I didn't waste time and went directly to look for Dr. Jiménez. I still had some time before clocking in.

The doctor, seeing my agitation, just asked me to go to the bathroom and pee inside one of the sterilized containers that were in the place, and that she would do the test.

I did what she asked, then she came in and performed the test. Normally, this was put in a type of dispenser that went to the nursing triage, where they were in charge of delivering the results to the doctor. But I needed more discretion than that.

My hands were sweating, as well as my back, my forehead, and I could feel the cold air from the air conditioning because of it.

Eventually, the doctor came out of the bathroom and handed me the test that showed two lines.

"It seems you'll have Omar Guzman's baby. I think his more than forty one million female followers will hate you. I'll give you an order for—"

"Code OB. Dr. Jiménez, report to emergency," was said over the intercom three times.

She picked up the phone and asked about who else was available to go assist with the emergency.

Hanging up, she turned to me. "Go change. Wendy is assisting a cesarean, and the others are with other patients. Then we'll continue with your consultation."

I nodded and ran to the nurses' station to change my clothes and meet the doctor at the elevator.

Upon arriving, I was able to witness the cruelest and saddest scene I've seen in my life.

"Luna Succolu, twenty-six years old, has three bullet impacts, one in the chest, another in the shoulder, and one in her lower abdomen. She is thirty-seven weeks pregnant and is losing a lot of blood."

The doctor looked at the scene with horror. Her face looked very familiar to me, but I didn't know where I'd seen her before.

"Phoebe, get me an operating room. Call Dr. Rubiales and Dr. White. Tell them we have a Code OB. That I need them, right here." The doctor continued giving instructions.

The doctors didn't need to be called, as both almost at the same time appeared in the room. Fortunately, there was an operating room available on the same floor. I was running from one side to the other, along with two residents who were helping to prepare the operating room with the necessary equipment.

"If you wish, you can return to the obstetrics room. This is very strong for you to see at this moment," said the doctor while she was washing her hands and sterilizing to enter the operating room.

"I'll assist you. I'm fine," I assured her. She nodded, and I entered the operating room with her.

The operation began; the place was crowded with doctors, and not much time passed when everything began to alter.

The doctor managed to extract the baby, but its abdomen had been impacted by the bullet in its mother. The baby had no vital signs, and they tried to perform resuscitation, but it didn't respond.

Among all those present, we were being as professional as possible so as not to break down in the face of the situation.

Dr. Rubiales began to operate to extract the bullets from the mother, but the internal bleeding and damage were too much, and no matter how much they did to save her life, they didn't succeed. Both had lost their lives because of those bullets.

I remember that the first to leave the room with frustration was Dr. Jiménez; I went out behind her and saw her throw her cap and her face mask to the floor and walk from one side to the other until she broke down in tears.

My body was trembling at all that. I didn't understand who in their right mind would do something like that to a pregnant woman.

"Jiménez, we must inform the family members," said one of the other doctors who assisted in the operation.

"Yes, give me a few minutes, Sergio."

He nodded and waited for her in silence. When she recovered, I walked with her to the waiting room where a young man was pacing from one side to the other, holding his head. A lady was crying, embraced by a man sitting in the chairs.

The doctor gave them the news, and the man walked backward, covering his mouth and falling into one of the chairs.

"No! My girl, my Luna," sobbed the woman. She released herself from the older man and went directly to the younger one, who seemed lost in his pain.

She hit his face twice, but the man seemed to have no more will than to release his crying.

"I warned you; I told you that coming to this country and to this damn city would bring problems. That damn woman killed my daughter and my grandson. All my sacrifice to make them have a life away from all the trash of her father, and you and your mistress do this to her. I will never let you live in peace, Charles; the death of my daughter and your son will be your cross as long as we breathe the same air."

"She wanted to know what caused her sister Rebeca's death; I just wanted to help her," said the man, drowning in tears; the woman again gave him a couple of slaps.

"And you fell in love and got into bed with a woman you shouldn't have! You made Luna suffer in the process and look how your way of helping her ended. You helped her find death for her and my grandson! Your son! My two daughters died in this damn hospital. Damn the day I asked your father to take care of my Luna! Damn the day I accepted that you marry her!"

It was at that moment that I realized it was the same Rebeca who tried to kill Alan. Rebeca had a twin who sadly had just died, and along with her, the bloodline of a man who had caused a lot of pain to many families in this hospital, Ibrahim Succolu. The previous director of this hospital, who ended up being a human and organ trafficker.

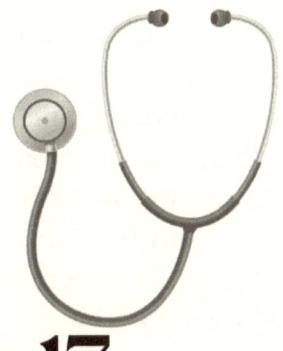

Chapter 17

Phoebe

We withdrew from the room, leaving the family members crying in peace and with their guilt. It wasn't until I reached the maternity floor and saw a woman smiling with her baby in her arms that my hormones clashed in my brain. How could life be so unfair? My eyes began to burn, and it was hard to breathe.

"Phoebe?" asked one of the girls at the triage when she saw me holding tightly onto the stand. I felt dizzy and very nauseous. "Phoebe!" Seconds later, everything was spinning, and I fainted on the floor.

For a while, everything was black. But then I heard a voice calling me from afar. "Phoebe, Phoebe…"

"Let her rest." The voice of Dr. Jiménez.

I opened my eyes and saw Aida and the doctor around me; I was on a stretcher.

"Oh, no. Phoebe, you're going to kill me with fright," gasped Aida.

"Phoebe, you had a drop in blood pressure. You need to start taking care of yourself, especially at this stage; I understand that what was experienced down there was very strong for you."

I nodded while trying to sit up, however, Aida pushed me by the shoulder. She shook her head, looking at me with super intense eyes.

"Many times, it's the way destiny plays with us," I tried to explain. "I remember I was feeling fine, but upon going up and seeing how they were taking a happy mother with her baby in the wheelchair and then the injustice we witnessed down there. That family... I'm very sorry."

"Well, but now I have to take care of mini Omar or mini Phoebe," said Aida, putting her hand on my abdomen. I loved her; I never imagined I could have an almost sister-like friend in her.

"I agree with you, Aida," the doctor said before turning to me. "I just gave you three days of leave to rest. When you feel ready, you can go home."

"How exciting! I'll be an aunt," Aida chimed. "Noah will go crazy when you tell him. Omar!"

I took her hands in mine. "Calm down, no one should know about this yet."

"Why? Omar deserves to know he's going to be a father."

"I understand, and you're right, but I don't know how it will make me look if I tell him that now; the man hasn't written, called, or visited for almost two weeks. How do you expect me to tell him he's going to be a father? What will he think of me? He'll think I didn't take care of myself because I wanted him to solve my life. For wanting to grab onto his fame. People will say I did it to trap him, and I don't think I'm sure if I want to have his entourage of followers on top of me."

It wasn't until Aida started laughing that I realized I was talking more to myself than to her.

"Well, we'll see about that later. For now, rest, and in a while, we'll go home." I nodded and closed my eyes for a moment.

Half an hour later, we were arriving at the apartment, and seeing Noah watching a replay of Omar's match was a blow to me. I went directly to my room and laid down on the bed, no longer able to control my tears.

"Your mom had a bad day at the hospital. We should let her rest," I heard Aida tell him patiently and then ask him if he wanted to eat a hamburger.

After two or three minutes, I heard the door close, and I cried, feeling the same way as when I arrived in Madrid alone and with a baby in my womb. The difference was that before, I had no one but my baby and my Aunt Salomé. This time, I had a good man who wanted to take care of me, my son, and who would be very happy to take care of this baby: our baby.

And I stupidly have been pushing him away and rejecting him. Now it was I who had to bring him back into our lives, but it would be step by step.

"Hello, little one. You'll have to wait a moment for your father and your brother to know you're on the way. It's not about denying you; just give me time to announce your arrival," I said, touching my belly.

I closed my eyes and started thinking about how to talk to Omar. I needed to start redeeming my mistake of pushing him away. But eventually, as I lay there, I drifted off to sleep.

"Are you sure she's okay? She never cries," I heard my son's voice ask.

"Yes, honey. Go brush your teeth and get ready to go to bed. Tomorrow is a school day," Aida said before his footsteps moved away, and I opened my eyes.

"Thank you," I murmured.

Aida caressed my cheek. "You know you would do the same for me. I'm going to leave now because I have to assist with an operation tomorrow morning. Don't hesitate to call if you need anything."

I nodded and sat up to give her a hug. I took the opportunity to say goodnight to Noah and take a bath, as well. Then I looked for something to eat and laid down on my bed again.

I would use these days to try and clarify the mess in my head and in my heart.

It would be a lie if I said that being close to Omar bothered me; who in their right mind could resist a man like him? What bothered me was the bunch of emotions he made me feel, how good a man he was, and what I least wanted was to smear him with my trash.

I was not foolish; when exposing my public life, things about my parents could be exposed, and then the situation with Steven. The last thing I needed was to feel guilty for ruining my son's idol's career.

I may be very determined, cold, and even fierce for many things in my life, but these things were dominating me. I couldn't continue like this anymore.

The two nights were very difficult for me, as I almost didn't sleep, because I had already made a decision, and that was to give Omar Guzman a chance. I wanted to know more about that enormous sweet wolf who didn't even let me think when he's near me.

On the morning of the third and last day of rest, I returned to the apartment after dropping Noah off at school. I breathed deeply, took my phone, and dialed his number. It didn't ring more than three times before the call was already being answered. I wanted to be brief; nerves were eating me up, the hand holding my phone was trembling, and like it, my whole body. I didn't know if it was the famous butterflies or the nausea that caused me to feel this commotion in my stomach.

The intention was to schedule for the next day, but the plans changed for that same night. I accepted because, truthfully, I did want to see him, and if I could recharge energy by being hugged or feeling loved by him, I was willing for it to be that same morning, and he wouldn't have refused, but I didn't want to seem so desperate either.

Gradually, I was coming to accept the idea that I was pregnant; I was drinking more water and trying to take my vitamins punctually. I smiled, caressing my belly when the doorbell rang.

"Have I told you I hate Dr. Reed?" Aida slammed the apartment door behind her, the sound echoing through the small space. Her purse hit the floor with a loud thunk, followed immediately by her keys, which she threw down with enough force that they skittered across the tile.

Her face was flushed red with anger, and she kicked off her heels so aggressively that one flew across the room and knocked over a small plant. "That man is absolutely insufferable!" she continued, her voice rising as she stormed toward the kitchen.

"Why?" I asked, unable to understand what she was doing at this hour in my apartment when she had been on shift for only a few hours.

"Because it turns out he was going on vacation today and didn't have the decency to say it yesterday. He made me go early all the way there to tell me in a phone call that he was giving me the day off for not notifying. He told me to take this out of one of his drawers and told me this was his way of apologizing." She held out an envelope.

I raised a curious eyebrow. "What is it?"

She opened the envelope and took out two tickets for a basketball game. I couldn't help but laugh out loud.

"I don't like basketball. Through Noah, I learned what an offside position in soccer was. And you know what the worst part is?" she complained.

"What?"

"That they're for today and will be wasted. Because who will I go with?" she said, and an idea occurred to me.

"You could go with Noah," I suggested.

She looked at me with a smile. "Yes! I'll use my day to go shopping for groceries, deep clean my apartment, and possibly get my hair done a bit differently."

"Yes, you should take advantage of this day off."

She left my apartment excited, and in the blink of an eye Noah had already returned, and I already had more or less prepared what Omar and I would have for dinner.

The time when Omar would come for me was approaching, so I went to correct my pronounced dark circles a bit. It was an almost impossible mission, and in the end, it wasn't achieved; I confirmed it a while later when I left my room, and Omar looked at me in detail with a bit of confusion.

Aida and Noah left the apartment almost immediately. I was sure to get a scolding from the inquisitive Aida afterward.

Omar stayed in the living room while I went directly to the kitchen to prepare dinner. The truth was that I couldn't find words to tell him what I wanted to say, while at the same time, if I started to open my mouth, there were many possibilities that I would talk too much, and I didn't want a word vomit that would lead me to make more mistakes.

He took the initiative to approach, and as expected, I let myself be carried away by that tranquility that his arms make me feel.

I confessed what I had stuck here in my chest, and it was his kisses and words that made me feel that I was in my safe place. Omar was that person to whom I should always return.

"So? What was the important thing you were going to tell me?" he asked.

"Isn't confessing what I feel important?" I retorted, trying not to talk about that topic. The truth was that I didn't know if it was good for his family to know that information.

"It is, but I don't know why, by the way you're trembling, I feel there might be something else you want to tell me."

I paused, trying to think of something. "Yes, the truth is that there is something else I should tell you… Rebeca Succolo, the woman who tried to murder your cousin Alan and Susy, had a twin sister," I said quietly.

"Let me call my Uncle Iván, and I'll help you prepare dinner." He took out his phone and walked to the living room. "How did you know?" asked Omar.

"She was the pregnant woman who died due to three bullet impacts three days ago in the hospital."

Chapter 18

Omar

I expected her to tell me anything, except that it was something like that; however, that information could be of interest to my Uncle Iván. That family had been responsible for hurting his career, his life, and his family, under threats and blackmail.

I didn't hesitate, and when I told him what Phoebe narrated to me, he told me that they had already been notified and that the problem was bigger than they expected. They had now discovered that this organization had continued operating in the shadows and under new leaders. They were hoping that the latest events would lead them to find the culprits or the leaders of this nest of criminals and murderers.

I hung up the call and approached Phoebe. I couldn't imagine how difficult it must have been to experience something like that; although she had already mentioned it, hearing her describe the details made an impression on me, too.

"Is that why you're like this? Your eyes shine saying you're better than ever, but your dark circles tell me you haven't been doing well," I commented.

"It's everything that has happened in the last few days. I must admit that you not calling affected me a lot," she said, making a pout, then turning to continue with the food.

I positioned myself behind her, surrounded her with my arms, and peppered several kisses on her cheek.

She laughed because with my hands, I began to tickle her abdomen. "Omar, stop."

"Alright, now tell me how I can help you. What are you thinking of preparing?" I asked.

"I thought you liked to eat seafood. Not to brag, but it's my specialty. Accompanied by a red rice that my Aunt Salomé taught me to prepare. I think it's traditional in Mexican cuisine and it's delicious," she said, licking her lips.

"Yes, I love it too. My family, even being 75% Spanish, we enjoy our 25% Mexican heritage very much," I said, and she raised an eyebrow. I elaborated, "My paternal grandmother and my grandmother Lorena were Mexican. She emigrated with her family to this country when she was just a girl. It was my grandmother Lorena who passed her roots to my grandmother Jimena, and since then, tacos have been her weakness." I shrugged.

"Wow, who would have thought," Phoebe said, and I approached to give her a kiss on her forehead.

I couldn't control this desire to caress, kiss, and be close to her whenever I had the opportunity. We continued talking about her life in Madrid and how Noah discovered his passion for football.

"So Noah was that boy?" I asked excitedly.

She nodded and invited me to walk to Noah's room. I saw a frame with my shirt inside.

"Yes, I remember he insisted on me taking him to the stadium to see the Madrid derby, and luckily, the only available tickets were behind the players' seats. When you threw the shirt, it bounced on my face, and although the man next to me tried to snatch it, Noah took it forcefully, telling him it was his with tears in his face, and the man had compassion for my son and let it go. You didn't even notice, because when Noah was going to show you, you had already entered the locker room."

I nodded my head in thought. "Indeed, there have been several stories that have connected us for some time."

But then her head snapped up. "The rice is burning!" she shouted when the smell reached us in the bedroom. We both hurriedly returned to the kitchen.

Frowning at the food, we decided it was a lost cause.

"What do you think if we order something? That way, I can sit with you on that couch over there, while we kiss like two teenagers," I suggested as she turned off the stove.

"I think I like that idea, but it will just be kissing," she said.

I couldn't help but laugh and lean next to her ear. "Unless you want to do something else, for which I am more than willing. Besides, it's not as if we haven't done it before."

"Don't try to run, number ten. We're going to go little by little, or it's better not to try," she chided, and I nodded.

"It will be as you want, my sweetheart, now come here," I crooned, taking her hand to walk to the couch.

We ordered food similar to what we were going to prepare, and while we waited, we melted into such a burning kiss that it was impossible to keep my body from not reacting. This time it was Phoebe who straddled me. My hands traveled to her soft and tempting behind. She rocked her hips, grinding against me, and to my mind came the first time we spent together. I separated my mouth from hers and kissed her neck.

"I won't be able to stop myself if we continue this way," I said, then ran my tongue over the lobe of her ear, causing her to bite her lower lip.

I squeezed her behind, and this time she moaned, seeking my lips, and again we devoured each other with need. Just when I turned my sweetheart to lay her on the couch, the doorbell rang.

"Saved by the bell, sweetheart," I chuckled, standing up.

"Or cursed by the bell," she retorted, and we both laughed.

I let in the delivery person and gave him a very good tip. We ate and put on a romantic drama. I had never liked Korean romances, but the movie was so good that we watched it from beginning to end, and in my case, without getting bored. Phoebe rested her head on my chest, and I could hear her sigh in the most tender scenes.

"I'll help you clean the dishes," I said when I saw her almost falling asleep.

She nodded, and I started to clean up all the mess in the kitchen.

The apartment door opened a little while later, revealing only Noah. He smiled when he saw me, and then his gaze went to his mother, who was peacefully sleeping on the couch.

"Aida?" I asked curiously, seeing that he came alone.

"I don't know. Downstairs, there was a man sitting next to the entrance with a bottle in his hand and the hood of a sweatshirt covering his face. Aida told me to enter and that she would help the man. That's what she must be doing."

That could be very dangerous for a woman to do, but then I remembered that being a nurse, she would have her way of helping to persuade and help the man.

"Noah?" said Phoebe, waking up.

"Mom, the game was incredible. The game was super close, with a one-point difference, and in the last second, Zaragoza threw a basket to score the last three points. It was super exciting! I would like to learn a bit of basketball. Do you think it's possible?" he asked, and I approached them.

"Yes, and you'll love to know that the coach of Zaragoza Basket is my Uncle Jerónimo. So if you want to see the team train, I don't think they'll deny us sneaking in." At my words, he nodded enthusiastically.

"Is there anything your family isn't involved in?" my sweetheart asked with a small touch of amusement.

I puffed my chest proudly. "It's hard for me to tell you exactly, because even in NASA, in Formula 1, in the best runways, courts, constructions, fabrics, and more, you can find a Galeano behind."

"Your family is incredible, Omar," complimented Noah.

Just then someone knocked on the door, and he opened it.

"Hello, I'm sorry, a person needed a little help down there. I just wanted to confirm that Noah was already at home. Goodnight," said Aida, peeking through the door.

"Yes, thank you very much, friend. Goodnight," said Phoebe. The door closed again.

"Will you stay to sleep?" Noah asked, turning to me.

I looked at Phoebe, but she didn't say anything, just shrugged her shoulders.

"How about we have a movie marathon?" I proposed, and both accepted. "But I'll choose the movies." Now both were surprised.

The three of us settled on the couch, and I had both of them stuck to me, one leaning on each side. Before the end of the first movie of "The Lord of the Rings," both fell asleep. I kissed Phoebe's head to wake her up, but I had to caress her arm a bit to achieve it.

When she got up, I decided to take the little one in my arms to his bed. When I came out of his room, Phoebe was standing. I came over to give her a hug and kiss before pulling away.

"For when is the first court summons scheduled?" I asked.

She frowned slightly. "It's for next week."

"If you need anything, don't hesitate to let me know," I said, and she hugged me again.

"You've already done a lot, asking your Aunt Luz to take my case," she murmured against my chest.

"That's the least I can do, sweetheart. Now I'll leave," I said, caressing her hair.

Her lips drew into a pout as she pulled back to look at me. "You're leaving?"

"I haven't been authorized to stay and sleep. The owner of the house didn't say yes or no."

She stood on her tiptoes just to give me a kiss. "You don't need permission. I want you to stay with me. I think we left an unresolved matter a while ago."

"But Noah?"

"We'll have to implement the adrenaline of doing it in silence so as not to be heard by him," she said, and without further ado, I kissed her as we clumsily walked to her room, where we made sure to lock the door. Then we enjoyed and loved each other in the silence of the room.

My sweetheart ended up completely exhausted, and I was happy to be able to sleep in her bed, by her side, hugging her soft and curvy body and inhaling her sweet scent.

I closed my eyes, hoping that this time I could wake up beside her.

The rays of the sun were beginning to appear in the bluish morning twilight. I opened my eyes, and she was so beautiful.

I looked at the time and realized it was barely five-thirty in the morning. I got up and went to the bathroom to clean off a bit of the overflowing love on my body. I changed and approached my sweetheart, giving her many kisses on her face.

"Enough, my sweet wolf."

"Yes, that's me. I'll go to my apartment and bring something for breakfast. I'll be right back," I told her.

She nodded but didn't let me get away, as she wrapped her arms around my neck.

"Don't go," she whined.

"I don't want to, but I also don't want my stay to bring you problems or misunderstandings with Noah. I'll be back in a while with breakfast. Also, I want you to come with me to my father's birthday party tonight. I'll formally introduce you to my family."

"But we're nothing more than..."

I put a finger to her lips. "I know we said we would get to know each other better, but I can't avoid the fact that you've been my family since the day I first saw you."

"Omar, haven't you noticed something that has happened all three times we've been together?" she asked.

"Apart from how crazy you drive me and that every time we are together like this," I said, seeking to touch her pussy with my hand, "I fall more in love with you."

"Alright, will I see you before eight? Today I have to return to my work after three days."

"You've been at home all these days?" I asked, and she nodded. "And why didn't you call me earlier?"

"These three days helped me decide what I want to do, especially what I want to be with you," she said, then yawned.

"Alright, yes, I'll come before eight. I can spend the day with Noah, if you don't mind."

She shook her head. "I'll feel a little jealous, but nothing more."

"You had me all night for yourself," I said, giving her a kiss on her lips. "You can't be so selfish with our son." She looked at me in a way that I couldn't name her expression, then just nodded and settled back on the bed. I gave her one last kiss on her forehead before walking to the apartment door.

When I opened the door, I heard Aida's voice in the hallway. "I won't say anything if you don't either. Goodbye." Then I heard the door close, and I went out.

I didn't want to make her uncomfortable or embarrassed with my presence if she had spent the night with someone.

It wasn't my problem, but it became a problem the moment my eyes collided with that person who was waiting for the elevator.

Steven was exactly in the clothing that Noah had described to me the night before.

What was Aida doing with Steven?

Chapter 19

Omar

I don't think he saw me, as I diverted to go up the stairs. The last thing I needed was to create a problem for my sweetheart. I waited a few minutes until I managed to go down to the parking lot.

I didn't see anything else that seemed suspicious. The only thing I could do was call Alexis; I needed reinforcements to know a bit more about what had just happened.

"No wonder the sky is falling over my head in Madrid right now," said Alexis. "What a miracle that you're calling me and especially at this hour. What did you do?"

I rolled my eyes. "I need you here," I said, starting my car.

"My flight leaves in a couple of hours. I already had it arranged to be at your father's party, but if it's something urgent, I'll go now."

"I forgot you were coming, and yes, I'll wait for you in the afternoon."

"You're going to leave me wondering—" I cut him off by ending the call.

I knew that if I told him something, he would come earlier, and I want to spend some time with my family without him hovering over me all the time like a vulture.

I quickly arrived at my apartment, called my father to wish him a happy birthday, took a shower, and once ready, left my apartment, went to buy a wide variety of dishes for breakfast, and a coffee just as my sweetheart liked it.

"Good morning, Omar," Noah greeted me as he opened the door.

"Good morning, champ." I looked around for my sweetheart, but she wasn't in the kitchen or the living room. The door to her room was closed. "Your mother?" I asked, and Noah shrugged his shoulders.

"I told you she had me worried. She's been very strange, and she never answers me when I ask her if something's wrong. Now she's sleeping."

I looked at the time, and it was already late for her to still be sleeping if she had to get to her shift.

"Your mom saw and assisted in an emergency with a mother and her child. Sadly, both died, and that's why your mother is a bit depressed. It can't be easy to experience something like that. It's the worst part of her job. Just as it can make her happy to help beautiful babies be born, it must be very sad to witness the death of one and the mother. Now the only thing we should do is try to cheer her up and get her out of that sadness or any other problem that has her that way."

He nodded and helped me take the food trays out of the bags.

"Today is my father's birthday, and I would like us to go together to look for his gift. How does that sound?" I asked, and he nodded enthusiastically.

"Now I'll go wake up our princess," I said, and he smiled.

"Omar," he said before I left the kitchen.

"Yes?" I turned back to look at him.

"Nothing. I think it's still too early to say it," he said, and I messed up his hair.

"Little one, you know you can tell me anything, right?"

He nodded with a smile and took a plate with pancakes, bacon, and scrambled eggs, and walked to the couch where he was watching his cartoons.

I knocked on Phoebe's bedroom door, but I didn't receive a response. I entered, and she was still sleeping. I approached her quickly and began to kiss her cheek and neck until she began to move.

"Sweetheart, don't be scared, but your shift starts in forty-seven minutes," I said, and she pushed me to get out of bed super quickly. She stood up, and I had to hold her since she had done it so quickly that she got dizzy. "You shouldn't get up like that. Sit for a moment and then continue to the bathroom."

"No, I'm fine now. I have to go to work," she exclaimed, separating from my arms and then entering the bathroom.

I left the room to have something ready to eat. It didn't take her even twenty minutes, and she was already drinking the coffee I had brought. Her hair was damp, and she had a high ponytail.

"See you in the afternoon. Behave with Omar, Noah," she ordered.

He nodded, and I approached to give her a kiss on her lips, but she turned to look at Noah, so her cheek was the recipient. However, she turned, looked at me, smiled, and gave me a short kiss on the lips.

"I'll see you in the afternoon, sweet wolf," she said before leaving the apartment.

The most correct thing would be for me to take her to work, but I didn't know if being seen together could affect the case with Noah.

The day passed as it should; Noah went with me to the gym, to eat, to buy my father's gift, and we bought something for everyone.

When Phoebe arrived, we had already prepared a restorative bath in the tub for her and a dress from her closet that Noah and I chose. We waited patiently watching a couple of FIFA matches until my stunning sweetheart came out of that room looking majestic. Her makeup was impeccable, and that dress, although it didn't show anything, hugged all her curves and molded them to perfection.

I had to maintain my composure and even look elsewhere so as not to lose control in front of Noah.

"Thank you for your attention. I loved your choice of dress. Now let's go, or we'll be late," Phoebe said, walking toward the door.

I looked at the time, and she was right; we were already almost half an hour late, and it was almost half an hour to get there. My mother was definitely going to kill me.

Upon arriving at the party, everyone's eyes were on us. I cared very little; most of the guests were my family. My parents, grandparents, and cousins came to greet us. We lost sight of Noah when Ariana, the little daughter of my cousin Ángel, took his hand and another little one who I knew was the younger brother of Susy, Alan's wife.

"I'm sorry, Ariana is in her most social moment, and she likes to include all the children," said Clara, and all the adults who saw the scene laughed.

"I just ask God that this doesn't turn into a love triangle later on."

"Grandma," exclaimed Ángel, looking at my grandmother while laughing.

"I won't be here to see it, but my instinct doesn't fail me."

The celebration was very lively. Alexis had come accompanied, which made everything a bit easier for me, especially in not having him stuck to me like a tick. I asked him what I had already thought about in the morning; now, I was just waiting for news.

"It must have been something very sad, the truth," I heard my mother say when I returned to the table where my grandparents were.

"It was, more so for the little one. He was an innocent being," said Phoebe, and at that moment, I knew what they were talking about.

"Yes, but thanks to that, it was discovered that this organization was still operating, and we are after all those involved."

"What intrigues me the most is, who can be so cruel as to kill Luna while pregnant?" asked Phoebe.

"You would be surprised by the number of brutalities we have seen over these years, but what happened yesterday was something we wouldn't wish on our worst enemy," said my grandfather Manuel.

"What happened yesterday?" I asked.

"Minutes after you called your uncle and he called me, the discovery of two bodies was reported, a man and a woman. The woman was known in the underworld as 'the Hyena' and was in charge of connecting organ buyers directly with people who turned out to be compatible. She was a woman who, when seen on the street, you could say is completely ordinary, the daughter of a former leader, forty-four years old, who thought she had control of everything but didn't imagine that her actions might bring competition.

"We still don't know from where or whom the order came; the only thing we know is that she, like Charles, appeared together completely dismembered. I'm sorry if I'm being very explicit with this, but everything indicates that both were tortured while they were still alive. Their organs were ripped out and left beside the bodies. It seems there was a note, but I don't know what it says. We haven't received more information to tell us more."

Phoebe was very affected by his words, to the extreme of wetting my shirt with her tears. I didn't hesitate as I hugged her. I offered her my consolation in the face of the impression of knowing what was the end of the murderers, one more than the other, but equally murderers.

"Stop talking about things of that type. I'd better propose a toast for my husband," said my mother to change the atmosphere that was drastically experienced after that conversation.

"Phoebe, you haven't drank anything. Is everything okay?" asked my grandmother, offering a glass of wine to her.

My sweetheart was about to take a sip of her glass when Alexis called me to introduce me to some people I had never seen in my life. I looked for Phoebe, but I couldn't identify her; Noah was playing with the children, but she wasn't there.

"Do you know where Phoebe is?" I asked my Uncle Jerónimo, who was talking with my father.

"I saw her along with my sister, your mother, and Aitana going up the stairs."

I didn't waste time and walked in search of my sweetheart. Through the hallway of the second floor, their voices could be heard until I reached the door of what is my room when I came to this house, and I heard Aitana's voice.

"But don't take too long to tell Omar. He deserves to know, and if you don't do it soon, from my own experience, I can tell you that things don't turn out well."

Chapter 20
Phoebe

Seeing them both like two princes waiting for me at home and having everything ready for me when I arrived from my workday was very sweet. I was feeling very emotional and attributed it to pregnancy hormones, although anyone in my place would feel that way being received at home this way.

I enjoyed the slightly warm water for a few minutes and then began to prepare to go to the birthday of my baby's future grandfather. How strange it felt, but it was something I had to get used to.

Regardless of what happened between Omar and me, I knew my baby would have a very good family to care for him or her.

I looked at myself in the mirror and hoped that my belly wouldn't start to grow until all this was over. I hoped that in one or two more months, everything would be back to normal.

A part of me wanted to believe that Steven truly wanted the best for the child and that he wouldn't continue with his lawsuit. I was willing to allow visits, but we would see what dirty tricks he and his lawyer would weave next week.

"For one night, forget about your problems, Phoebe. Enjoy this new family that life is giving you on a silver platter," I said out loud to myself.

When I came out ready from the room, the reaction of both Omar and Noah was very funny. Both were completely stunned looking at me from head to toe, while they had the video game controllers in their hands.

Minutes later, we were entering the Guzman house, and indeed, our arrival had caused a bit of commotion among the adult guests and the little ones; even Noah was kidnapped to play.

Omar got up from the table to talk about something with his assistant, and Omar's grandfather began to ask me what I knew about the murder of Luna Succolu and her baby.

It was still a delicate topic for me, and what impressed me more was remembering that man crying over the death of his wife and son, and now he was dead along with the murderer of his family. I internally thanked Omar's mother, who proposed a toast for her husband, completely changing the subject.

"Phoebe, you haven't drank anything. Is everything okay?" asked Grandmother Jimena, extending a glass of wine in front of me.

Again at that moment, Alexis appeared, a man who didn't please me at all, and took Omar with the intention of introducing some people.

"Don't think that your behavior goes unnoticed," said the grandmother, causing my heart to accelerate because, when Omar left, I immediately put the glass on the table instead of drinking.

"No!" gasped Aitana, the grandmother, and Mrs. Patricia.

"It's best if we go to a place where you can tell us everything," said Mrs. Patricia.

I nodded; we all stood up and walked inside the house to one of the rooms.

"Are you pregnant?" asked Aitana when the door closed behind us.

"Yes, I just found out four days ago. I'm still coming to terms with the news."

"It can't be. I'm going to be a grandmother," exclaimed Mrs. Patricia with excitement, approaching me to touch my abdomen.

"Does Omar already know?" the grandmother asked, and I shook my head.

"No, and for a moment, I ask you not to tell him anything. The idea is not to tell him until the trial over Noah's custody is over. Apart from that, we are giving ourselves a chance and need to get to know each other a bit more. You'll understand that my situation is not easy, and all I want is to do the right thing."

"But don't take too long to tell Omar. He deserves to know, and if you don't do it soon, from my own experience, I can tell you that things don't turn out well."

My heart almost stopped when I saw Omar on the other side of the door.

"What's happening here?" he asked.

It was his mother who saved me by saying they were talking about my feelings for him. The three of them left the room in a hurry.

"You know you can talk to me about anything, right?" he said as he approached me to wrap his arms around my body. "I would love to be able to throw you on the bed and make you forget everything, but I couldn't do it at this moment. Later, I'll make love to you in such a way that every time you touch your skin again, you'll have me in your mind," he declared, filling my face with kisses.

He fulfilled his word of making love to me that night and the four that followed. I could only say that if this would be my life, I couldn't wait to get married already.

Another week passed, and Omar literally lived in my apartment. Alexis was very much on top of Omar due to a campaign he was recording in Madrid. It bothered me that just one day before my court date, Omar had to go on a trip, leaving much silence in his absence.

"Are you ready?" asked lawyer Luz before we entered our appointment with the judge.

"Yes," I said, and she opened the door.

Upon entering, Steven and his lawyer were already there, but I ignored his greeting and anything that might come from a man like him. We settled in.

"Good afternoon, everyone. My name is Estefanía Triviño, and I will be the judge in charge of what is discussed and disputed here, making it clear that any decision I make will be exclusively for the benefit of the minor in question."

My hands were sweating, and my legs wouldn't stop moving. Lawyer Luz looked at me and smiled comfortingly.

"Plaintiff's attorney, present your claim and what you request to resolve the case." The judge gave them the floor first, and that was something my lawyer had already made me aware of.

It hurt a lot how Steven's lawyer labeled me as being irresponsible or a bad mother to Noah just because I spent many hours working at the hospital. He exposed my latest scandal with Omar not being married, and thus began to come out with a lot of things that were not true at all.

"My client had an accident less than a year ago that has permanently made it impossible for him to have children. In this envelope, you can find the evidence of what we are talking about and the examinations that my client has undergone in recent times. That is why he wishes to give an exemplary home and the best quality of life to his only son, apart from the fact that my client's family gives Mrs. Phoebe a monthly allowance for the child's expenses."

Lawyer Luz took my hand under the table when, without wanting to, a tear ran down my cheek as a result of the anger I felt at that moment. I wiped it away immediately, and my gaze was fixed on Steven who, like the good coward he was, wasn't looking me in the face.

"Okay, if there is nothing more to say from the plaintiff's side, Lawyer Amador, how does the defendant respond?"

She released my hand and passed an envelope to the judge, just as the other party did. Giving all the evidence and talking about how everything was from the beginning. Where Noah's schedules, my schedules, and other things that the other lawyer also had filled his mouth with were delivered.

"What draws my attention, Your Honor, is that the plaintiff's side has not talked about this." Luz delivered the document that Steven signed, giving total custody of Noah to me.

"What does this mean, counselor?" asked the judge.

The lawyer looked at Steven, and he just shrugged his shoulders.

"They made me sign that document under deception. Had I known what it was about, I wouldn't have done it," said Steven, and I shook my head.

"You can argue those accusations at another time, sir, because according to the evidence presented, it is clear that this will not be closed in a mediation. The case will be handed over to a social services lawyer who will be responsible for ensuring the best for the minor.

"If none of you wish to add anything else, we will see each other in court in two months; meanwhile, the social services lawyer will contact you lawyers to continue with the case. Now, the most important question. Mr. García, do you wish that while this mediation is being done, the child in question be under the care of social services?"

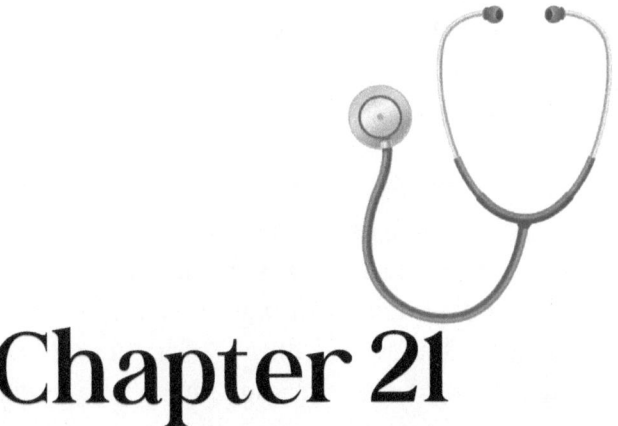

Chapter 21
Phoebe

Steven looked at me, and I shook my head, believing he could see the way I was pleading with just a look. He immediately addressed the judge.

"Yes, I don't think my son is well or safe in that place."

"No... no!" I shouted.

"Calm down, Mom. You're dreaming," said my Noah, touching my cheek with his hand. I took his hand to bring him to my body, hugging him tightly and distributing kisses on his face.

Yes, that last part had been a nightmare. Steven said no, that it was fine for the child to be with me until the process was finalized. Luz encouraged me, saying that decision could be a point in my favor.

"And it's the only good thing your father has been able to do," I said under my breath, and Noah looked at me with curiosity.

"Will you tell me what happened?" he asked. I shook my head.

"No, it's better that you don't know. I don't want you to get involved and that head of yours to start imagining things it doesn't need to. The only thing I ask is that we continue our life as usual."

"Okay, and have you heard from Omar? I called him a while ago, and he didn't answer me."

I smiled and caressed his cheek. Omar called me during the meeting, but I couldn't answer the call. When I left, I called him, but he didn't answer. I didn't worry about calling him again because he sent me a message saying he would be recording a couple of things and would call me as soon as he could.

"He must be busy. Remember that he went to work."

"I'm upset because he left on a day when he should be with you," Noah said, crossing his arms with all the righteous indignation an eight year old could muster.

I had to bite my lip to keep from smiling at his serious expression. The way he stood there with his little chin jutted out, looking like a miniature adult ready to lecture someone twice his size, was absolutely adorable. A warm bubble of laughter threatened to escape my throat.

"Oh really?" I managed to say, trying to match his serious tone while my eyes sparkled with barely contained mirth. The corners of my mouth twitched upward despite my best efforts to stay composed.

His freckled face was set in such a determined frown, his green eyes flashing with protective anger on my behalf. It was like watching a kitten try to be fierce—endearing and amusing all at once. I had to look away for a moment to collect myself, pressing my hand to my mouth to hide the smile that was definitely showing now.

The fact that my eight year old son was essentially scolding a grown man for not treating me properly was both touching and hilarious. I felt that wonderful lightness in my chest that comes from unexpected joy, the kind that makes you want to scoop up your child and squeeze them tight.

"I know, honey, but he only knew the date a few days ago, and he's had this commitment for months. We must be aware that Omar will not spend all his time with us. Now he does because we are enjoying his summer months, but the days will return when it will be difficult to see him because he will be training and attending matches, and we must understand that."

Noah nodded his head, seeming to agree with me. "Will we move to Madrid with him?" he asked, and the truth was that I didn't have an answer to his question.

"I don't know, honey," I admitted.

"But what if Omar asks you?" he asked me.

I shrugged my shoulders. "Even if he asks, I have to see many factors, and the most important is that we must finish with your father's custody petition."

His face twisted in disgust. "I don't like that you say that man is my father. He's not."

"Noah, even if you don't like it, he won't stop being your father. His blood is the one that runs through your veins, and you have his eyes. It's difficult to deny it; I understand that you don't like him because of how he has behaved with us, but it's bad to have resentment, rancor, or even hatred for our parents," I said, taking his hand.

"You never talk about your parents. Were they bad to you?" he asked, and I shook my head.

"Let's prepare dinner because tomorrow is a school day, young man," I changed the subject. I stood up, feeling slightly dizzy. It seemed that dizziness appeared only when I stood up very quickly.

"Mom, a few days ago, I had a dream, and I hadn't told you because they say that dreams shouldn't be told if they are to come true, but this one really made me very happy," Noah said, and I could see how his expression confirmed it.

"Tell me what it is that made you so happy."

"I dreamed that I had many siblings and that we lived in a huge house with many courts for different sports. We were all children, Mom, and we played football with Omar and his dad, and I called Omar 'dad' and his dad 'grandpa'," Noah said, and my eyes filled with tears.

The happiness on my son's face was incredible, and it hurt me not to know what was going to happen with this whole situation.

My relationship with Omar was still something that was in limbo, because apart from spending almost all the time here with us, we hadn't given 'us' a title. He hadn't asked me to be his girlfriend, and although there was a marriage proposal in the air, neither of us had touched on the subject again.

"Would you like to have siblings?" I asked, turning my attention back to Noah.

"Yes, I hope that very soon you have many babies here," he said, touching my abdomen. "Omar and I would take good care of them."

"We'll see what God says, honey." I was dying to tell him that very soon he would become a big brother, but I figured it was better to wait. My Noah didn't have much of a filter, and for the moment, it was better to continue keeping my little one a secret.

We ate dinner while watching a movie. Then I helped Noah prepare his uniform and tidy up his room a bit. We read a few lines from his favorite book, Moby Dick by Herman Melville.

After making sure he was asleep, I took my phone and called Omar.

"Sweetheart, I was about to call you. How are you? How was the first meeting? I've been anxious and worried all day," he said when he answered.

I couldn't deny that he seemed really concerned by his tone of voice.

"Well, it went well. The judge heard both sides, but Steven..." I began to tell him everything that was said and debated. "Now we have to wait two months to know what will happen."

"Wow, that long?" he asked, and although he couldn't see me, I shrugged.

"Yes, according to your Aunt Luz, it's normal because they will begin to investigate with the social services lawyers."

"I imagine how difficult that moment was for you, sweetheart, and here I am without being able to hug you, kiss you, rest my chin on your head, and tell you that everything will be okay. I hope to be able to return tomorrow afternoon and talk about some things. Discuss our future together." Those words, his words, always had the power to make me sigh and fall more in love.

"Okay, I'll go rest because, although tomorrow is my day off, I want to make the most of it to do certain things. Do you know what time you fly back?" I asked; it had occurred to me that I could prepare something special for when he returned, but with time, and without burning the food again.

"I don't know, but I hope it's not before noon. I'm already dying to be with you and Noah. Yesterday I could hardly sleep; I needed the warmth of your body beside me."

"You're a liar," I said, feeling my cheeks starting to burn.

"I'm only telling the truth, my love," he said, and I sighed like a teenager.

"You always are a sweet wolf," I said, smiling and caressing my belly, thinking about what it would be like when he found out about the existence of our little one.

"Always yours, baby. For now, I'll let you rest. See you tomorrow. I love you, sweetheart."

"I love you, little wolf. Good night." Yes, this wasn't the first time he told me he loved me and also not the first time I responded; the first was a few days ago, but it always felt as exciting as the first time.

Half an hour later, I prepared to sleep, and as had been happening to me in recent days, I fell asleep as soon as I made contact with the pillow.

Knocks on the front door woke me up a while later. The knocks were insistent to the point that Noah also appeared rubbing his eyes in the living room.

"Who is it?" I asked; I didn't even know what time it was.

"It's me," said Aida from the other side of the door.

I opened it without hesitation, and she came with her phone in her hand and her pajamas.

"What's happening, woman? You scared me," I exclaimed.

She didn't say anything when she saw Noah; she merely put her phone in front of me.

The image surprised me a lot, but the headline affected me much more.

"Omar Guzman is seen with a beautiful blonde, very affectionate. Has he moved on from the curvy woman in Zaragoza?"
"The bachelor continues his antics."
"The number ten forward of the Colchoneros team has made the news again, and not for his participation in the new campaign, but for being seen with a tiny and slim woman, activating rumors that perhaps he is not ready to assume responsibilities such as having a family and settling down."

Those were just a few lines, as there was much more written there. At the same time, more photos appeared. Omar was hugging a woman, kissing another woman, and twirling another woman in his arms.

The phone began to tremble in my hand. I felt somewhat dizzy, but upon seeing Noah's eyes on me, I calmed down and handed the phone back to Aida.

"What's happening?" he asked with curiosity.

"Nothing, honey. It's getting late for school; go get ready."

He nodded and went back into his room.

"He's an idiot," I said about Omar, hitting the sofa where I had collapsed, tired of it all.

"I'm sorry, friend. I didn't want to wake you up like this, but you needed to be informed in case downstairs is full of reporters or journalists," said Aida, giving me a hug.

My eyes burned with tears; I bit my tongue trying not to cry in front of Noah. I didn't want to transmit all this to my son—well, my children.

"I knew something like this could happen, but I need him to explain. I must give him the benefit of the doubt before thinking or seeing more," I said these words more to myself.

Aida nodded and helped me get to my feet. "Go lie down; I'll help you with Noah. I'll take him to school."

I didn't refuse. I needed to think and try to keep in line so many emotions that were bad for my baby.

"I'm ready, Mom," said Noah, coming to my room.

"Have a good day, honey. Your Aunt Aida will take you, and I'll pick you up in the afternoon, okay?" I forced a smile.

Noah nodded his head in affirmation, and after giving him a kiss on the cheek and a hug, he left hand in hand with Aida.

Minutes later, the silence inside my apartment was deafening. I took my phone, and the first thing I did was call Omar. I needed explanations, and only he could give them to me.

To my misfortune, the one who answered the phone was none other than Alexis, Omar's representative and assistant. From our first meeting, it was clear he disapproved of my relationship with Omar—whether he saw me as a gold-digger, a distraction from Omar's career, or simply an inconvenience, I couldn't tell. But his hostility toward me was unmistakable and seemed to go beyond professional concern.

"I need to talk to Omar," I requested.

"Omar is busy at the moment," he said, but in the background, I heard Omar's unmistakable voice saying something that broke my heart.

"Get a car to take her to her hotel, then pick up her things and bring them here. She will stay here with me for a while. What are you doing with my phone?" Just at that moment, the call ended, and I sat down trying not to think about anything, but how could I avoid not thinking the worst?

A woman was in Omar's apartment at seven in the morning? What was she doing there? The answer caused me a lot of pain in my chest and even a strong urge to vomit.

I ran to the bathroom, throwing my phone on the bed, and emptied my stomach. When I came out, I realized I had two missed calls from Omar, and they would continue. I wasn't going to answer the phone; I laid down on the bed and cried, hugging the pillow. I felt mocked, used, and publicly humiliated.

The phone was ringing, and this time it was Omar's mother. I didn't answer her either. I didn't wish to talk to anyone right now.

Chapter 22

Omar

I hated leaving my sweetheart alone a day before the first legal mediation. But it reassured me to know that she was in good hands with my Aunt Luz.

The recordings for the campaign would begin that same day, and it was a contract we couldn't lose. Besides, canceling it wouldn't benefit my image and could cost us several thousand euros.

"A day or two that you don't spend with that woman and her son won't be the end of the world," said Alexis, and I couldn't hold back.

I grabbed him by the collar of his shirt and brought my face close to his.

"I told you once, Phoebe is not just any woman; she is the woman, my woman, the one I want in my life. I don't care what you want and think about that. I remind you that you are my representative, and I consider you my friend, so learn to distinguish what your place is and your limits on how far you should and can get involved.

"Her name is Phoebe, and her son's name is Noah. Remember that for the next time you mention her because otherwise, I'll forget who you are." I released him and glared at him.

He glowered at me. "And as your representative, I tell you that being with that woman is not good for you. I did what you asked me to do with her neighbor, and the only thing that happened between Steven and her was just that night. The guy has been looking for her these days, and she has refused to see him again. It seems she sacrificed herself to give you two your moment.

"I also learned about her past; do you know what kind of parents she had? Do you know the problems you're going to get into if the creditors of those people find out that Phoebe is their daughter? Your career will go down the drain! Just because you decided to fall in love with the wrong person." He was about to continue, but the gesture I made made him back off and shut his mouth.

"I don't care what you think of her," I snapped. "That is the woman my heart chose to love, and that won't change until life says otherwise. I've never had this type of problem with you, and I hope it stays that way. Don't overstep your boundaries."

"Yes, yes, okay. Now you can go eat; in two hours, you must return to the set to conclude with this location."

I turned around and headed to a hotel restaurant where the recording for the men's underwear advertisement was taking place. I tried to call my sweetheart, but when I saw the time, I realized that she might still be in the meeting. So I decided to send her a text message to tell her that in a little while, I would be busy again.

The day passed more slowly than I would have preferred. I wanted to finish everything and take a direct flight to Zaragoza. I had already spent a terrible night trying to sleep alone; I had been resting with Phoebe's warmth by my side for five days, so it was very difficult for me to fall asleep.

"With this, we have concluded, gentlemen. You did a very good job," said the commercial director to all those involved.

After that, I finished changing and left the hotel quickly.

"Do we have anything else pending in Madrid in the coming days?" I asked Alexis, seeing that it was barely evening; I could arrive today if I found a flight.

"No," he responded simply.

"Okay, get me a flight that leaves from here no later than noon to arrive in Zaragoza early."

He nodded, and we continued walking to the car.

I felt a small hand caress my back, and I was about to respectfully move away. When I turned around, I realized who it was, and I couldn't help but kiss her cheek and hug her tightly to the point of making her spin with me.

"Sonia! When did you arrive? What are you doing here? Do my parents know you're here?" I exclaimed as I put her back on the ground.

Sonia was the daughter of my grandfather David and his third wife, Sofia Mejía. Sadly, my grandfather David died nine years ago, and her mother was still alive and lived with her in Chile.

"I arrived three days ago; I didn't want to announce anything, you know it's better that way," she said.

"What a surprise. It's been, what, eight or ten years now?"

She continued to caress my back. "My nephew is always so sweet, how about you take me to dinner? My group seems to have left me alone," she said, looking towards three people who were behind her a moment ago.

"Of course, let's go, and along the way, you can tell me about your adventures in Chile and Antarctica."

"Aren't you going to introduce us?" said Alexis at my side.

"Yes, Alexis, my rep. Sonia is my aunt on my grandfather's side," I explained.

She extended her hand and smiled. I could see the wretch winking at her.

"Let's go. I'll take you to a new restaurant," said Alexis, opening the door for my aunt.

"What an attentive representative you have, Omar. I can see why you appear in the best campaigns and projects," she exclaimed, praising Alexis's work.

We all got into the car that took us to the restaurant on one of the rooftops in the center of Madrid. The place was very elegant.

"I don't think I'm dressed for a place like this," she remarked, taking my arm.

"You're perfect; don't worry," said Alexis, flattering, who didn't want to vanish as he usually did when I came alone or accompanied by a girl.

This time he wanted to join us during dinner and even suggested that we go to my apartment, which was nearby, to have a drink and continue listening to Sonia's exciting stories and adventures, because there have been many.

"Make yourselves comfortable. I'll be right back, I have to make a call," I said when we arrived at my apartment.

"Me, too. Excuse us, Sonia," said Alexis, leaving the apartment.

Seeing that, I had no problem sitting in the living room in front of Sonia and calling my sweetheart. The call was brief because she was about to go rest, and I just wanted to leave everything to go to her. I sighed when the call disconnected.

"My nephew is so tender; he seems like a teenager in love. Who is she? The girl with her son?" she asked, and I nodded with a smile on my face.

"Yes, and the truth is that I am a teenager in love."

"I'm glad to know that," she said with a bit of sadness.

"And you are in love?" I asked, furrowing my brows at her expression.

She shook her head. "With my work, it's impossible to achieve a bit of stability. I'm traveling the world now, giving conferences on the latest research we've done, and it's not possible."

"It seems that studying Marine Biology has its disadvantages," I said, and she nodded.

"Yes, but not as many as those of a football player. You have millions of people on top of you, and in my case, people don't know I exist, and that's better."

"Is that why you wanted to go study so far away?" I wondered.

"Yes, but I also did it for my mom. When my father died, she became very depressed and swore she saw him everywhere, besides she told me many stories about her past and said she wanted to seek peace in a place far from Spain. I couldn't refuse that, and we've been fine, although she's already getting sick and is losing her hearing," she said, and I sat next to her to give her a hug. "I understand it's the law of life to lose your parents, but I don't feel prepared to say goodbye to my mother."

"I understand. Will you go see my father and my Aunt Regina?" I asked, and she nodded.

"Yes, in fact, starting the day after tomorrow, we have a day off; at 10 a.m. tomorrow I have to be at the conference room at the Madrid Zoo Aquarium. It will be a doctor's visit for one of the animals, but at least I'll be able to have lunch with my siblings. I talk with your father once a week, so I've already seen that it's from the Guzman side to be tender and attentive."

"With great honor," I said, taking a sip from my glass.

Alexis returned and throughout the night was almost throwing himself at Sonia. Between drinks and chats, it was two in the morning when we finished, and Sonia's hotel was on the other side of the city.

"I say it's time for you to go to your apartment, and you, miss, can go rest in the room here. I'll pass you a set of clothes so you can rest comfortably," I said, walking to my room to bring her what I promised.

"Thank you. Good night to both of you. Sleep well."

We said goodbye and each found our way to bed.

In my case, I took a shower and laid on the bed. I hugged the pillow and sighed, thinking of my sweetheart, and that tomorrow I would squeeze her again until I fell asleep drowned in her delicious lavender scent.

There was a coffee aroma in the environment, and the sun was shining scandalously through the window. Lately, I had been sleeping too much; I hadn't been able to wake up at five in the morning as I used to do for days. It seems I should resort to my alarm clock again.

I left the room minutes after doing my personal cleaning. I looked for my phone in the room and couldn't find it.

Upon seeing Alexis standing with his back in the middle of the living room, I gave orders so that Sonia could use my apartment during the time she is in Madrid.

Alexis turned around, and I observed that my phone was in his hand.

I took it from his hands and looked at the calls; my sweetheart had called, and this idiot answered. I called her twice, and she didn't answer either time.

"What did you tell her?" I said and gave him a direct punch to the jaw.

"I just told her you were busy," he defended, cleaning the blood from his lip. "It's not my fault the woman gets hysterical." He shouldn't have said that; I gave him a second blow that sent him to the floor.

"Oh, no… Omar," Sonia's voice cut through my rage just as I was raising my fist for a third blow. Her tone was sharp with alarm, stopping me mid-motion.

"What's happening?" I demanded, turning toward her.

She approached me with evident concern etched across her face, her eyebrows drawn together in worry. Her hands were slightly raised, as if she wanted to reach out but wasn't sure if she should.

"It's better that you see it for yourself," she murmured as she handed me the phone.

They were photos that were taken yesterday when I met her and were taken completely out of context, implying we were lovers. My blood began to boil as I saw the amount of stupidity written in the headlines.

"According to his manager, he is not ready to assume responsibilities such as having a family and settling down," I read aloud. My gaze went to the idiot lying on the floor. "It was you, wasn't it, you son of a bitch?"

Chapter 23

Omar

I didn't know how many punches I gave him. I was only aware that Sonia pushed me to the floor to prevent me from continuing to hit him.

"Omar! Stop it now. You're going to kill him!" yelled Sonia, falling on top of me.

"You're fired, you damn idiot," I snarled. "Phoebe hasn't interfered at all, so you have no right to do this to her. I'm not stupid; I know very well that you did this to bother her."

Sonia went to where he was to help him up.

Alexis spat blood. "Yes, I did it, because that woman is not good for you."

"No! She is not the problem. The problem is you, who always wants easy work without problems. You did the same to that boy… and remember how far your actions went. But I'm not him, and I gave you the opportunity to be my representative because you were my friend; however, I've already seen that with you, friendship is worth nothing. Because a friend would be happy to see the other happy.

"We all have a past, and although we would like to erase it, we have to learn to live with it. Phoebe has no fault in having the parents she does. I remind you that one doesn't choose that detail, just as you can't live with the fact that your father is homosexual and fell in love with one of your friends."

I stood up and returned to my room. The phone vibrated in my hand, and I answered without seeing who it was.

"Oh, Omar, what did you do?" cried my mother's voice. "Who is that girl? Her face can't be seen well in the images."

"It's Sonia, Mom. We met on the street, and I greeted her; that was all. Everything was taken out of context because of that damn Alexis," I growled, looking for clothes in my closet to change. I needed to leave Madrid as soon as possible.

"I called Phoebe, but she didn't answer me. It's better that you fix this misunderstanding because if not, I'm going to cut off the sack that hangs between your legs."

"I'm on it, Mother; I'm leaving for Zaragoza as quickly as possible."

"You'd better. Phoebe already has enough on her plate without you giving her more. I hope her health isn't affected because of your idiot assistant. I'll go see her and explain."

"No, I appreciate your concern, but this is something I have to do. You would help me a lot by getting a flight or a way I can get there as soon as possible."

"Okay, I'll send you what I find now."

I ended the call, and after ensuring I had everything necessary, I left for the living room. Sonia was already there with her clothes from the night before, placing ice in a cloth for Alexis, who still had the nerve to be sitting on the couch.

His nose and lip were bleeding, but beyond seeing his cheeks slightly swollen, I didn't see anything that should be a cause for concern.

"Why haven't you left? Get out!" I shouted, and he shook his head.

"No, I want to help you solve the problem I got you into."

I scoffed at his audacity. "You've done enough. I don't need you to try to fix anything," I said, looking between the two. "Sonia, I'm on my way out to the airport. I can drop you off at your hotel, so none of this harms you and what you came for."

"No, it's fine. I just ordered an Uber."

"No, I'll take you. I'm very sorry you had to witness this," said Alexis.

"It would be the least you could do after also trying to damage her image, knowing she is another member of my family. I'm sorry, Sonia. I'll wait for you in Zaragoza; the offer for you to continue using the apartment stands. Make yourself at home," I said, approaching her to give her a hug and a kiss on the cheek.

"Omar," insisted Alexis, walking behind me. I stopped but didn't turn around. "I'm very sorry."

"Yes, me too, for trusting someone I shouldn't have." I threw open the apartment door and left. As I walked to the car, my mother sent the flight itinerary.

My security personnel took me to the airport, where I only had to check in, and they got me to the jet that would take me to Zaragoza. During the flight, I thought about how Phoebe would be, what she would be thinking about all this; I called her countless times from the airport and before boarding, but I didn't get any response.

My heart was beating strongly in my chest; I could feel her pain imagining her little face upon seeing the images, believing herself mocked by me.

Upon arriving in Zaragoza almost at noon, a car was already waiting for me, and I went directly to her apartment. I pressed the access code at the entrance, and it seemed invalid. I tried it more than four times, and the same thing happened. I called her number and didn't receive a response. A lady was coming out, and I had the hope of entering, but she stood in front of the door until it closed.

"You have nothing to do here. Go with your new girl and leave that poor young woman and her child in peace. I have the tragedy of knowing those of your kind, and you are spoiled children who believe that by having everything, you have the right to come and hurt others."

She turned around and continued on her way. I didn't care about her words because I hadn't done anything wrong, and it wasn't as she thought.

I stood there for I don't know how long; five people upon seeing me did the same as the lady. They didn't let me in, until my sweetheart appeared. Her face was pale, and her eyes were swollen, which she tried to hide with sunglasses.

"Sweetheart," I said, and she said nothing. After closing the door, she just continued on her way. "Phoebe, let me explain. She is…"

She stopped and turned around.

"I'm not interested in what she is, what you have done, and much less what you want to explain to me. From the beginning, it was clear that something between us simply cannot be. Stupid to think it would be the opposite. I'm going to ask you, no, I'm going to demand that you stay away from us; go back to your world there in Madrid, it's clear that we are nothing but obstacles for you."

She ran to the trash can at the entrance and emptied her stomach. I approached her, but she removed my hand.

"Don't touch me," she said and began her walk to Noah's school.

I followed her at a prudent distance, saw how she talked with Noah for a moment, and I could observe the tears on Noah's face. I couldn't help it and approached to ask what was happening to him.

"What happens is that Noah told his classmates that you were going to be his father, and today they all made fun of him," she snapped, standing up.

"I trusted you a lot, but you're a liar. I don't want to see you again," said Noah, giving me a push before walking away from me.

Phoebe sneered. "This is what happens when you fill a child's mind and heart with illusion, and then everything turns out to be a lie."

"Phoebe, please let me explain; she is my Aunt Sonia," I tried to defend.

She laughed bitterly, passing by my side.

"I'm serious; she is my father's sister, daughter of my grandfather David and his wife. She has lived in Chile for nine years. The photos are real; yesterday I found her on the street and greeted her with enthusiasm, as I would with any of my family. I don't have eyes for any woman other than you," I said just when I could perceive the sound of a flash in our direction.

"Whether what you say is true or not, I won't know, and much less should I care. The best thing for us is to say goodbye here and now."

"I'm not going to give up so easily," I insisted. "I'm going to prove to you that what I say is true. I can't live without you, without you both. I love you, Phoebe. I have since the day I saw you. I don't regret anything we've experienced; please don't push me away from you."

"I love you too, but it's the best for everyone, Omar. Otherwise, we would only hurt each other more, and believe me, the last thing I want to do is hate you."

She turned and followed Noah at a quick pace.

Chapter 24

Omar

As I said, I wasn't going to give up so easily, but it was very difficult for me to have access to her and Noah. I sent them presents that were returned, and each time that happened, it hurt me more because I knew they wouldn't give me the opportunity to explain myself again. When sadly, I hadn't done anything to deserve this treatment.

As my mother told me that day when I arrived at her house: This was the price of fame; something so minuscule was capable of hurting everyone around me.

The days went by, and Sonia came to Zaragoza; she felt very bad for me about what had happened. She even offered to talk to Phoebe, but I refused. I had learned that mistakes could not be corrected by pointing to others; this problem wasn't created by me, but it involved me, so I didn't want anyone else to intervene.

Alexis called me non-stop, but he didn't receive a response from me. When it was work-related, he communicated via email, and yes, through the intervention of my father, he continued to be my representative. But nothing more; friendship and trust were non-existent between us.

Three and a half weeks had passed, not to say a month.

To everyone's surprise, Alexis gave some statements where he made my relationship with Sonia very clear, saying he regretted having made that comment, finally trying to explain a bit of what had happened. I thought that would give me the opportunity to explain myself to Phoebe, but it wasn't so.

"Have you tried going to the hospital?" my mother suggested, and I affirmed.

"Yes, I wait for her, but she evades me, and the truth is that I feel it's time to give up."

"No! I forbid you, Omar. You must continue insisting; you haven't wanted anyone to interfere and help you, and although I respect that, I don't share those feelings. A lot of time has passed, and I'm going to help you. Leave it to me; meanwhile, get the biggest bouquet of flowers they can sell you."

I looked at her without knowing what kind of method she would use to make Phoebe agree to talk to me.

Two hours later, my mother was already saying that I should be at the cafeteria at one in the afternoon. It seemed strange to me, but I wasn't going to contradict her. People were looking at me since I had a bouquet of flowers next to me and was standing right at the entrance as if I were waiting for someone.

When I saw Phoebe enter the door, I stopped breathing. She looked thinner and thinner, and her face was still pale.

"What are you doing here?" she asked, and I didn't know what to tell her.

"I need you to listen to me; I can't take it anymore," I said, getting on my knees in front of her.

She looked around, took the flowers, and nodded. She offered me her hand, and we walked to a table, where we sat down, and I didn't miss the opportunity. I could talk, explain everything that had happened.

"I want to be with you; please don't push me away anymore. I'm about to go crazy if I don't have you by my side."

She sighed and looked at me with tears in her eyes. "It will be difficult to regain Noah's trust," she said, and I smiled because that meant yes, she was giving me a chance.

"I'll do anything to regain his trust, and yours, sweetheart." I stood up to hug her and kiss her, but when she was standing, she got dizzy, and I held her in my arms. This must be something serious now; whenever she was near me, something happened to her.

"It's not normal for you to be pale, vomiting, and about to faint all the time," I said as I helped her sit down in the chair.

"It's normal when you're pregnant, Omar."

"Even so, I think you should see a..." Did she say pregnant? I lowered down to her height. "Are you pregnant?" I asked in case I had heard wrong, at the same time taking her hands.

"Yes, I'm two months pregnant," she confirmed, and I smiled so widely that my cheeks hurt.

I hugged her tightly, and between smiles, my eyes began to sting to the point of shedding a couple of tears, which I didn't worry about wiping away when I pulled away from her to see her face.

"Really?" I asked, still unable to believe it.

"Yes. It seems it was impossible not to end up in this state when we have never been careful," she said, and I mentally kicked myself; I had never paid attention to that detail. Even in that, Phoebe made me lose my sanity.

"I'm sorry, darling. I should have been careful and—"
She put a finger to my lips.

"I think we are more than aware that this is not only due to your lack of sanity but also mine. I realized it from the first time, but with all the media stuff that day, it completely slipped my mind, and then the second time, I took a pill, but with the possibility that it wouldn't work due to our first time, and it seems there was nothing that could be done to avoid it," she said, caressing my cheek.

"How long have you known?"

"I've known since the day of the Luna Succolu incident."

"Is that why they gave you days off?" I asked, and she nodded, making connections of many things at that moment. "Is that why you called me?" She nodded again. "That means that if you hadn't been pregnant, would you not have called me?"

"It's possible I wouldn't have, but I would be lying to you if I said that every night I didn't think about you, that I didn't feel a tremendous need to know about you, to see you; I looked at your social networks all the time. I needed that time to realize that I had never wanted something for myself as much as I want you."

"Why have you hidden it from me all this time?"

"I didn't want you to feel obligated to be with me because of the baby. I wanted to get to know you a bit more, and yes, that's very childish of me, but understand me. Look at the situation I'm in with Noah; I can't handle a new disappointment and have the story repeat itself for me. I can be very strong, but falling in love and being rejected again, I couldn't bear it."

"I understand your fears, your distrust, but your lack of confidence bothers me. You know that what we had was magical from the beginning; my feelings for you were sincere and honest from day one."

"I know, but you must understand that for a woman whose heart has been broken, like mine, it's very difficult to believe when good things happen around her. You are a dream come true for any woman, and for me, you become more of a fantasy."

"Well, you have very good fantasies, sweetheart."

"Silly," she said, pushing me slightly.

"So my little one has been here for two months already, and I didn't even know?" I said, touching her abdomen.

"Yes, and your mom, your grandmother, your sister, and even your father know it."

"Well, the typical Galeano tradition. Hiding pregnancies from their parents."

She looked at me without understanding.

"I'll explain it to you in more detail when we get home, and you rest."

"No, don't become overprotective because I won't be able to stand it," she protested, and I raised an eyebrow.

"Well, if you know me as a sweet wolf, then you'll also know me as your overprotective man. How did Noah take the news?" I asked.

"He doesn't know." That completely surprised me. "But he suspects it. So much so that the day before what happened, he told me he had dreamed of you, your father, and that he had many brothers. I didn't tell him because he was always in communication with you, and he would let it slip without hesitation."

I smiled at that because it meant that Noah would take the news very well. But then another thing filled me with anxiety.

"Have you had any check-ups?" I asked; I needed to know.

"I have an appointment for my first ultrasound today with the doctor in…" She took her phone out of her pocket and looked at me again. "One hour."

"Well, then let's eat something while we wait. I imagine you were here to find something for lunch, and I'm making you hold off on hunger," I said, and she laughed out loud and shook her head.

We ate, talking about what had happened all these days that she hasn't allowed me to be close to her. The situation and the turn that the case with Steven was taking bothered me a lot. We stood up, and when we were leaving the cafeteria, Aida was approaching with an envelope in her hand and a lost look on her face.

"Aida, is everything okay?" Phoebe asked with concern.

"Yes, I was coming to find you. I need to talk to you. It's something really important."

Her friend's voice was too bright, too forced—the way people spoke when they were trying not to panic. Aida's hands were fidgeting with the hem of her shirt, and she kept glancing toward the windows as if expecting something terrible to appear there.

"You're worrying me, Aida." Phoebe studied her friend's face more carefully, noticing the tension around her eyes, the way her smile didn't quite reach them. Aida was practically vibrating with nervous energy, shifting her weight from foot to foot like she couldn't stay still.

"No, in fact, it's something that could help you find a bit more peace, although it's about to drive me crazy," she said, and this time I could see her more affected.

"Let's sit down for a moment so we can talk. We're in the middle of the entrance," Phoebe suggested, and we settled at the nearest table.

"Now, Aida. Tell me what's happening. You're making me nervous. What do you mean that what's happening to you can help me?" my sweetheart said, and I could see that she was indeed getting anxious. I took her hand, trying to calm her.

"I'm pregnant," she said, and Phoebe looked at her and smiled a bit disconcerted.

"Congratulations, but I don't understand."

Aida wiped away a couple of tears. "I'm pregnant by Steven, Noah's father."

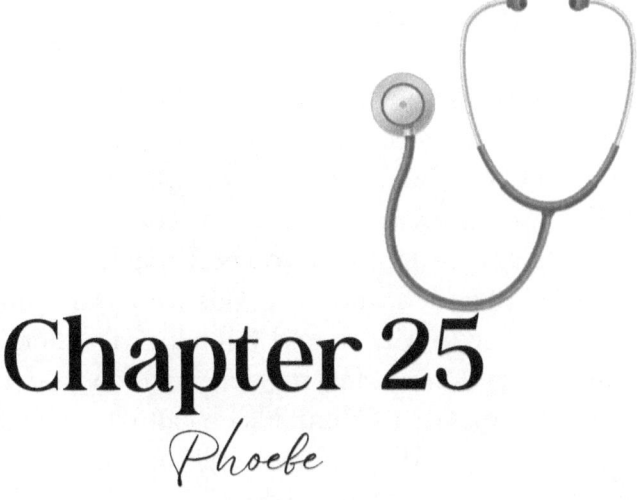

Chapter 25

Phoebe

The phone wouldn't stop vibrating, and I knew I had to act before everything got out of control. I didn't need Omar at my door all the time.

Being with him was a mistake. We didn't fit into his life, and it was better to push him away before anything else. Eventually, I would have to tell him about my pregnancy, but I would wait until everything was resolved with Steven.

"Phoebe, how can I help you?" said Mr. Ernesto, the building maintenance manager, when I called him.

"Good morning, Mr. Neto. I wanted to bother you with something," I said, trying to sound as calm as possible.

"Yes, of course, if it's in my power, with pleasure," the man said kindly.

"I would like to change my access code," I said; Omar knew it and would have access to enter the building.

"Of course, send me the current code by text message, and I'll send you a new one."

"Thank you very much, Mr. Neto. You're a star."

"You are more so and deserve something better. Don't get discouraged; sometimes things happen for a reason.

By the way, I'll send a message saying that Omar Guzman is prohibited from entering."

I smiled shyly. Everyone knew what had happened, and I felt very embarrassed.

"Yes, and again, thank you very much."

The call ended, and my hands were trembling as I wrote the message to Mr. Neto. I felt a lot of anger, but I had to calm down. I could feel my abdomen contracting, and that was my signal that I should keep calm, or my baby could be the most affected since it was still very small.

"I'm sorry, but I have to do it," I said, speaking to my belly.

I took a bath and went to the kitchen to force myself to eat something; without any appetite, I ate and stayed in the living room for a moment thinking about what to do now. I was worried that this would affect my case with Steven.

Eventually, I took out my phone and called the lawyer; it was a relief to know that this wouldn't affect me, while she tried to tell me that there has to be an explanation, and the truth was that I had to tell her I was running late to pick up Noah before she continued to intervene for Omar.

Finding him at the entrance of the building was hard, plus seeing him trying to explain regardless of people looking at him. I was furious, and that feeling only grew when, upon arriving at Noah's school, he ran into my arms crying, telling me how his classmates made fun of him, telling him that he would never have a dad like Omar.

Omar was there, and although it hurt me a lot to see how Noah reacted, it hurt me more that all this had not only affected me but had also emotionally affected Noah. My children were the most sacred thing I had, and I didn't mind defending them from anyone, including their fathers.

Two weeks later, to say that this didn't have an impact on Noah and me would be lying; however, little by little, we were getting out of the sadness that all this was causing us.

The explanation that Omar gave me didn't feel credible; reporters investigate, and then there was the fact that Alexis had stated that Omar wasn't ready for the responsibility of a family. Omar's mother, grandmother, and sister spoke to me to ask how I was, but none of them tried to talk to me about what happened; they only asked about the baby, about me, about Noah, and if I needed anything.

On the other hand, Omar tried to approach us, but neither of us wanted to see him, much less talk to him.

The first meeting with the social services lawyer was being held at our house, and I thanked God that Noah was as calm and normal as possible answering the questions.

There came a time when the social worker asked to speak with him alone, and I didn't hesitate. I left the apartment to give them total privacy. Aida was watering her small plants that decorated each side of the door.

"How is everything going?" I asked. Lately, Aida was increasingly busy at the hospital, and I saw her less than before. Sometimes I felt as though she was avoiding me, and that made me feel a bit sad.

"Everything is going well, I'm just tired. I just came from the hospital and found my babies thirsty," she said with a smile, concluding by sprinkling water on another plant.

"Lately, you've been very distant. Are you sure everything is alright?"

She nodded. "Just matters of the heart, nothing you need to worry about." Bingo, someone had hurt her.

"You know that whenever you want to talk, I'll be here for whatever you need."

She approached and hugged me. "I don't deserve you," she said, embracing my body with greater force.

"You're not okay. Something happened," I noticed, and she moved away, wiping the tears on her cheek.

"Yes, something happened, but I don't feel ready to talk about it. I can only tell you that I'm very afraid," she admitted.

I was about to ask why, but then the door of my apartment opened with the lawyer and Noah.

"Go, we'll talk later," I affirmed and returned to the apartment.

The lawyer gave me a document with the date of the meeting that Noah would have with the judge in charge of the case. It was three days before the scheduled date for the initial hearing.

A week and a half passed. The symptoms of pregnancy were increasingly difficult to hide: vomiting, dizziness, and a lot of sleep. Aida told me it was normal, but she also had me worried; I didn't want to insist on what was making her so distressed, but it reassured me that after that small exchange outside our apartment, she went back to being a bit like before.

It was a normal day at the hospital until I received a call from Mrs. Patricia.

"Good morning, Phoebe, how are you?" she asked.

"I'm very well, ma'am."

"I was calling to ask if I could talk to you for a moment. Perhaps during your lunch hour." She possibly wanted to talk about Omar, and although I didn't want to, I had to do it.

I was already two months pregnant, and my emotions were becoming more intense with each passing day. I missed him, and possibly he missed me too; he hadn't given up, and seeing Alexis's statement in recent days has filled my head with the thought that I owed him the opportunity to explain in detail what happened. I would do it, but only when he came to look for me again.

"Yes, my lunch hour is fine. Could you be here at one in the afternoon in the hospital cafeteria?"

"Yes, of course. I'll be there."

I smiled as I hung up.

"Phoebe, don't forget that at two-fifteen you have your appointment with the doctor for your first ultrasound," said Wendy next to me.

I nodded; I had an appointment to meet my little one. With excitement, I took the tablet and went to visit two of my patients.

Lunch hour eventually arrived, and I went to the cafeteria.

I never imagined finding Omar with a bouquet of flowers in his hands, much less that he would kneel in front of me. I could no longer delay our conversation, much less our relationship, which, if it were to begin, should be as sweet as honey.

What happened next was something that should have happened weeks ago, but I loved Omar's reaction to the news of my pregnancy.

He didn't hesitate, didn't doubt, didn't shout, didn't faint; he gave me the most genuine reaction I had ever seen. He hugged me with a wide smile that lit up his face, which was moistened by the tears that ran down his cheeks. It was impossible not to feel love, tenderness, and peace.

Peace because I no longer had to hide that secret, and tenderness because Omar, from that moment on, already loved and cared for our baby.

After lunch, we were about to leave for the maternity floor to wait for our turn and be able to meet our little one together, but Aida appeared in front of us with her face completely disjointed and with an envelope with the clinic's letterhead in her hand.

She immediately approached us and began to explain what was making her feel so bad. I was prepared for anything, except for what left her lips.

My head didn't understand. From the moment she said she was pregnant, I stopped reasoning because I didn't understand how her pregnancy benefited me, nor did I know who the father of her baby was.

"I'm pregnant by Steven, Noah's father," she said, and I looked at Omar as all the blood left my face.

"Could you leave me alone with her for a moment?" I asked, trying to control my rage, and he nodded.

He moved away a bit from us, and I put my attention on Aida.

"Why didn't you tell me? When and how did it happen?!" I shouted, and she continued playing with her hands.

"I didn't know how to tell you. It happened the day of the basketball game. Steven was drunk; when I approached to help send him home, and Noah was no longer by my side, he began to mention your name. Saying he would take Noah away from you if you didn't leave Omar…"

That's how she gradually gained the courage to tell how it had all been, and I couldn't judge her. My hatred for Steven only increased.

"I felt a lot of disgust and guilt; I thought you would hate me. I'm very sorry for having betrayed our friendship. I broke many rules and your trust." Seeing her in that state made me feel bad. Truly, she wasn't having a good time, and that could harm her and her baby.

"Yes, it hurts me that you hid it from me, but at the end of the day, it's your life and your business. Steven is no one to me, other than Noah's father. It hurts me that he has hurt you too; I don't blame you. There's no doubt that everything Steven touches, he damages. However, I still don't understand how this benefits me."

"He claims he can't have children, doesn't he?" she said, and I nodded. "Well, with me, several things are proven: one, his immorality in being unfaithful to his wife, and I am willing to undergo an amniocentesis to help confirm the relationship between my child and Noah."

Chapter 26
Phoebe

"No, I don't agree with that. An amniocentesis is very risky for the baby, and you know it's only done if necessary."

"I know, but even if I say I'm pregnant by him, proof will be needed to show that it's his child. I know, understand, and will assume the risks involved in the procedure," she said, and I shook my head.

"No, I'm sure the lawyer will be able to prove it; we can wait until the baby is born. I would never ask you to undergo a procedure like that without it being necessary. I understand that you want to help, but we'll find a way to do it without having to put your baby at risk. What have you thought about doing?" I asked, and she lowered her head.

"Steven is a married man, Phoebe; there's nothing I can do. After we do the procedure, I'll go to Barcelona and raise my baby there."

"Did you fall in love?" I asked, and she nodded her head in affirmation.

"I had never felt like this with anyone; I think that's why I made that tremendous mistake," she said, and I smiled bitterly.

"I don't blame you; Steven is an idiot and many things, but I would have to be blind not to see that he's just what the doctor ordered," I said to release her from the tension. Who was I to judge her knowing my past? I felt very bad that she'd gotten involved in my problems and now with a baby.

"Excuse me?" I heard behind me.

Aida looked at me, frightened. "I'll see you at the apartment. I need to get back to work," she said, disappearing from the cafeteria.

"I said that the father of my son, Noah, was just what Aida's doctor ordered," I said, and Omar approached and hugged me.

"And how did your doctor prescribe yours?" he asked, and I wrapped my arms around his neck.

"Just like the man that my eyes are looking at right now, that my arms are hugging, that my body is brushing against, that my lips want to kiss, for whom my heart beats uncontrollably, and who has left a little piece of himself inside me," I said as my hand caressed his hair above the nape of his neck.

He didn't say anything, just kissed me. It wasn't until we heard some applause that we stopped kissing and saw his parents and grandmother in front of us.

"She just needed a little push and a little white lie. Although it wasn't a lie. Here I am; I arrived late, but Omar got ahead of me," his mom said, and we all laughed.

"Well, it seems that the whole family came to see the show," I remarked, and Omar's eyes widened.

"We're going to be late," he exclaimed, and I nodded.

"What show?" asked Omar's father.

"Phoebe has an appointment with her gynecologist to meet our baby," said Omar, caressing my abdomen; we all smiled. "You have to explain to me why you applied the Galeano tradition and hid from me that I was going to be a father."

"We understood Phoebe, and it's not as if much time has passed. The important thing is that you found out from her and not from any of us. We are indeed good at keeping secrets," his grandmother added.

"Sorry to interrupt, but... can we continue talking later? After this, I have to run to pick up Noah," I said, and his family nodded.

As we walked toward the elevators, Mrs. Patricia, or Patricia as she asked me to call her, offered to send someone for Noah. Grandmother Jimena again told me that they were there for whatever I needed. The truth was that this family was really something.

"So, the girl is truly Omar's aunt?" I asked, looking at Roger; it felt strange to treat them this way, but it also felt good.

"Yes, my sister moved with her mother when my father died. Normally, we are the ones who go to visit them, but the day she met Omar, she was in the city for a conference. She is a marine biologist. She was here days after the incident, but Omar wouldn't let us intervene."

My gaze went to Omar, who just shrugged his shoulders. We soon arrived at the maternity area. Wendy approached me quickly.

"We've been looking for you in every room. Dr. Jiménez is already waiting for you," she said and was surprised to see the people around me.

"I'm sorry, my lunch was a bit more extensive than normal. I'm going to the doctor's office right now. Thank you very much, Wendy," I said, walking to the doctor's office with everyone behind me.

I knocked on the door, and Jiménez was surprised to see that I had company.

"Well, we'll have a full office," she said, somewhat intimidated.

"If there's no problem with you, of course," said Patricia, looking at Omar and me.

I shook my head. "I have no problem with it," I said, and with that, Jiménez started the consultation with her routine questions. She was slightly surprised by my weight loss. I had lost five pounds since the last time I came to see her.

"But is that normal?" asked Omar, concerned upon hearing that it was a lot of weight.

"Yes, it's a lot, but it's also normal in the first months, especially when there is a lot of nausea and vomiting."

"Yes, many times I have to force myself to eat something because everything gives me nausea, and what doesn't, I'm throwing up minutes later. I know it's normal in pregnancy, and although there are medications that improve the situation, I don't want to take any of that," I commented, and she nodded.

"Yes, I understand your opposition to medications during pregnancy, but this time I think it's necessary that you have the pills, at least not for daily or continuous use, but for days when you haven't been able to retain anything in your stomach for at least two hours. Or look for some more natural options," the doctor said.

"It's time to pass on the recipe, Patricia," said Mrs. Jimena, sitting in a corner of the room.

"Well, then let's move on to the best part," Jiménez said.

I put on the gown, and after everyone was present, the transvaginal ultrasound began. Omar was a bit surprised to see what the doctor was using to perform it, and just when he was about to say something, his mother covered his mouth, avoiding embarrassment.

"I'll explain later," she said, causing everyone in the room to burst into laughter.

The doctor began to look at the small monitor, while we looked at a larger one right in front of us. Omar held my hand tightly and with the other caressed my hair when I lay down on the stretcher.

"Yes!" shouted Patricia. I looked carefully at the monitor, seeing two amniotic sacs and a tiny one inside each sac.

"There are two?" asked Omar, looking at the screen.

Jiménez nodded her head in affirmation.

"That's right, we have two babies. Let me take measurements and…"

My hand released Omar's hand abruptly, and in the next second, the dry sound of his body hitting the floor was heard. Had Omar fainted?

"Help him, please," I asked.

The doctor stood up and walked to a small container with cotton balls and alcohol. She approached Omar and placed the cotton at the level of his nose. Omar began to regain consciousness, and his mother started laughing.

"It's something in Guzman men, dear. Don't be scared," she said between laughs.

"I only fainted once," said Roger to his wife.

"There are two! There are two!" shouted Omar, standing up and coming to me to give me a kiss on the lips, and then he went to his parents. "You're going to be grandparents of two children." And then he went to his grandmother and hugged her.

"I've never had such an effusive father. It feels very good to know that the little ones are coming into the world being loved and desired from the first moment. Now I'll finish the examination, and then you can go." It was Jiménez's words that echoed in my head and heart.

Seeing the smiling faces of Omar's parents and grandmother, feeling Omar's cheek on my forehead while we watched our babies on the monitor was something very unreal for me. Although I had already had the opportunity to know what pregnancy was like, I had never felt the warmth of a family. Patricia's hand caressed my arm, and she smiled widely at me. Reality and emotion overwhelmed me.

"Don't cry, Phoebe. Everything will be alright; you're not alone. This time you have people who are willing to give everything for you and your children, my grandchildren. That includes Noah; that boy stole our hearts from the moment we met him," said Mr. Roger.

"Calm down, sweetheart. I'll be here with you and for you, always," said Omar, sealing that promise with a kiss on my lips.

The examination ended, and everything was fine. Against my wishes, I had to follow the doctor's instructions. I needed to eat better, and even more so now that I knew that not just one baby depended on me but two.

I ran to the nurses' station for my things, then met Omar in the lobby where he said goodbye to his family, and we went out to look for Noah.

"When will we tell Noah?" he asked, and I sighed.

"I think for the time being, we should wait. I would like first for you to regain his trust. Then we can give him the news."

"That seems perfect to me." He raised my hand to his lips and left a kiss on the back of it.

For some strange reason, I could feel that from that moment on, our relationship could be cemented and become more solid; it was just a matter of trust. I had to leave the insecurities and complexes that frustrated me so much aside.

Omar loved me and had already shown it in various ways. Why couldn't I give myself the opportunity to trust in something as beautiful as his love?

Noah was a bit quiet on the way from school to the apartment. I knew he should have a conversation with Omar, and so it was after snacking.

While they were doing that, I left them for a moment to call the lawyer, and I told her what was happening with Aida, her baby, and Steven. She said that if that was the case, she would immediately ask to postpone the hearing. She told me that to do that procedure, we would have to wait until Aida was between twelve to fifteen weeks of pregnancy. That I should talk to her to make a letter stating that she was doing this of her own free will to keep everything in order and legally sound.

The amniocentesis was a very risky procedure and consisted of inserting a needle into the pregnant mother's abdomen and extracting a sample of the amniotic fluid. Normally, it was a procedure used to identify genetic diseases if the doctor deemed it necessary.

That same night, I let Aida know, and she accepted without any problem. We hugged because my heart didn't want to allow her to do something like that, but I knew how stubborn Aida was about something.

The days went by.

The judge agreed to postpone the hearing for the time needed, but not her appointment with Noah; that remained scheduled for the planned date.

Omar wouldn't leave my apartment; he showered me with attention, and as much as I told him not to get me used to it, I knew he did it because in a few weeks, he would have to fly to Madrid and start with his commitments in the League.

His relationship with Noah improved since that night they talked; however, Noah still held it against him for having hurt me.

"How did my little ones wake up today?" said Omar, lying on my belly. He had gotten up to exercise, and here he was, talking to our children and my stomach, as the smell of food was ever present at that hour.

"We woke up well, although dad got a bit excited yesterday," I said, and he opened his eyes wide.

"Did I hurt you?" he asked, evidently concerned.

I shook my head. "No, but that game with your fingers unlocked a new addiction in me," I joked, caressing his cheek.

"That was the idea, for you to enjoy it, to enjoy me, and to feel that way; sexy, beautiful, exquisite, delicious," he said, lowering the sheet a bit to expose my breast, which he didn't hesitate to squeeze and bring to his mouth.

"Little wolf," I moaned, scratching his back with my hand.

"Don't do that, sweetheart. You'll wake my beast, and we have to get out of bed because you have your three month appointment."

We got ready, left the room, and Noah was looking at my bottle of prenatal vitamins.

"When were you going to tell me that I'm going to be a big brother?"

Chapter 27
Phoebe

"I wanted it to be after the hearing against Steven. I also wanted you to be good with Omar and for the risk period to pass," I said subtly.

His face didn't seem to be happy, and a chill ran down my spine. My heart started beating faster as I watched his expression darken, and I found myself unconsciously taking a small step back.

"So I am going to be a big brother?" he asked.

My gaze went to Omar. He took my hand, and then I looked at Noah.

"Yes, you'll be a big brother," I said. I didn't know what his reaction would be; his face didn't tell me anything.

It wasn't until he ran to me and hugged me that my lungs could finally release air and let me breathe.

"Thank you, thank you, thank you. When will the baby arrive?" he exclaimed, pulling back from me with tears in his eyes and looking to Omar to answer his question.

"They'll arrive in about six months," he replied, and Noah hugged him, taking him by surprise.

"Wait, did you say 'they'll arrive'?" my son commented. We both nodded.

Omar explained, "All indications point to there being two babies growing inside your mother's womb."

He looked at us in complete astonishment, and I could see how his little eyes began to fill with tears, and they had a strong impact on me and caused the same reaction.

"My dream will come true. I'll have many siblings," he cried, hugging my body tightly.

I looked at Omar, who was watching us with a smile. He joined our hug, caressing Noah's back.

"That means that if you hurt my mom again, there will be no forgiveness for you," said Noah, looking at Omar with his eyebrow raised and with his index finger up.

"I've never done that; I know you still don't believe me, but time will tell and confirm what I told you the other day."

Noah nodded to his words. "Where are you going? I thought today was your day off," he questioned upon seeing us ready to leave. "You need to rest and not move much," he commented, and I wanted to eat him up with kisses.

"We were thinking of taking you to school, and then I'll take your mother to the hospital; she has an appointment with the doctor," Omar said.

"Can I go? I want to meet my little siblings. Can I?" he asked hopefully, and I nodded. One day that he didn't go to school and stayed with us wouldn't hurt anything.

Hopefully that doesn't bring us any problems in the future. Especially with the custody battle.

"Yes!" he shouted.

We had breakfast amid laughter, and Noah talked about a plan for his siblings. He was so excited about being a big brother that he was already saying they would be boys. Even a curious theory came to light.

"I think my brothers should have names that are four letters. A while ago, I heard my teachers say that the best things only have four letters in their name, and my brothers are the best thing to me."

Could he be any sweeter? Omar messed up his hair and nodded.

"I agree with the little one. There are many names that only have four letters; we can look for names that go perfectly with them, whether they're boys or girls."

"No, they will be boys," Noah insisted, and again a new fear was unlocked.

"We'll see what the ultrasound says later, but if they're girls, you'll be the one to defend them from anyone who tries to bother them, just as you've looked after your mother," Omar pointed out.

"In my dream, there were only boys, but Mom had a huge belly."

I choked on a bite of watermelon. Omar got up concerned as the coughing didn't cease. I drank a bit of juice and raised my arms to help my lungs.

"There, sweetheart, breathe," he soothed, making circles on my back.

"We'd better go, or we'll be late," I said, looking at the wall clock after picking up the plates from the table.

We left the apartment, meeting Aida leaving at the same time. We greeted each other respectively, and I signaled for Omar to go ahead with Noah.

"How are you?" I asked, seeing her all pale.

"I think you already know how I am," she said, and I nodded.

"When I come back, I'll prepare a tea that Omar's mom gave me for that. It will give you more appetite and calm the discomfort," I offered.

"I'll thank you for it. Will you be busy at twelve?" she asked, and I shook my head. "Could you accompany me?"

"Of course. Let me know, and I'll be there," I said, approaching and hugging her. "Has he tried to communicate?"

She took her phone out of her pocket and showed me the many missed calls. The truth was that I didn't understand Steven; he called Aida non-stop, but he hadn't tried to approach Noah once.

"When I answer, he just stays quiet, as if he doesn't know what to say. That's why I prefer not to talk to him; it just makes me feel bad. I'm very sorry I failed you," she mumbled, and it hurt me a lot to see her so sad.

I started thinking about how I would feel being in her shoes. Being alone with guilt, and with a little one in the womb. I took her hands.

"Aida, I'm not upset or hurt by your actions. It hurts me because you're going through this situation, and it's very similar to what I went through with Noah. I don't want you to feel that you've betrayed me. It hasn't been like that; Steven stopped mattering to me many years ago, and I'm no one to judge you.

"You're almost my sister, Noah's aunt, and I love you very much. Besides, I gain nothing by giving you a couple of spankings if you already know that Steven is not a good man. I don't want you to feel alone because I'm going to be here for you, just as you have been for me and Noah in these last years."

I wiped her tears and gave her a hug. I stayed with her until she calmed down and offered to take her to the hospital with us, and she accepted.

"Omar, will you leave for Madrid next week?" asked Noah, and Omar nodded. "Will you come to visit us, or will we go to visit you?"

I looked at Omar, not knowing how to answer that.

"When the time comes, you'll move in with me in Madrid. I don't plan to be far from you now that the League is starting. My Aunt Luz already told me it was possible, so long as the necessary changes of residence are made, that she would take care of that. For the time being, I'll go and look for a house where we can live comfortably."

I exhaled in relief because Omar seemed to have everything under control, and in the rearview mirror, I could see Noah smiling happily about returning to the city that gave us a lot of peace and where he was born.

We soon arrived at the hospital and said goodbye to Aida. We went to the office, and many of the nurses on my floor were surprised because some didn't know Noah.

The consultation was beautiful, just like the previous one, but with the special moment that Noah got to know his little siblings, and of course, my little one didn't understand what was being talked about.

"But are those babies? They're just two white dots," he said, furrowing his brows as he tried to understand what he could see on the screen.

The doctor smiled. "The babies will grow and develop, and that's why your mother's belly is going to grow little by little, and they'll get bigger. Parents, everything is going perfectly; keep it up."

"Thank you, Doctor," I said, leaving the office when we were finished. Aida called me soon after to tell me that Jiménez had advanced her appointment.

"Could you take Noah to the cafeteria?" I asked Omar.

He nodded with a wide smile and ushered Noah away while I took the opportunity to accompany Aida at her appointment.

"Calm down. Everything will be fine," I reassured her as the doctor began to ask the necessary questions and interrogations.

Jiménez instructed her to go to the exam table to start the ultrasound. To say that was an easy moment would be a lie. Aida was a complete sea of tears, and I understood her completely because I had been in her shoes.

Finally, Aida asked about the test she wanted to do. For a moment, the silence in the room was uncomfortable. Jiménez paid close attention to Aida's explanation.

"The most prudent thing would be to wait until after the twelfth week. Before would be very imprudent; both of you know this, as well as the risks."

"Is there a non-invasive test?" I asked, and Jiménez nodded.

"A blood test can be performed, but we must wait a couple more weeks to obtain a reliable result. Particularly because it's not from father to child, but between siblings."

My gaze connected with Aida's. "We can wait until—"

"No, I need us to get this over with as soon as possible. I have already made the decision, and I'm not going to change it."

It's at this moment that I felt like giving her a slap. "Aida, your baby could be in danger. I don't care how long we have to wait."

"And I already told you that for me, the best thing is to finish this as soon as possible."

"Don't you want this baby?" I asked, and her face shuttered in shame.

"Of course I do, but…" She couldn't continue, the words lodging in her throat.

The doctor added, "These are the options you should consider."

"You don't understand; in my family, there are genetic diseases, and my biggest fear is that my baby will have them. I want to know if my baby won't leave me at birth or after a few years. This goes far beyond doing it solely to help you."

I immediately remembered she lost two of her siblings to that disease, especially hydrocephalus; that was the reason she decided to study pediatric medicine.

Jiménez proceeded to ask what kind of disease, and it was spina bifida. She mentioned that it's now possible to perform an operation during pregnancy to repair the spinal cord.

"I know, that's why I also want to do the exam."

If that was one of her reasons, I supported her one hundred percent.

"If that's the case, we will still carry out the necessary blood tests next month, and if we don't see anything alarming in your tests, it will be up to your criteria and desire whether the test is performed or not," said Jiménez before we left her office.

"Everything will be fine," I said to Aida, giving her a hug. She reciprocated, and we said goodbye to continue with our day.

I met with my guys in the hospital cafeteria, and at Omar's suggestion, we went bowling, ate pizza, and ended up in the living room of our apartment watching a movie. Noah fell asleep, and me and Omar went to our bedroom.

"I couldn't make any comment on the subject because it wasn't appropriate, but I agree with Noah and his teachers; the best things are four letters," Omar said, giving a kiss on my bare shoulder.

"Life?" I suggested, earning me a kiss on the neck.

"Yes, but the most important one. Do you know what it is?"

"Omar?"

"Close, but it's *love*, the feeling that has united us all," he said, hugging my body, making my back stick to his bare chest. "Come, I'll help you take a relaxing bath, and we'll rest," he said, and I nodded.

I let myself be, his hands were like embers on my body, impossible not to end up wrapping my legs around his waist, enjoying that delicious swaying that sent us to another reality, one in which only he and I existed.

The days passed, and the time came for Omar to return to Madrid.

It was very difficult to say goodbye, but we had promised to visit him on weekends and on days we were free, and he would also do the same on his free days.

Noah was my little guardian and even made sure that I ate and took my vitamins. Aida had also become my priority, as she was more anxious every day.

During that time, I received visits from Omar's parents, his grandparents, and even his sister. With Aitana, I was able to build a bit of trust. First, it was by phone, then she visited me. On one occasion, I was able to attend to one of her friends, Dana, who had fainted in her store, and she asked me to take care of her when I arrived.

At first, I couldn't because they came through the emergency room, but when performing routine tests, it was revealed that she was a few months pregnant. So we had to attend to her and perform an ultrasound.

The girl was really scared, but we were able to get her to calm down. She would be living in the city, so I offered my support and made myself available if anything came up and she had any doubts or fears about her pregnancy.

Grandmother Jimena also recommended her to me, as she was an assignment from an acquaintance of hers, one that seemed to be a very important family.

A month and a week passed since that day with Aida, and I was feeling very well. I had requested a few days off since Noah was on holiday, and we were in Omar's apartment. Alexis was still his representative, but he no longer involved himself in our relationship; he apologized to me for what he did. A huge wall had been raised between them, and it was very uncomfortable. I could see how Alexis tried to establish a conversation, and Omar simply dismissed it.

"Hello, Aunt. Is everything alright?" I heard Omar answer the phone while we were enjoying the sunset on the rooftop. Omar handed me the phone, and I looked at the identifier with the name of Lawyer Luz.

"Hello?" I asked.

"Hello, Phoebe, how are you?" she asked me, and her way of greeting unsettled me since she did it in a somewhat altered manner. Not as she always did.

"I'm very well, and you?"

"Is Omar with you?" asked Luz, and I looked at Omar, who was sitting next to me.

"Yes, is something wrong?" I asked; I could feel my stomach numbing at the possibility of some bad news.

"Aida has already undergone the test, but there were some complications."

Chapter 28

Aida

"I'm not leaving here without talking to her! Without telling her the truth," said the man that Ernesto was insisting on moving away from the entrance door to the apartment building.

It was past nine at night, and I was returning from the basketball game with Noah. I had sent Phoebe a message to see if I wouldn't be interrupting anything, but upon finding this situation at the entrance, I thought I could use my persuasion on the man who was wearing blue jeans and a black sweatshirt with the hood up, hiding his face.

"Noah, go up carefully. I'll be up in a moment; I'll see how I can help Ernesto."

Noah nodded and went up without looking back.

I approached and could see that the man was about to hit old Neto. Regardless of the significant difference in our height, I grabbed his hand firmly, preventing him from delivering the punch.

"Aida, it's better if we call the police," said Ernesto when the man tried to throw me to the ground.

"You don't understand; I need to talk to Phoebe," insisted the guy as he stumbled, and due to the darkness of the street, I hadn't been able to see his face.

"Phoebe Santiago?" I clarified.

"Yes, I need to tell her many things. I need her to understand, I need to see her, I need her and my…" he said but stopped when he recognized me.

I didn't know what to do; this guy was definitely Phoebe's ex, but I was sure he was referring to something important. Possibly something Phoebe needed to know, but I couldn't take him to her apartment if Omar and Noah were there. It could be a huge problem.

"Ernesto, would you help me bring this man to my apartment?" I asked, and he looked at me with a raised eyebrow.

"Are you sure about that? Do you know him?" he said, and I nodded.

I didn't need to get any closer to the man to know that he was drowning in alcohol.

"Yes, he's Phoebe's ex, and we don't want to create more problems for her than she already has. For Noah's sake, it's better if he doesn't see him like this."

He hesitated, then said, "Alright. Let's go before someone else comes."

We proceeded to move the man's body, who was babbling a bunch of incoherencies on the way through the elevator. I opened the door to my apartment, and Ernesto helped me throw him onto my sofa.

"If he gets aggressive, it would be better to call the police," he suggested.

"I don't think that will be necessary. He's about to fall asleep, and I need him to tell me why he came in this state."

He nodded and proceeded to leave the apartment. I went right behind him to Phoebe's home and made sure that Noah had arrived safely. After confirming that, I returned to my apartment.

"Let's see what information I can get out of you, Steven," I said and approached to remove the hood of his sweatshirt.

Upon doing so, I became aware of his features; the only time I had seen him in person, I couldn't see him well because I tried to prevent Noah from seeing the exchange between them. Then just those photos that appeared in the social pages with a designer suit and his perfectly combed hair.

His freckles, his full lips...

"If Phoebe heard you say that, she would slap you," I said out loud to myself.

The man was very handsome and was beginning to accelerate my heart in a very strange way. I sat down beside him.

"Steven, Steven. Steven!" I called him, but he seemed unwilling to get up.

I went to the kitchen to find a bottle of water. I called him again, and getting no response, I let a bit of water fall on him. He shot to his feet as the water filtered through his nostrils, sputtering.

"Don't bother me; let me sleep," he said, rubbing his face.

"What is it that you have to tell Phoebe?" I demanded, and he shook his head.

"Do you care?" he asked, removing his hands from his face and looking at me with strangeness and a hint of amazement.

"If you tell me, maybe your words will reach her," I said, trying to persuade him to say something. He let himself fall to the floor, walked on his knees and hands, to kneel in front of me and rest his head on my legs.

"I would tell her that everything was a lie from the beginning. That I didn't want to do many things that I did. That if I'm away, it's for the best... You have a very sweet aroma," he whispered, and his hands caressed my legs.

A shiver ran through me; I tried to stand up and couldn't. As I fell, he opened my legs and slipped between them.

My heart began hammering against my ribs so hard I was sure he could hear it. Cold sweat broke out across my forehead and palms as the reality of my situation crashed over me. I was trapped, completely at his mercy, and with the worst possible person. My breathing became shallow and rapid, each breath feeling like I wasn't getting enough air.

My hands trembled uncontrollably as I pressed them against his chest, trying to create some distance. Every muscle in my body was tense, coiled like a spring ready to snap. The metallic taste of fear filled my mouth, and I could feel my pulse throbbing in my throat.

"Please, let me go," I said, fighting to keep my voice steady even as it threatened to crack. I forced myself to speak calmly, knowing that if I showed panic, if the situation escalated beyond his control, things could get very ugly. But inside, I was screaming, every instinct telling me to fight or flee while knowing I could do neither.

My mind raced through every possible escape route, every potential consequence, while trying to maintain the facade of calm that might be my only protection.

I tried to push him away, but his hands surrounded my back and brought me to his body, leaving my face trapped in his neck; his overwhelming scent and closeness provoked countless sensations in my stomach. His hand left my back and caressed my hair, making me look up.

Our eyes connected for a moment; his were red and full of tears. It was evident that he was drinking to suppress the pain of whatever was haunting him.

"I just want you to help me forget all this pain I have in my chest. Don't reject me; I just want you to love me…" His words disarmed me, but no, I couldn't. He wasn't just any man wanting to spend just one night with me.

He was my friend's ex, the father of her son, and if that wasn't enough, he was drunk, and I was conscious at that moment.

"No, it's better if you call someone to come pick you up," I said, trying to get out of his grasp, but he didn't let go or move away; he did the opposite, and his lips connected with mine.

I pushed him and slapped him, taken aback by what he'd done.

"We can't do this. I only brought you here to know what's going on and why you said there were things Phoebe should know. It's better if you leave," I said, and he shook his head like a scolded child.

"I'm tired. The cage I live in is suffocating me. It hasn't let me breathe for more than nine years, and now everything will be worse," he said with tears running down his cheeks. "Can't I desire something for myself?"

His forehead rested pitifully on my shoulder.

"You've been an idiot, and whatever you're going through, you've brought it upon yourself," I scoffed, rolling my eyes.

"When you love, you have to let go. I wanted a different life for the only person who loved me with all my garbage. Our cruel destiny was to be born into the families we were." His warm breath and the moisture of his lips made contact with my neck.

I closed my eyes; this man was clouding my reasoning. "No, Steven, this is not right."

"Nothing we do is right, but this is the most perfect," he drawled as his hand took one of my breasts.

I knew I was going to regret it, but the heat and what that man was making me feel was something I was interested in discovering. Between kisses, we laid down on the living room carpet.

I didn't resist anymore, and it was something hallucinating.

The way he thrusted inside me, a perfect mixture between a beast and a gentleman, how he caressed and stimulated my body, and how he made sure that I enjoyed it before him was something very strange and divine at the same time. It was the best night of my life, but I was spending it with the wrong person.

We eventually reached my bed, and without knowing how many times he had taken me—and died from exhaustion—I fell asleep on his chest.

"Who are you?" was the shout that abruptly woke me up. I was still naked, so I got up and looked for my robe. "Aida? You're Phoebe's best friend. What the hell is this?" Steven spluttered from beside the bed.

"Do you need an explanation? We spent the night together. You arrived at the building making a scene, and after you mentioned that you wanted to tell Phoebe the truth, I brought you here to see if you could tell me more, but you see, we ended up committing a crime," I said as he put on his clothes.

"Yes, because I thought you were her. That you were Phoebe!"

I smiled to mitigate the strong blow I felt in my stomach. "It's better if you leave," I said, and he tried to approach.

"What things did I tell you?" he asked with a bit of concern.

"Don't worry. Whatever you told me will stay here," I deflected, walking away from him.

"Why do you assure me of that? You are her best friend," he scoffed behind me; I shook my head, and both guilt and reality hit me very hard.

"The best friend who let herself be carried away and seduced by the father of her son, her ex, and on top of that, a married man. Believe me, I'm the first person interested in her not knowing. Her friendship is worth much more than what happened between us. Pretend it was with her that you had sex. That way, you don't add more pain to your miserable life. Please, it's better if you leave."

I could feel my eyes stinging because of the tears. This could not be happening.

He stared at me, mouth agape. "I'm sorry, I…"

"You don't have to apologize; I assume the responsibility. I brought you here, and I wrongly agreed to your request to make you forget your pain and dry your tears." I walked to the entrance and opened the door for him.

He looked at me without knowing what to say, much less what to do. He passed in front of me, crossing the threshold of the door.

"Aida…" He tried to speak, but I didn't let him. What could he possibly say that would make this better?

"I won't tell her anything if you don't either. Goodbye.

I closed the door, pressed my back against it, and slid down until I was sitting on the floor, letting out the hurricane I felt in my chest. I hit the floor twice with my fist, trying to appease what I was feeling.

"I deserve it; I shouldn't have been so weak and let myself be carried away by what that guy provoked in me at the moment. How will I face Phoebe now?" I sobbed.

Eventually, I stood up and looked for my phone. I was running late for my shift at the hospital; I would try to repress what happened so that it wouldn't affect my relationship with Phoebe.

Two days later, I received a call from an unidentified number. I didn't take the call, believing it would be from the bank. I remembered that my credit card had passed its payment date. Two hours later, there were several more attempts, which I also couldn't answer because we had a scheduled operation at that time.

I arrived at my apartment, and again my phone vibrated, so I didn't think it was bad to know what all the insistence was about; at that moment, I would schedule the payment if that was the reason.

"Hello?" I said.

"Hello, Aida."

The familiar voice hit me like a physical blow. I jerked the phone away from my ear, staring at the screen in disbelief. My eyes widened as I checked and double-checked the number, my brain struggling to process what I was seeing.

"Steven? How did you get my number?" The words tumbled out before I could stop them, my voice pitched higher than usual with shock. My free hand flew to my chest, where my heart was now racing.

I felt my mouth go dry as a wave of confusion and alarm washed over me. This was impossible—I had been so careful, so protective of our privacy. My mind immediately started spinning through possibilities, each one more unsettling than the last. How long had he had my number? What did he want? How had he found us?

I found myself pacing without realizing it, my legs suddenly restless with nervous energy. The phone felt heavy in my trembling hand as I waited for his response, dreading whatever came next.

"The important thing is that I got it. I would like to talk to you about what happened. I've remembered certain things from that night, and I would like to clarify some of them."

I had to sit down because I couldn't handle his words.

"I don't think we have anything to talk about; we both agreed that we were going to try to forget. That it was for the best. There's no need for you to call me or look for me. You're a married man, and I don't need more problems than I already have."

"I know, but since yesterday, my mind has managed to remember, and I haven't been able to get you out of my head."

"Have you gone crazy?!" Then an idea crossed my mind. "Ah, I get it now. You'll take on the task of trying to 'win me over' just to get to Phoebe and Noah, but no, that won't work for you."

"You're mista—" I didn't give him the opportunity to speak; I cut the call and continued with my life.

And so it was; I stayed away from Phoebe and Noah for a few days, as it was very difficult for me to keep a secret like that.

Steven began to send messages and call me late at night. I could also see him when I left the hospital on the third day. A part of me said to answer him and yell at him to stop contacting me, that he wouldn't achieve anything with me; another said to listen to him.

However, another little voice in my head told me not to give him any opportunity at all. Doing so would be breaking the promise I made to myself and to my mom.

What was my promise?

Not to get married or try to form a family, so as not to live through the same pain she experienced.

I was the only surviving child of her three children, the product of her first marriage. My father was her teenage boyfriend, but she lost him in a robbery at their family store one month before my birth. My uncle, my father's brother, was the one who took care of us, and little by little, a romance formed between them.

From that love, my first brother, Elías, was born. I was six years old when my little brother was born with Down Syndrome.

My mother was completely devastated because, unlike many cases where the baby manages to lead a completely normal life, grow up, and live an adulthood like anyone else, my brother's case wasn't one of those, since days after birth, an anomaly in his heart was discovered.

We lost my brother after four years by his side. Two years after his departure, my mother became pregnant again, but this time the situation was much worse; she was afraid, cried a lot, and I, being a thirteen year old girl, could see how hard it was when, at seven months of pregnancy, the doctor told her that her baby also had a congenital disease.

This was the cause of many fights, discussions, and tears for everyone, especially for my uncle and her.

Simón was born, and between heart failure and a disease known as spina bifida, he also died after a few months of struggle.

My mother was completely devastated and was even more so when, a year later, my uncle decided to leave her. She was no longer the same, and it hurt me to see her like that, but I understood her; three fourth of her heart had been torn out.

From that moment on, I promised myself that I wouldn't suffer like her.

Months after finding ourselves alone, she asked me to go to her mother's house and stay there for the night. I didn't want to leave, but my grandmother came to pick me up.

The next day, she took me back; we had keys to the door of the small apartment where we lived. So, we just entered and looked for my mother. We found her lying in bed, hugging three photographs, with two letters on the bed.

My grandmother approached and tried to wake her up, but it wasn't possible; my mother had purple eyes and mouth. Her chest wasn't moving.

She had left me alone, wanting to join her other children and my father. Possibly they will tell me that for a child, then fourteen years old, it must have been difficult, that I should have broken down in tears over the loss of my mother, but no. I remember very well that I looked at my grandmother; she was crying, but I smiled and said:

"She's happy now, with my dad and my brothers. Let's let her sleep with them."

My grandmother raised and cared for me until her age no longer allowed it, and I had to work to provide for both of us.

In the letter, my mother made me promise not to suffer trying to find happiness beside a man and children. Because in that path, she had only found pain, and she didn't want that for me. That my happiness should come from being able to enjoy the world, travel, meet people, and love myself much more than anyone else.

That's why I decided to study medicine and be able to use my energy and love to bring happiness to my little patients, just as I did with my brother Elías, and in the few times I could with Simón.

While studying, I could see that congenital, genetic, and hereditary diseases went almost hand in hand. So my brothers' diseases could be more genetic than anything else. Therefore, there was a huge possibility that my children would also have it.

In the present day, four days had passed, and strangely, I received a dinner invitation from Omar's representative.

I resisted doing it on a previous occasion until he went to the hospital and waited for my departure time and wasn't willing to receive another refusal from me.

"I just want to know more about Omar's partner. How can I be a good representative for him if I'm not prepared to help him?" said Alexis as we sat down to dinner. He chose a somewhat fine restaurant, and I thanked God that I didn't like to leave the house wearing my nurse's uniform.

"But if it were necessary, I think Omar would have already told you. If he hasn't commented on anything about that, it's because you don't need to know it." I knew that what he really wanted was to know the dirty laundry of Phoebe's life.

"Yes, but Omar has always been reserved about all that. The press is always digging through people's mud, and it can be very harmful to her, especially now that, through Omar, I know she's fighting for the custody of her son with this guy. What's his name?" Alexis asked, and I remained silent. "It's Steven, isn't it? And I think you know him very well, don't you?"

I began to get nervous at his insinuation.

"You spent a night with him, or are you going to deny it? I promise not to say anything, but only in exchange for obtaining the information I'm requesting. Especially the fact that you're betraying your best friend."

"You're an idiot," I sneered, hitting the table, causing several people to turn and look at us.

"I am, but it's because I know very well how to handle my clients and know the people around them. Besides, Omar is also my friend, and I worry about him twice as much. Now I'm all ears," he said, leaning back in his chair, taking his drink, and looking at me with a raised eyebrow.

Sadly, I found myself in a situation where I could have run out after emptying the water glass over his head, but I knew that would only make things worse.

In the end, realizing that he was possibly just being sincere in his attempt to protect Omar and Phoebe, I ended up telling him everything and had to comment on what kind of situation was happening with Steven so that there wouldn't be more speculation about it.

After our meeting, he and Omar went to Madrid, where a strong controversy erupted that hurt Phoebe and Noah a lot. I felt bad for not being able to be with her, but I truly had many commitments at the hospital. I should have been with her and supported her; however, I was also aware that what she needed least were more traitors around her.

The days continued their course, and Steven kept insisting. On several occasions, he waited for me outside the hospital, offered to take me home, and I obviously refused. On one occasion, he brought me flowers and smiled every time he looked at me.

I hated him. Especially for provoking all this turmoil inside me.

"Please, I just want to talk to you," he said, exasperated. He took the courage to grab my hand, but I immediately moved away.

"What do you want, Steven? I've told you a thousand times to stop calling and looking for me. I don't understand all this insistence. I already told you that I'm not going to help you go against Phoebe, so don't continue."

I turned around to continue on my way, but he hugged me from behind. I remained motionless for a moment; it wasn't until I felt his nose inhaling against my neck that I separated and slapped him.

"What's wrong with you?" I snapped and turned around again to leave, almost running at this point.

"What's wrong is that I can't stop thinking about you, that I've become your shadow, that I've dreamed of you every day in these two weeks since we were together. I'm going crazy wanting to know what you're doing, how you are, and if at any moment you've thought of me and that night together."

My heart was pumping very hard in my ribcage at his words, but I wasn't going to fall for this.

"There are mistakes that can't be made again, and that's what you were to me, Steven, a mistake. Something of one night, but nothing more. Now, please, don't look for me again." I turned around, and this time I did manage to continue on my way.

I got into a taxi, and the tears just came out, without me being able to control them. For some strange reason, those words I said hurt me more than him. Had they been too harsh? I wouldn't know.

The days passed, and there was something very strange. I felt very tired and was very hungry. I took an inventory of my symptoms and noticed that my period hasn't come; I looked at my calendar, and it almost took my life away. I realized that I had forgotten my appointment to get my contraceptive injection two months ago.

A shiver ran through my body, and I was about to go crazy. That night, I ran to the nearest pharmacy and bought three pregnancy tests.

I arrived at my apartment and went straight to the bathroom to take them. They were like a slap in the face, all coming out positive. That night was hell for me; it was a complete disaster. I couldn't sleep, I cried, and I felt like the worst human being on the face of the earth.

Then I took a breath and tried to find the good in the situation, but I couldn't. One of the most unsettling things was realizing that I was pregnant by Steven, my friend Phoebe's ex and Noah's father. I was going to have a child, and that child would be Noah's half sibling.

A child of a married man who had become my stalker. A child of a man who claimed to have been sterile for a year, and that's where I found the light to what was happening.

That same morning, I visited the hospital laboratory and requested a blood test.

The answer was the same: positive. It was then I gathered the courage to talk to Phoebe; I couldn't keep quiet anymore. Although this truth could cost our friendship, it could also be an opportunity to dismiss what Steven was claiming.

I looked for Phoebe all over the hospital and found her in the cafeteria with Omar. I didn't want to ruin their happiness, but this was something that couldn't be postponed.

I expected her to shout that I was a traitor, a liar, and other insults that I deserved, but no. She took it much better than I expected, and that gave me a lot of peace.

That same night, Steven called me, and I answered. I wouldn't tell him about my pregnancy; eventually, he would find out, but I was in a situation where I needed to know if this baby would have the opportunity to live or if I was just waiting to lose a baby.

Performing an amniocentesis was the only way to know if I could let my heart fall in love with the little one growing inside me. I was aware of the risks of the procedure and was going to assume them in order to know if the baby would be born well and, incidentally, help my friend keep her son.

"Steven?" I said, but he didn't say anything. "I'm going to hang up."

"No, don't hang up. We're just in silence for a moment."

I tried not to cry, but it was impossible. I began to sob, and just when I was about to hang up, I heard him sob too. I stayed and continued listening to him; apparently, he was also fighting with his own demons.

The call had already marked an hour long.

"Goodnight, Steven."

"Goodnight, my star." He was the one who cut the call; again, this sensation of pain and not knowing what to feel overwhelmed me.

"Am I falling in love with Steven?" I closed my eyes and let myself be carried away by the god of sleep.

The weeks passed, and everything remained the same. I received calls and messages from Steven. The day of my first ultrasound, I was dying of fear. Fear of falling in love, and against all odds, that happened anyway. Hearing his little heart while holding the hand of my best friend, who was smiling at me, was something that left me speechless.

I had to talk to the doctor so that she would have knowledge of my family history, and it was very painful to remember, but it was something she had to do.

Phoebe and Noah traveled frequently to Madrid to see Omar, as he was already back on the field. My emotions only became more and more overwhelming.

Eventually, the day of the test that would be performed at twelve weeks had arrived. Phoebe's lawyer and Omar's grandmother were my companions that day.

"Does it affect the test that Noah isn't here?" I asked.

"No, Noah's sample was already taken in the morning before they went to Madrid; we're only waiting for yours," the doctor said.

I nodded, and Omar's grandmother took my hand. "Don't be afraid. Good things will come your way for the good deed you're doing. Your baby will be very well. It will be a healthy and strong boy; you'll see," she assured me.

I was terrified; the worst that could happen was that I would lose my child, and trying to remove those thoughts from my head, Dr. Jiménez and Wendy arrived to begin the procedure.

I closed my eyes tightly when I felt the cold prick of the needle. The rest passed in a breath.

"If you feel any discomfort, whether it's pain, burning, or unusual vaginal discharge, you must tell us, okay?" the doctor said, and I nodded my head in affirmation. "We'll give you something to help you rest."

Dr. Jiménez left the room, and after a moment, I was about to fall asleep.

A discomfort in my belly woke me up; it was very difficult to ignore when the moisture between my legs was abundant. I brought my hand to the place, and upon withdrawing it, I could see blood staining the palm of my fingers.

I pressed the button to call a doctor with the other hand.

"I'm so sorry, my life, don't leave me," I cried to the baby inside me, caressing the small protuberance in my lower abdomen.

"Aida, what's happening?" Wendy entered the room first, with Phoebe's lawyer right behind her.

"I'm bleeding."

Chapter 29

Omar

Finding out I was going to be a father was life changing, but discovering there were two little lives waiting for me doubled the wonder, the fear, and the love in my heart.

Fainting was certainly embarrassing, but I wasn't the first it had happened to, nor would I be the last.

It has been very difficult being apart, and I needed to change the situation soon. I lived in anguish thinking about whether Phoebe was eating well, if she felt well, if between work, coming and going with Noah, the hearing, the situation with Aida, all the pregnancy symptoms, plus our distance, would have her very overwhelmed. The last thing I wanted was for her to get sick or for something to happen to her with so much stress.

For this reason, whenever they came, I tried to attend to them as they deserved. Today the weather was very good to spend the afternoon on the terrace. Until my phone rang, and it was my Aunt Luz.

Her call was an omen of bad news; the insistence on wanting to talk to my sweetheart surprised me. After seeing Phoebe's gestures and words, I confirmed it.

"But what happened to her? Oh no! Did something happen to her baby?" She stood up and began walking inside the apartment. She listened attentively to what they were telling her, and tears started to form in her eyes. "Poor thing, I have to go see her. I should have stayed to be by her side," she said, then continued listening.

I took her hand and led her to the sofa. I didn't want those strong emotions to overload her and make her feel bad.

"Yes, I'm returning tomorrow to be at the courthouse on Monday. Thank you for keeping an eye out. Please call us if anything else happens." She handed me the phone, covered her face with her hands, and began to sob.

"What happened, sweetheart?" I asked, caressing her back, trying to calm her down.

"Aida's baby is in danger. It's not known yet if she lost it or not. I need to return to Zaragoza. Also, at the judge's request, the hearing has been moved up to Monday, and I don't think the results will be ready by then."

I took her hands and gave a kiss on both. I hugged her and kissed her forehead. "Let me find someone who could send them."

"No, it's already too late. Noah is with your aunt at the aquarium; I don't want him to worry about this. Could we leave together after your game tomorrow?"

I nodded. Fortunately, it was a local game and early in the afternoon.

"Try to calm down. I don't want you to get upset," I said, putting my hand on her belly.

She put another one on top of mine and laid down on the sofa. "Aida can't lose her baby; it would be very sad. She has already suffered a lot since she was very young. Why does life have to be so unfair?" she cried, hiding her face in my chest.

"Nothing will happen to them. Both she and her baby will be fine. Tomorrow we'll go visit her. When Sonia and Alexis return with Noah, I'll ask Alexis to schedule our departure. I don't have to report until Tuesday in Barcelona."

My relationship with Alexis was strictly professional, and now that Sonia had given him the opportunity to win her over, he came more often. Sonia was wanting to settle in Madrid after receiving a job offer the previous time she was in the city.

They returned with Noah, and in private, we had to explain to them what was happening.

"I'll prepare everything for tomorrow right now," said Alexis, to which I just nodded. He left, and only Phoebe, Sonia, Noah, and I remained.

"Aren't you going to tell me what's happening?" asked Noah, seeing that his mother was crying.

"Nothing bad is happening, champ," I explained. "It's just that your mother is a bit nervous. They have moved up the hearing to Monday. Let's give her space and not get overwhelmed. Hopefully by Monday, she can have the peace she needs."

He hugged his mother, and after eating, we went to rest.

The next morning, I said goodbye to my sweetheart, who had woken up to prepare a coffee for me and a tea for herself. She was very anxious, and that left me worried.

I arrived at the stadium and concentrated on the game just when I saw them in the stands chanting my name; the team won two goals to one.

Upon finishing, Alexis guided me to the car where Phoebe and Noah were already waiting for me.

We landed in Zaragoza before seven in the evening. My mother and father received us and offered to take care of Noah so that we could go to the hospital and see how Aida was doing.

"You're hiding something from me, and I don't like it," said Noah, crossing his arms with evident annoyance.

"Aida is sick, Noah. She's in the hospital. Tomorrow, if she feels better and everything goes well at the hearing, I'll take you to see her," said Phoebe, caressing his cheek.

"Are you going to see her now?" he asked, and she nodded. "Tell her I love her very much and that I hope she gets well soon."

Phoebe leaned in to give him a kiss on the forehead, and then he took my mother's and father's hands to walk to the car.

"Don't you want to rest a bit?" I suggested.

She shook her head. "No, take me to see her before they don't let us visit her anymore."

I nodded, taking her hand to help her get into the car. We arrived at where Aida was, and my Aunt Luz was with her.

"How is she doing? How's the baby?" asked Phoebe, her voice worried.

"They've managed to save it, but Aida will have to spend some time in bed until the danger passes. They've suggested that she spend a few weeks in the hospital for monitoring, and if they deem it appropriate, they'll send her home."

At this, Phoebe breathed more calmly.

My aunt continued, "She hasn't woken up since they brought her here. I have to leave to prepare everything for tomorrow; I also have to add the DNA test to the list of evidence that will be presented."

"Will we have the results in time?" asked Phoebe, and she opened her purse and took out the envelope.

"I sent the samples to my trusted laboratory; the DNA test is already ready, but the others requested by Aida are not yet. It seems that some take a little longer. I'll leave before Tiago goes crazy if Leila wakes up," she said, referring to her husband and her little granddaughter.

"How is Ian doing?" I asked, and she shrugged her shoulders.

"It has been very difficult for him, but we have tried to follow all the psychologist's advice. A few days ago, he went into Leila's room and caressed her cheek, so with a few small approaches, we are achieving something. He religiously comes to his therapies and spends all his time at home. Zafiro has been a great blessing in our lives. She has managed to bring my two sons closer together."

Her phone rang, and she left the room, waving her hand in farewell.

"Zafiro... isn't she from psychology?" asked my sweetheart. I nodded.

The conversation couldn't continue because Aida began to move, and Phoebe approached to take her hand.

"Aida, how are you? How do you feel?" asked my sweetheart.

"I think I'm fine. I feel a bit uncomfortable and sore, but I think that's normal after everything," she said, letting a tear escape to roll down her cheek. "My baby must already be in a better place, isn't that right?"

"Your baby is still here with you, Aida. Now no crying, only smiles. Remember that your emotions also affect him or her."

"Really?" she said, and we both nodded.

"The only thing is that you'll have to be under observation for several weeks, and then, if it's prudent, you can go home."

She sighed. "Yes, that's the least of it. All I want is to see my little one."

We stayed a moment longer until the nurse told us that Aida needed to rest and that visiting hours were over.

"We'll come back tomorrow afternoon; the hearing is in the morning. It has been moved up, and the DNA results are already in. Now we'll just have to see what happens tomorrow."

"What will happen is that you'll keep custody of Noah. Man's justice cannot go against divine justice. I'll be here; I'm not going anywhere."

Phoebe leaned in to give her a kiss on her forehead and to leave a small and delicate caress on her abdomen.

We went to find something to eat and then headed to her apartment. But neither of us expected that Steven would be there waiting for us.

"Could I talk to you for a moment?" he asked Phoebe and me.

I wasn't going to get between them; in the end, they were Noah's parents and should try to get along, although to me, Steven didn't deserve the time of day from either of them.

"I have nothing to talk to you about. The only thing we'll talk about will be about Noah, and we'll do it tomorrow in front of the judge," she snapped, turning her back on Steven.

"The death of your Aunt Salomé. It wasn't a simple accident. That was the work of Pablo García, my father."

At this, Phoebe spun to look at him. "You're so vile that you're using that lie to get my attention. Why after all this time do you want to talk right now?"

"Because I'm tired of being the bad guy for you when it hasn't been that way. Trying to get close to you has only brought misfortune."

Phoebe took a step towards him, her hands clenched into fists at her sides. "What do you mean by that?" she demanded, her voice sharp with fury but trembling slightly at the edges. Her jaw was tight, eyes blazing with indignation, yet there was something uncertain flickering beneath the surface—a wariness that made her shoulders tense.

Her breathing had quickened, and she could feel her pulse hammering in her throat. The anger was real, burning hot in her chest, but it was tangled with an uncomfortable knot of anxiety. His words had hit too close to something she didn't want to examine, and the combination of rage and fear made her feel unsteady on her feet.

She lifted her chin defiantly, trying to project strength, but her free hand fidgeted nervously with the hem of her shirt.

"My father and mother are behind the death of your aunt and... your parents. Before, I didn't have evidence, but now I do, and that's why I'm here to help. Phoebe!"

"Sweetheart! Love!" I shouted at the same time as I held her before she fell to the ground. I rounded on Steven in a rage. "You damn idiot, if anything happens to her or my children, I'll kill you!"

"She's pregnant?"

Chapter 30
Phoebe

The strong smell of alcohol was what woke me up. My head hurt, and I felt dizzy.

"What happened to me?" I rasped, seeing Steven on the other side of the room.

His words before I fainted came back to me, and I sat up abruptly.

"Lie down a moment longer. Your blood pressure is somewhat elevated," said a man with a medical bag.

I laid back down, but the urge to cry overwhelmed me. I couldn't believe that his parents had committed such an act. Why?

The man insisted, "You need to calm down. A pregnancy like yours needs to be handled with greater care. I don't mean to frighten you, but you must try to control yourself."

"Don't overwhelm her anymore, Uncle," Omar chided.

"I'm sorry, Omar. I understand what's happening, but she needs to face the reality that everything else must take a back seat right now. The priority is her and those babies." The man was scolding me, and upon looking at him in more detail, I realized it was Mr. Iván, Alan's father.

"I'm very sorry," I said between sobs. Omar sat beside me and hugged me.

"It's okay, sweetheart," he soothed, but I shook my head.

"No, I need to know what you told me, Steven," I said, making the guy look at me with surprised eyes. I didn't realize that Omar's father, Mr. Iván, and a man I didn't know were there, but who was looking at us with great seriousness drawn on his face. "You said you came to talk to me, and then you said..." I trailed off, looking at those present.

"They already know. That's why they're here. He is Marco, and he's in charge of the Eagles. Do you remember? I told you about the organization. More than helping you, he's here to help this idiot," said Omar, pointing to the serious man and Steven.

"We had already taken on the task of investigating everything behind the Garcías at the request of Mrs. Luz. There were several blind spots in our investigation, and with the information provided by him," he said with disgust, looking at Steven, "we can now turn the case over to the prosecutor's office."

"What will happen? What would be the next step?" I asked.

"Nothing on your part. The only thing that couldn't be guaranteed is the freedom of the young man here present."

"But... I... I didn't do anything," stammered Steven, completely tormented by that possibility.

"He who is silent about a crime becomes an accomplice, and although you were threatened to keep quiet and coerced by your parents, it's not something for me to judge. That will possibly be decided by a judge when the trial against your parents and their crimes begins. For now, it's better not to waste any more time; I will immediately go deliver all this information, thus not giving your parents time to escape. Tomorrow, I imagine they will be present at the hearing. We will keep them under surveillance from now on." With that, the man left the apartment.

"We will leave too. If you need anything, don't hesitate to call me. Noah was so tired that he fell asleep after a bath. He didn't find out about my departure or any of this, so you can be at ease," Mr. Iván said, and I nodded.

"Thank you very much, and I apologize for all the trouble," I said, looking at the two older men.

"You're a member of our family now, Phoebe, and taking care of each other is our duty. Don't put too much pressure on yourself with things you can't change. People won't change if you ask them to. They will change in their own time and when they've already been hit hard. Isn't that right, Steven?" He turned and walked to the door, opened it, and turned back towards us, focusing his gaze on Steven. "You were a good boy when I met you. What happened to you?"

Without saying more, he left the apartment with Mr. Roger trailing behind him.

"I think I should leave too," said Steven, evidently affected by Mr. Iván's question.

"No, whatever you told them, I need to know it too."

We stared each other down, and in his, evident shame was what dominated.

"You're not well, and the last thing I want is for that to affect you and your children. Congratulations, by the way," he expressed with a crooked smile.

"I agree, sweetheart. You can talk tomorrow after everything," Omar said.

I shook my head. "No." I crossed my arms, glaring between them.

"Fine." Steven approached and sat in the chair in front of me. "A few days before you arrived with the news of your pregnancy, my father had told me that he was receiving text messages and calls from a man asking for money, supposedly charging for his 'sex toy'; he was referring to you. That same day, I went to your father and confirmed it was him.

"He told me that if I didn't give him money, you would disappear, that we were from two different worlds, and that he had so many debts that he was thinking of offering you to one of his creditors. So I gave him the money he asked for. My father found out and demanded that I break up with you. I told him I wasn't going to do it, and he threatened to kick me out of the house and leave me without money, without university, without a future since I had chosen someone else, turning my back on the family.

"That's why I didn't look for you during those days; I was thinking about what to do," he said, and to my mind came those two days when he didn't call me, nor did he answer me, and that's why I had to go to his house to look for him. He continued, "Then you showed up at my house and said you were pregnant in front of all my friends, my parents, and my grandmother. I must admit that my actions were immature, full of rage and helplessness for not knowing what to do, how to react.

"I cornered you with harsh words and humiliations, to the point of pushing you and you falling into the pool. Upon hearing you, I remembered that you couldn't swim, and seeing that everyone was just enjoying seeing you in that situation, I couldn't take it anymore and jumped in after you to help you."

Warm tears silently ran down my cheeks. I didn't want to interrupt him, but more questions arose within me.

"You could have just said it. Called me and told me what my father was doing. Why did you keep quiet?" I demanded, feeling how Omar was holding my hand tightly.

"That day when you were about to leave my house after having fallen into the pool, I wanted to tell you everything, but I couldn't. The best thing for you and Noah was to get away from me. Then everything got complicated. My grandmother demanded that I apologize to you and take responsibility for the baby. With so much insistence, I went to your house and saw your father leaving nervously; I entered your house and saw you on the living room couch, wet, unconscious, and with your lip split.

"I called emergency services, and they came to get you. While waiting, I saw a photo of you and your Aunt Salomé. You had told me about her; I remembered she lived in Madrid, and I thought that if she knew what was happening, she might help you. So, I called her from your phone."

It's true, Steven called me and seemed to have the intention of telling me something, but he didn't. Everything he was telling me seemed to make sense. I didn't understand at that moment the appearance of my aunt when I was in the hospital. Now I knew the reason.

"At the hospital, I made it clear to your parents that I would not take responsibility and that they shouldn't try anything because what I could do was put them in jail for extortion. I left the hospital until your Aunt Salomé arrived. When I returned to my house, my grandmother and my parents were waiting, wanting to know what had happened, so to leave you in peace, I lied to them.

"I told them you had lost the pregnancy; they believed me because they never asked anything about it again. I continued with the party, drowning my sorrows in alcohol and drugs; I no longer had the only person who calmed me by my side."

After a long moment of silence, I finally blurted out the question I'd always wondered, "Did you love me?"

Chapter 31
Phoebe

"Did you love me?" I asked again, because if he had loved me, he would have acted a thousand times differently. At the same time, I felt stupid asking something like that.

He smiled and nodded, even as Omar squeezed my hand.

"I don't know if it was love, but you were very important to me, so much so that I hated sharing you. That's why when I had the opportunity, I took advantage of it to keep you away from the perfect Alan Galeano."

Omar growled and gave him a dirty look.

"Not all of us were born into the best family, Omar. Phoebe and I had shitty parents, while you guys were a pack that, beyond popularity, was loved by everyone, and your parents cared about you and your well being. The envy I felt was enormous, and that's why I didn't hesitate to hurt your cousin Alan. I'm sorry, because at that moment my actions affected you too," he said, trying to approach me.

Omar raised his hand to keep him away. I leaned into him for support when Steven continued speaking.

"Going back to the past, when you left for Madrid, I was very happy for you. You had managed to escape from that hell your parents had subjected you to. Years passed, and for me, life was shit, but I had to mature because, thanks to your aunt, I knew I had a son who had inherited my hair color. I would send your aunt a little money for his expenses, even though she said she didn't need it, but she didn't refuse to receive it either."

My chest ached to know that. All that time it had been Steven's money. That's why when he died, his lawyer told me his bank account was my inheritance.

"Then my parents found out, not because I maintained contact with your Aunt Salomé, but because your father came back looking for money. He came to my house, and everyone found out about Noah's existence. My father asked Salomé for her information in exchange for giving him money, and… from what I understand, she refused to tell him where you were, as she denied the fact that you were with her. Weeks later, the accident happened. I didn't know he was involved in that until a few days ago."

I frowned, taking this all in. "I remember she was very nervous and told me that my parents had been calling her. That it was better not to leave the house together. I had changed my hair color, and my body had changed a lot since I moved. So, I didn't need any kind of disguise to go out with her; However, she was an innocent woman who didn't deserve to die like that," I said, hugging Omar.

"My father sued your father and found some of his creditors to have him killed in prison. As for your mother, you already know," he said, and I nodded.

"What I don't understand is why there is so much hatred towards me and my family."

"When my grandmother found out about Noah's existence, she told us that if we didn't find the boy and bring him to see her, she would donate all her assets to a charity. You can imagine that didn't please my father. That's why he took on the task of finding you, and before he did, I preferred to do it myself."

"And what happened with the legal power of attorney you gave me?"

"That was my father's move. Believing he would earn your trust, to wait for the slightest mistake on your part and do what is being done right now. All he wants is to obtain control and power over Noah's inheritance. The day I came here, I was influenced by the rage of knowing that once again, a Galeano was trying to steal what at that moment I still considered my property."

"Phoebe is no one's property but her own. The only thing you share together is the connection you have through Noah!" Omar shouted as I tried to hold him back.

"I know, to the point that I stupidly thought that only with her could I have a family," he said, looking at the ground.

"What I don't understand is why you told me you wanted to have a child with me if you supposedly can't have any more."

"I didn't know. The week the lawsuit was filed, I found out I couldn't have more children. Let's say the woman I have as a wife made me take that test. Since we've been married for almost three years and still have no children. She has undergone tests, and they haven't come back bad, so only my part remained. Thinking back, I remembered an accident I had at an equestrian field with one of the horses, and I ended up in the hospital, but they didn't tell me about possible sterility at that time."

I looked at Omar, and the huge doubt fell into my head again. "So, better to take my son away from me and give him to another woman?" I scoffed, shaking my head.

"No, quite the opposite. If I'm doing all this, it's to free us all from their ambition." There was still something that didn't quite add up in his story.

"What made you change your mind?"

"I didn't have the evidence to prove their crimes, but now I do. I also found out that my father has a relationship with the woman who claimed to be my wife. He forced me to marry her just to have her under the same roof, pretending it was an arrangement between both families' businesses. Plus,,,"

He walked to the shelf under the television and took in his hands a photograph where Aida appeared tickling Noah, both with wide smiles. I looked at Omar, and he smiled at me.

Steven continued, "I think I fell in love with your friend, Aida, and no, it wasn't premeditated. The truth is, I don't even know how things happened, since it only took one moment together for her to burn everything inside me. She doesn't deserve garbage like me, but I can't help looking for her, thinking about her, calling her."

"If that's not love, I don't know what it is," Omar remarked.

"I don't understand much about how this love thing works. Because that's what I thought I felt for Phoebe, but what I feel for Aida is different; it's much stronger and more intense than anything I've ever felt. It's as if a magnet were drawing me to her."

I remained silent, analyzing his words. There was no doubt the man was an idiot. Aida was just as in love as he was. If only he knew that his sterility was a fraud. No doubt tomorrow would be a very interesting day for him.

After a few minutes where we just looked at each other in complete silence, Omar decided to speak.

"I think we've had enough for today. Tomorrow will be tough, and Phoebe needs to rest."

Steven sighed. "We'll see each other at the hearing then. I want to say that, if I don't get custody, I would like to be able to approach Noah, if the judge and you allow it."

"We'll see what happens tomorrow," I said stiffly.

With that, he nodded and left my apartment. Omar closed the door with the bolt and returned to my side.

"Why didn't you tell him anything about Aida?" he asked.

"The last thing she needs right now is more emotional burden. Tomorrow he'll realize everything when your aunt presents the evidence about that."

"It will be a hard blow for him."

"It could be, but every act in our life has consequences. Now let's just hope everything goes well tomorrow."

Omar heated the food we brought, and after forcing myself to take a few bites, we went to sleep.

The next morning, we got ready to leave. I was confident and calm. As Mr. Ivan said, there are things I can't control, so they shouldn't be a reason to burden myself more physically and emotionally.

We arrived at the family court, and at the entrance to the courtroom was Steven's entire family. As we sat down, I could see the malicious smile of the man who once said he would take care of us. It sent a shiver down my spine.

We stood up to receive the judge on the bench. The secretary read the case number and why we were there. Then the judge said the following words:

"The court is now in session."

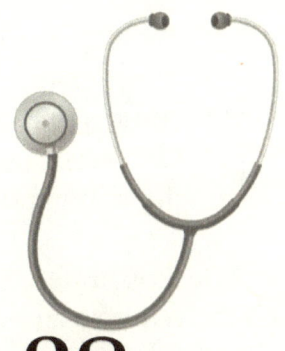

Chapter 32
Phoebe

"First of all, I would like to clarify that everything discussed in this session will be strictly to guarantee the emotional and physical stability, as well as the welfare and benefit, of the minor, Noah Santiago."

The judge gave the floor to Steven's lawyer, who once again presented the same argument from the previous meeting and concluded his statements. Then, it was Attorney Luz's turn.

"Your Honor, this morning I sent a request to incorporate new evidence for this case," she said, and my heart began to pound strongly in my chest.

"I have received them, and I'm interested in knowing what the plaintiff has to say about this," the judge replied.

Steven's lawyer seemed unaware of what it was about. A young woman appeared to shuffle through papers and handed him a manila envelope.

"Counselor, while the lawyer reads what you requested, could you tell us what all this is about?"

Attorney Luz stood up. "Of course, Your Honor. It's a DNA sibling test conducted at Synlab Laboratory, one of the most prestigious in the country."

The atmosphere among all those present became tense, especially Steven, who looked at me in such a way that I thought at any moment his eyes would pop out of their sockets.

She continued, "Mr. García claims he cannot have children due to an accident a year ago, but according to this test, this is not true. A few months ago, a young lady shared an intimate encounter with Mr. García and is now pregnant. The test was performed between Noah Santiago and that fetus. Since they do not share the same genes from both mothers, the test, which has been sealed from the laboratory and delivered to you, shows that there is a similarity of forty nine point ninety nine percent. Confirming that Mr. García lied about not being able to father more children, while at the same time maintaining an extramarital relationship."

Murmurs arose in the courtroom. Steven snatched the envelope with the test results from his lawyer's hands, then fell heavily onto his chair. I focused my gaze on the judge, feeling Steven's intense stare on me.

"Where is she?" Steven asked anxiously, while looking for Aida or a familiar face among those present.

"You were unfaithful to me, Steven? How could you? I love you," cried Steven's devoted wife, standing up.

"Order in the court. Who are you looking for, Mr. García?" asked the judge.

"You, be quiet," said Steven's father, grabbing the woman's arm to seat her. "Don't say anything," he scolded Steven.

He stammered, "The mother of that child, I… I need to talk to her."

"That will not be possible, Mr. García. For safety reasons, the young lady wishes to keep her identity anonymous. The question here is: Do you confirm that this information is true?"

Steven didn't hesitate and nodded, confirming the lawyer's statement.

"Alright. Anything else, Counselor?" the judge asked.

"Yes, Your Honor. I have also submitted several documents regarding an inheritance left by Mr. García's grandmother to the minor Noah Santiago, of which Phoebe Santiago, as his legal representative, is the executor."

The judge pulled out some documents from a folder and nodded.

"I wonder, Counselor, why in the first meeting I was not informed that the child is the heir to Mrs. Efigenia de García's assets? Assets that were granted when the lady was still alive. At the same time, Mrs. Santiago was established as the executor. Here I have documents showing that Mrs. Santiago has not used a single euro for her benefit. On the contrary, this money has grown due to investments and compound interest obtained, which will also benefit the minor when he comes of age."

As the judge finished saying those words, some men appeared in the courtroom, among them the man who was at my apartment yesterday.

"Your Honor, I would like a moment to speak privately with you about something related to this case," said a man who had some documents in his hand.

"Very well. We'll take a fifteen minute recess. If it's related to this case, the lawyers will need to be present."

"I have no objection to that, Your Honor." Attorney Luz followed them, and I took the opportunity to approach Omar.

"Everything is going well, sweetheart. Steven and his family don't stand a chance," Omar assured me, and I nodded.

"Beyond that, I'm worried about the danger we could be exposed to if that man is not arrested or something is done about him. You heard him trying to interfere between Steven and his wife," I said, and the affectionate wolf took my hands and gave me a kiss on the forehead.

"Steven can't stop looking at you. He wants you to tell him something about Aida or to tell him who it is. I don't think he's a faithful man, so his head must be figuring out who his lovers have been in the last few months," Omar added, and I shrugged my shoulders.

I didn't want to make eye contact with anyone from that family. Omar sheltered me in his arms, and I didn't push him away; I needed that security that only he gave me.

Finally, the door opened, and those who were absent returned. Steven's lawyer seemed anxious, and when he reached his seat, both Steven and his father asked him if something was wrong; however, the lawyer merely denied it and told them to wait.

"We will resume the hearing, trying not to forget the omission of information by the plaintiff's side. We will continue with the witnesses in this case. I want to say that I requested an interview with the minor in question, and so has the social services attorney. I would like her to come forward and give her opinion on this case."

The attorney approached the stand and began to describe the place where we lived with my son, how well mannered he was, how kind, sweet, and intelligent.

"I have been assigned countless cases like this, and mostly negligence is shown on the part of the father being sued; however, this is not such a case. I attest that the child is safe, cared for, and loved where he is. I not only interviewed the child but also several neighbors of Mrs. Santiago, and they all say the same thing about never having heard, seen, or known of any mistreatment toward the minor. I must say that Mrs. Santiago has done a fine job so far. Noah shows the necessary independence for his age, which is very difficult to find in most children these days."

I looked at the attorney, and she held my hand under the table.

"Thank you very much, Counselor. This case turned out to be much simpler than I imagined, but darker than I thought. When a case is assigned to me, I take my time to investigate, and there's no doubt that people are only moved by their ambitions, desires, and yearnings. In this case, it's clear that the biggest gain is the money that the minor brings with him and for his legal representative.

"I cannot base my decision on values or stability because it's clear that the plaintiff need things to work on. Because I will not overlook the fact that his company was going through a difficult time exactly a few weeks before the news talked about the lady's relationship with her current partner. As I said at the beginning of this hearing, the first priority will be to put the interests and welfare of this child," the judge said.

"Your Honor, please, I want to be part of my son's life," said Steven, standing up.

The judge looked at both of us and, after removing her glasses, spoke.

"Mr. García, while no one wins when family members are at war, the evidence that has come into my possession leaves no room for doubt. Mrs. Santiago will retain custody and parental rights over her son. Mr. García, if you again demand the intervention of the court or harass child services to investigate Mrs. Santiago regarding the care of her son, I myself will have you investigated for fraud, and I assure you it's not in your best interest to put yourself in that position.

"Fix your life and give love to your son, or rather to your children; that's what he needs most right now. For now, all visits will be at the discretion of Mrs. Santiago." With that, the judge finished, or so we thought. "Mr. Prosecutor, you may proceed when ready."

"Thank you very much, officers, please proceed," he said, and the men surrounded Mr. Pablo. "Pablo García, you are under arrest for first degree homicide against the humanity of Salomé and Leopoldo Santiago."

Chapter 33

Omar

"You're making a serious mistake. I had nothing to do with those deaths!" shouted the man as he was escorted out of the courtroom in handcuffs by the officers.

"I advise you not to leave the city, Mr. Steven. Your mother must be detained at this moment," mentioned the prosecutor, and Steven just nodded in confirmation.

"Go with him. You're his lawyer," remarked the young woman next to Steven.

"I'm sorry, ma'am, but that's not my area of expertise."

"Well, but you can help me with the divorce. I won't stay married to a woman like her."

His wife scoffed. "You were the one who was unfaithful to me, and now I'm the one you want to get rid of as if I were a piece of paper."

"Isn't that what you were? We got married by a contract, a paper, which I want to throw in the trash. Besides, you act offended because I fell in love with a woman who doesn't have even a single hair like yours. You've been sleeping with my father for years."

She let him go and took three steps back in shock.

He kept going. "I know everything, and you were the one who made me go to that damn doctor to tell me that 'I couldn't have any more children.' Do you need more reasons to ask for a divorce?!"

Steven walked toward the exit like a bat out of hell.

"I think it's time to go find Noah. Right now, I just want to hug him tight and give him thousands of kisses," said my sweetheart.

Her lawyer smiled. "Well said, Phoebe. Now all that's left is for you to let me know when you're going to put a ring on her finger, Omar."

"That will be very soon, Aunt. I'll let you know at any moment. First, I have to ask for permission and see if they accept me," I said, not missing Phoebe's gaze on me.

"I agree with you."

We all left the courthouse, heading toward the parking lot; however, upon reaching the entrance, Steven was waiting for us.

"It would be better if you don't harass my client, Mr. García," said my aunt, positioning herself in front of us.

"I don't want to bother anyone, I just need to know about Aida. Yesterday I was knocking on her door almost all night and calling her phone, but it's off. I've been calling her, and everything remains the same. I need to talk to her, please, help me."

His voice cracked on the last few words, and I could see the exhaustion etched deep in the lines around his eyes. Dark circles shadowed his face, suggesting he hadn't slept, and his usually neat appearance was disheveled—shirt wrinkled, hair uncombed, like he'd been running his hands through it repeatedly.

"Please," he repeated, his voice barely above a whisper now, and I could hear the raw desperation bleeding through his attempt to stay composed. "I just need to know she's okay. Something's wrong, I can feel it."

The way his shoulders sagged, the tremor in his voice —everything about him screamed of a man on the edge, barely holding himself together.

Phoebe looked at me and then at Luz. "Let me ask her if she wants to see you. Right now, she's a bit indisposed."

"Why is she indisposed? Are she and the baby okay?" he asked, and with that, he shut me up. Here I was thinking he might be a man with several lovers, but apparently, it was only Aida all this time.

"They're fine. She just needs to rest with no disturbances or stress, so it's better if I ask her if she wants to see you or talk to you."

"Tell me where she is," he said and tried to take her hand, but she moved away.

"You'll know, but only if she wants it to be that way. I'm sorry, Steven, but it all depends on her right now. I can't go against her wishes."

Finally, he gave in with a sigh. "I know it's very soon, but... would it be possible for me to talk to Noah?"

Phoebe looked at me, and I caressed her arm comfortingly.

"I'll talk to him about it. You'll have to earn his trust. I've always tried to make sure he doesn't hold a grudge or resentment against you, but he's no longer a little three or four year old; he's entering his rebellious stage, and it has to be how he wants it, otherwise, everything could go wrong."

"I understand." He handed her a card with his phone number. "I'll be waiting for your call. Please, don't take too long. I feel like I'm going crazy. I want to do things right with Aida and our baby, please tell her that." His eyes were beginning to turn red and watery.

Without saying more, he just turned around and walked toward the parking lot.

"Poor guy, he seems to really be interested in Aida," commented my Aunt Luz.

"Both of them. Aida is just like him, but for her, being with him would be betraying me. I've tried to make her not feel guilty about anything; my relationship with her hasn't changed. It's not as if Steven is important in my life and in my heart. We only have Noah and a past history," Phoebe explained.

"That's good to hear. It means I'm the only one in your heart," I said, hugging her body from behind.

"Don't think you're the only one; I share you with three other people," she retorted, and I smiled.

"And with the others who are yet to come. I don't have any problem if I only share you with them."

She snorted. "Get away from me."

"Don't you think it's too late to get away? Just be careful after this pair, because Galeano men seem to have that gift of getting you pregnant with just a look."

Phoebe, my aunt, and I started laughing. We said goodbye, agreeing to meet at my parents' house.

The smile that Phoebe had on her lips was contagious, at the same time making her look much more beautiful than she already was.

"Could you look at the road? You're making me nervous," she said when I was driving, and I took her hand.

"It's impossible for me to take my eyes off my delicious, sweet, and smiling sweetheart," I teased, making her laugh.

"You're a lost cause," she said, rolling her eyes.

"You're right, I love getting lost in you."

"Omar, behave," she scolded, and I winked at her.

"With you by my side, it's hard to control the wolf."

"The wolf will have to wait," she said, playing with me by moving her hand to my leg, almost brushing against my manhood.

I sucked in a breath. "That's playing dirty."

"What? I just want to calm the beast," she defended, removing her hand and looking out the window.

"Tonight, you won't escape from me." I began to caress her leg and slowly moved up, brushing against her center, but I continued upward until I took her breast in my hand.

She released a moan that wreaked havoc on my manhood.

I added, "I'm going to eat you slowly; my tongue will make you come so many times that you won't be able to stand it anymore, and you'll beg me to lose myself in you, and I will gladly do so. I'll take you in all the positions you love, and I'll do it until you end up fainting in my arms or on the bed."

"You're bad," she said when I removed my hand from her center.

I just shrugged. "You started it, darling."

"Would it be possible for us to stop by the hospital before taking the detour to your parents' house?" she asked, and I nodded.

"Yes, of course."

"I don't want to be anxious about this. I know Aida needs to know what happened at the hearing, and I don't want to keep her waiting for that. There's also the matter with Steven. I don't know why, call me crazy, but I feel like those two will heal each other. All that's left is to pray to God that their baby is born healthy."

I was in agreement with her words. I didn't know much about Aida's story, but being a young woman alone and without family, I could deduce that her childhood and her past were not easy at all.

My grandmother Jimena always told us that the best part of not having everything easy in life was learning to appreciate. Although we were born into a family with financial ease and much love, they always taught us to be aware of reality and never look down on anyone. On the contrary, we were told to be of help and support others.

When we arrived at Aida's room, she was already awake, waiting for Phoebe.

"What happened?" she asked.

Phoebe took her hand and smiled. "Noah stays with me," she said, and Aida sighed, touching her chest.

"That's good. What else happened? What did Steven say about the test? Did he ask about me?" she asked quickly.

The door to the room opened, revealing a sweaty Steven.

"How could I not ask about the woman who has driven me crazy with love and who is now expecting my child?" he said, walking to her side.

Aida looked at him in surprise and then at Phoebe. "Did you bring him?"

The three of us shook our heads.

"No, I came looking for you at the hospital, and they couldn't give me any information about you. I was leaving for the parking lot when I saw them coming, and I followed them. Something told me I could find you. I couldn't follow them in the elevator, but when I saw that the elevator stopped on this floor, I took the stairs and asked for Phoebe, and they told me she was here."

"You ran up the stairs because you wanted to know if Phoebe was coming to see me?" said Aida with a small smile on her face, while the man nodded enthusiastically.

"I've been calling you like crazy, and you haven't answered. I've been looking for you for days, and I haven't been able to see you. I didn't know if I should ask Phoebe about you, but... finding out that I'm going to be a father again made me want to look for you even under rocks. I needed to tell you that I can't be away from you anymore, Aida. I love you, I want to be with you and our child, and I'm asking you to give me a chance. I've been asking you since before knowing we're going to have a baby together."

She blushed. "I feel the same way, Steven, I really do, but I couldn't be with the person who has caused so much harm to my best friend."

"Oh no, no, miss. Don't use me as an excuse. From the beginning, I told you, I have no interest in this man. The only thing that connects us is Noah, but what connects you is that baby and the feeling you have. You just admitted it; it's mutual. I'll be more than happy if you are," Phoebe said.

She turned to Steven with a frown. "But you're a married man, Steven."

"And you can't imagine the way he asked for a divorce," said Phoebe, who began to explain, and I approached her, seeing that Steven couldn't speak.

"Sweetheart, I think that's for Steven to explain. I think our mission here is accomplished; Noah is waiting for us," I told her.

She offered an embarrassed smile toward Steven.

"I'll come to see you tomorrow. Take care of her, start doing your job well as a partner and father," she said to Aida while pointing to Steven.

"I will," he promised.

But then Phoebe paused. "Hey, I forgot to ask yesterday. What evidence did you have about the death of my parents, and why aren't you implicated?"

Steven looked at me, and I nodded. She deserved to know those people's intentions.

"As I told you, I didn't know, or at least I had no way to confirm my suspicions, and about the evidence. There is a video and a recording, a conversation between my parents where they talked about trying to do something in case they lost custody. The topic of your parents came up, and also a clarification from my father, where he explained that I didn't know anything, among other things."

Phoebe nodded, and to my surprise and everyone else's, she hugged him.

"I forgive you. I don't hate you, but I don't love you either. I thank you for what you did, though it wasn't in the best way, but it was what you could do for us at our age. I think we can have a cordial relationship; after all, we have Noah, you'll have another child, and possibly you'll marry my best friend in the future.

"Noah will be Omar's son and yours, if he so wishes. We'll all be a family, and there's no change; otherwise, I'll cut off your balls and yours too," she said, looking at the two of us. I instinctively covered my sensitive area.

"Those hormones, they need to be controlled," said Aida, making her laugh.

"Let them take everything from me if they want. The person who caused all these changes will have to face the consequences. Isn't that right, Omar Guzman Galeano?"

"Protect me, Lord, with your holy spirit."

Chapter 34

Omar

"Let's hope he protects you enough," said Aida, and at that moment, the doctor entered.

"Oh, we have a full room. How is everyone?" she asked.

We all responded in different ways. Aida introduced Steven as the father of her child.

"I'm very glad. Aida, I have the results of your tests, and you can relax. Everything is within normal parameters. There's no alteration of any kind."

Aida covered her mouth with one hand, while the other went to her abdomen. Her eyes filled with relieved tears. "Really? But…"

Steven approached and placed his hand over hers on her abdomen. "Could someone explain to me a bit about what's happening?" he asked, looking around at everyone.

"I'll explain in a moment. Doctor, I don't understand," Aida said.

"The only thing I can think of is that the problem might be on your uncle's side. Are you sure he's the biological son of your grandparents? It could also be a blood factor, or stepping a bit away from science, it was destiny."

Aida shrugged her shoulders. "I don't know, but I think I could investigate it."

"Either way, there's no need to be stressed and anxious anymore. Your baby will be fine."

"When can I leave?" she asked.

"It's best to keep you here for another week or possibly two. We need to be sure that your baby won't be in any danger later on," the doctor explained.

"I'm so happy for you, friend. I'm saying goodbye for the third and final time. We'll see you tomorrow," said Phoebe, taking my hand.

I said goodbye to them with a smile and a wave, as I was almost dragged out of the room.

"Let's go to the apartment," she suggested, and I stood frozen in place.

"We need to go get Noah, darling," I reminded her.

She pouted. "I wanted to do some things with you before we went to get Noah, but it's okay, let's go get him. I don't want to take advantage of your parents' trust," she replied, released my hand, and walked to the elevator.

For a moment, my chest ached with regret for making her feel hurt.

"We'll go to the apartment," I said, but she shook her head.

"No, it's better to go to Noah," she said without looking me in the eyes. Without saying a word, she entered the elevator.

I tried to approach her, and she wouldn't even let me touch her. We reached the car, and unlike the journey to the hospital, now she had her arms crossed and was looking out the window the entire time.

I knew a way to calm her down. Her favorite song—strangely, we had very similar musical tastes—so I played a song that detached her gaze from the window: "Flor Pálida" by Marc Anthony. When the chorus came, her gaze went directly to me because I sang the lyrics.

Finally, she laughed.

"I'm sorry, I don't know what happened to me; I think it's the pregnancy hormones. I was upset that you didn't want to sneak away to be alone with me," she admitted.

I gave another kiss to the back of her hand and caressed it with my cheek. "I know, it's just that I'm dying to tell Noah that he'll stay with us and that we can be the family he wished for."

"Noah always wanted a father, then you appeared in his life, and he only lived wishing for your love," she said, and I smiled at that.

"Only he desired my love? You've never told me what that little mind of yours was thinking when you saw me running on the field or in the moments when the camera pointed at me," I said without letting go of her hand.

"I always said you were a truly handsome man, and I must admit that I came to think you were even presumptuous or haughty. You always appeared serious in your interviews; if they only knew you're such a puppy when you're with us."

"Of course, I saved the best for you all—my family. And look what a beautiful family destiny had in store for me. It was well worth not despairing."

Her little eyes shone just like her smile. We sang a couple of songs until we arrived at my parents' house. As I parked the car in the driveway, Noah came running out the door directly to hug his mother. She covered him with kisses and hugs.

"No one will separate us, my child," expressed my sweetheart with tears in her eyes.

My mother came up to me, and I put my arm around her shoulder as we watched the emotional scene in front of us.

"Grandpa Roger is making a barbecue," Noah chimed.

Phoebe straightened up and looked at us, somewhat embarrassed. "Son…"

My mother explained, "Roger and I have asked him to call us grandparents if he wishes. Roger jumped on one foot when he heard him call him that for the first time."

"Let's go to Grandpa Roger," Noah said, taking his mom's hand and leading her inside the house.

"Thank you, Mom, for accepting my family," I said to my own mother, hugging her small body.

"Thank you for choosing the right woman for you, for knowing how to wait. Now you just need to take care of her, respect her, love her very much, and ask her to marry you. I don't want any more grandchildren coming before you're married." She gave me a pointed look.

"Someone's already thinking like a grandmother."

We both laughed and entered the house. We had lunch amid laughter and anecdotes from when I was a child like Noah and wouldn't let go of the ball even to sleep; eventually, my uncles and grandparents joined us. Then my father, Noah, and I played a soccer match against three of the guards, and I don't need to tell you who won.

Then I looked at my mother and Phoebe sitting in the patio chairs chatting with my grandmother.

"Aitana?" I asked my father.

"She's in love again."

"Ovidio?" I clarified, and he nodded. "And you're going to let her go back to him after all the harm he did to her and without having left that life?"

"We don't choose who to love, Omar. They chose each other. Besides, if that's what she wants to do and she's happy, who am I to interfere? Your mother and I have always been the least invasive in your private lives for the same reason. Your disappointments, your heartbreaks, your good and bad experiences—they're yours. We'll be there when you need and want us, but we won't stand in the way of your own mistakes."

"You're an excellent father, you know that?" I said, hitting his shoulder.

"Now I'm a grandfather, so you all will move to the background; you'll no longer be my problem, but that of your partners. My job will be to spoil and indulge all the mini versions of you that come along and to enjoy my princess."

A growl was heard behind us.

"I heard you, Guzman," said my grandfather.

We laughed and chatted a moment more. Noah was talking to my Uncle Tiago while making funny faces at Leila, my cousin Ian's daughter.

"Champ, come here," I called over.

Noah left them and walked up to me. "What's up?" he asked, out of breath.

"I need to ask you something."

He raised his eyebrows. "What happened?"

"I want your permission to ask your mother to marry me."

"Ahhh!" he shouted, drawing everyone's attention. Phoebe quickly approached, and Noah shook his head. "Yes, you have my permission, and I have the perfect idea for asking her to marry you. We need the entire Atlantico Madrid fan base to help us."

He instantly zipped his lips when Phoebe reached us.

"What are you two up to?" she asked suspiciously.

We both shrugged our shoulders.

"Omar told me that we'll have tickets and special seats for next week's match against Reyal Madrid," Noah lied.

"Don't scare me like that," she chided, and seeing that no one was going to say anything else, she walked away again.

Noah hurriedly turned to me. "Call Alexis; we have a lot of work to do."

"But first, explain to me what it's about so I can understand your idea."

The little guy began to explain, and I loved his idea. We also agreed on which day we could go look for Phoebe's ring. Night eventually fell over my parents' house, and we said goodbye to them.

"I don't want to leave," Noah whined. "Grandpa Roger said we would play on the new console he bought."

"You bought a PlayStation?" I asked, and he nodded.

"I want to be a modern grandfather, so I must learn to do what my grandson likes."

"No, Noah, we've imposed too much; let's go home," said my sweetheart.

"Not at all, Phoebe. Noah is a blessing for us. We've really missed hearing a child's laughter, cartoons on TV, and games in this house. Leave him with us; you two go rest," he said, winking at both of us. "Behave yourselves," he said, hugging Noah but shaking his head in amusement.

My sweetheart and I laughed, saying goodbye to Noah and my parents again before leaving the house.

"Now, my sweetheart, I'm all yours, and you're only mine. We won't go to your apartment; we'll go to mine. There you can scream without any fear of the neighbors hearing us."

"Have I told you that I love you?"

"No, but I'm sure that you do, and that's more than enough for me."

Chapter 35

Phoebe

Omar's free hand got lost between my legs. His fingers were gently stimulating my entire body. "I want you to scream my name while you immerse yourself in the most absolute and divine pleasure. Don't hold back until you reach your limit." His words did nothing but shake my body, igniting that overwhelming fire that only he could control.

"Could you wait until we get to the apartment?"

"I did, darling," he said, and I opened my eyes, realizing that we had already entered the building's parking garage.

I adjusted my pants while Omar got out and came to my door to help me out. He took my hand, and we practically ran into the building. We exchanged glances and smiles while waiting for the elevator.

It wasn't until it arrived and we entered that the assault began.

His lips crashed against mine, and I didn't hesitate to give him the access he liked. His tongue plundered my mouth while his hands slid down my back, one seeking the end of my shirt to slip his hand underneath until he reached to caress my breast, the other squeezing my backside with total need.

His body was so close to mine that I could feel how hard he was. I ventured to touch his cock through his pants. He moaned without separating our lips; my hand squeezed his manhood, and I was about to undo the button of his pants when the elevator reached our destination.

We entered clumsily due to the haze of pleasure. As the door closed, Omar tore off my shirt, removed my bra, and brought his mouth to one of my nipples; both eagerly awaited him as always.

My body always tingled from his way of playing with me. He moved the caresses given by his mouth up to my neck until he reached my mouth again. His hands now sought to remove my pants, and I pushed him down onto the couch.

I climbed on top of him, removed his shirt in the same way he removed mine, and kissed him desperately. His hands gently slapped my backside.

"I don't remember you being so gentle before," I said, caressing his chest and kissing his neck.

"I don't forget that you're pregnant, baby. It's true that I want to do many things to you that I'm sure you love, but I must take care of our little ones. They seem to go unnoticed; your pregnancy doesn't show, although I can see growth here," he said, squeezing both of my breasts.

"How wild my sweetheart becomes," I mused as I quickly took care of removing the rest of his clothes.

I got on my knees in front of him and could see how he bit his lower lip, waiting for my next move. I took his cock in my hands, making him throw his head back. Then my mouth began to suck as much of him as I could.

His hand was on my head, gripping my hair; however, Omar didn't exert any kind of pressure on my head, he let me take as much as I wanted and could of him.

After nearly bringing him to the edge, he helped me stand up.

"Do you remember the first time we had sex here?" he asked me breathlessly, and I nodded. "I want to do it like that again," he said, taking my hand so I would climb on top of him.

I didn't hesitate, and without giving him time for anything, I took his cock in my hand and lowered my body, slipping his manhood into me. We both moaned, and I bit my lip when I felt him raise his hips. I wrapped my arms around his head, and again he entertained himself with my breasts.

I began to move my body in the way he liked. I loved that Omar wasn't a one-time guy and much less one who put his pleasure above everything else.

"Let's go to bed, sweetheart. I want to eat and take my favorite sweet," he said, carrying me to his bedroom. He laid me on the bed but pulled back to enter his closet and came out with a tie in his hands.

Our gazes connected for a few seconds until he got back on the bed and raised my arms above my head, securing my hands with the tie. Without taking his eyes off mine, with that fire emanating from them. His thumb caressed my lower lip and then moved down to caress my erect nipples, where he again used his tongue to take me to the edge. The tip of his fingers caressed everything in his descent. I opened my legs gladly, waiting for him; his nose tickled my belly before reaching my folds.

His tongue slid up and down between slow movements, making me feel like a knot was forming in my belly and heat ran through my body.

I screamed my orgasm, and he didn't wait to give me what I so craved at that moment. He raised my left leg to hold it with his arm before guiding his manhood in and beginning his delicious thrusts.

The entire apartment was filled not only with our pants, screams, and moans, but also with the obscene sound of our bodies colliding. Omar was capable of giving me one orgasm after another until I lost count.

"You're insatiable," I exclaimed between moans when my backside hit his pelvis with impetus, gladly receiving everything this man gave me.

"I will never have enough of all this, sweetheart," he said, clutching my backside with his hands. His thumb ventured to caress my back entrance. I bit my lips expectantly of what he would do, but it didn't go beyond that. "This looks very tempting from my view, baby."

"Whenever you want, wolf," I said, turning my head in his direction.

His gaze became more lustful, his thrusts became faster, deeper, delicious, and I was about to follow him to the peak, and we made it. I collapsed exhausted on the bed, and he did the same on top of me.

"I love you, Phoebe. I love you madly," he said, placing kisses on my back. "I think we should stop; we shouldn't overdo it. Our little ones must be upset."

He slipped out of me, untied my hands, and lay down beside me.

"I love you, Omar," I said when he cradled me against his chest, his hand caressing my hair, and he placed the other on my belly, leaving delicate caresses.

Without being able to prevent it, sleep came over me, and I gladly accepted the invitation. Knowing that I was in the arms of the man who loved me and whom I loved. A man I never thought I would have for myself; however, here I was with him, he was mine, and I was his.

"How much time is left?" I asked, looking at the stadium screen. There were four minutes of additional time that the referee had given for the Madrid Derby to end.

The scoreboard said they were two against two. Reyal Madrid was giving them a battle. Omar scored the first goal and assisted the second. A tie was not an option; they needed to win to take the lead over Reyal Madrid in the standings.

"Three minutes and forty eight seconds," said my father in law nervously, biting the nail of his index finger.

"Come on, Omar!" shouted my mother in law when we saw Omar running with the ball from midfield.

"Go, Wolf!" I shouted too.

Omar kicked the ball to the other side of the field where another player guided the ball to the area where Omar was waiting. The player seemed to see Omar's position and kicked the ball to him; it was very high, so Omar jumped and with his head sent the ball to the back of the net.

The stadium erupted in joy. My wolf looked for me among the people and blew a kiss in my direction. A minute later, my image appeared on the stadium screens, and I applauded, celebrating the team. We were all wearing the Atlantico Madrid shirt with Omar's number and last name.

The last minute was dramatic as Reyal Madrid was attacking Atlético's goal, but without success. The referee blew the final whistle and gave the victory to the team.

I was dying to hug and congratulate my wolf, and it seemed he was more desperate than I was because he jumped over the division between the stands and the field. He came directly to me, took my hand, and invited me to come down. I went down with him, and his entire family was behind us.

Several journalists asked him for an interview, but he smiled and asked them to wait a moment so that he had to do something important.

He took me to the side of the goal post, right in front of the entire fury of the Atlético fans. Throughout the stadium, a song that moved me began to be heard; he had dedicated it to me a few days ago: "Eres tú" by Matisse and Reik.

I looked at him in amazement, and he pointed for me to look at the stands. From the bottom part, a gigantic banner began to unfold.

I covered my mouth when the first thing I saw was my name. I looked at Omar, and he gave me that smile that drove me crazy from the beginning. The people who still remained in the stadium began to shout, to whistle, and I felt so incredulous with what was happening that tears began to be part of the emotion.

The banner was completely extended, and it read:

"Phoebe Santiago,

Would you accept our #10 as your husband?"

I looked at Omar, who was already on his knee on the grass. He sang while taking my hand. "What do you say, sweetheart? Would you do me the honor of marrying me?"

"Yes! Yes! Yes!" the stands shouted.

"Yes, of course, yes," I cried in amazement.

Omar slid the ring onto my finger. Then he stood up to take my face in his hands and to kiss my lips, completely forgetting the place where we were and the number of people who were around us.

At that moment, it was just him and me.

Chapter 36

Omar

"How are my boys?" I asked, approaching the women of my life to caress my wife's belly. My sister had come for my sons' baby shower, and yes, they would be two little boys.

"You're only asking about your sons?" Aitana asked, and I shook my head. She was also showing a small pregnancy belly.

"How is my little nephew?" I said, rubbing her five month belly. The baby was already starting to move, and whenever I approached, he would kick.

She smiled. "He's doing very well. I still can't believe this house will be filled with only boys. The good thing is that I'll continue to be my dad's princess," she said, sitting next to my mother.

"Every baby is welcome in the family regardless of whether it's a boy or a girl," said my grandmother, patting my fiancée's belly.

The wedding hadn't taken place yet. After I proposed to my sweetheart, many rumors arose, and the news of Phoebe's pregnancy became public. People cruelly accused her of getting pregnant on purpose just to force me to be with her. As much as I tried to persuade her, I couldn't change her mind. We reached an agreement that the wedding would be two years after our children were born.

Among the other things that were agreed upon was that although we would marry for love, she requested that a prenuptial agreement be signed, and I wasn't in agreement.

Weeks later, after trying so hard to change her mind, I decided not to insist anymore; I just wanted her to enjoy her pregnancy without problems or pressure, and that's what I did. We've enjoyed every moment of this pregnancy thanks to her and Noah accompanying me everywhere.

The training sessions, tours between matches, and events I have to attend haven't interfered with our relationship. The media has left us to live in peace since Alexis threatened to sue if they continued causing trouble for my pregnant woman.

"I think it's time for me to go lie down for a while," said Phoebe, standing up.

"Is everything okay, Phoebe?" I asked in concern, and she nodded.

"Yes, it's just that I still have things to pack, and I feel these babies could come at any moment. I've been having discomfort in my lower back and some light contractions. Since they're twins, it's normal for the delivery to come early."

We were in our home in Zaragoza; I had bought a large house very close to where my parents lived and another in Madrid to live with more space that my children would need later on.

"When did you start feeling like this?" I asked, making her sit down again and kneeling in front of her.

"This morning, but please stay calm. I should remind you what I do for a living, and I know when it's the right time to go to the hospital or seek medical help. For now, I would like to rest and make sure everything is ready, so when the time comes to go to the hospital, it's not chaos."

I nodded, and when she tried to stand up, I helped her do so and walked with her to our bedroom. My mother and sister followed us.

"Do you need help with anything?" asked Aitana, and Phoebe nodded.

She began to explain where some things were that she needed to pack in her bag, while my mother gave her words of reassurance, telling her that she wouldn't be alone, to stay calm.

However, the one who was panicking was me. I left the room, leaving them alone, and went to say goodbye to the remaining guests, then I headed directly to the kitchen to get some water.

My father entered at that moment and looked at me with a raised eyebrow.

"What's happening to you?" he asked, and I waved him off. "I know you, son. You're scared, right?"

I nodded slightly. "I'm just afraid of not being good enough for them. I don't want to make mistakes and have Phoebe suffer because of me again."

He smiled and hit my shoulder. "The simple fact that you're afraid and worried tells me that you'll be the best father for your children. I remember feeling the same way when your mother had you all. The difference is that the entire pregnancy with your sister and you was very difficult for her to bear. So my fear was not only if I was enough for you and for her, but that I could lose her due to some complication.

"While bringing a child into the world is not easy for the mother, no one tells you about the emotional pressure that falls on the father. It's at that moment when they put your child in your arms where all fear and doubt go away because you realize that you would be capable of anything to provide what they need. You are not alone; you have a family that will support you, advise you, and be available when you need them. You are a good man, of whom I am very proud and—"

"Omar!" My mother's shout was heard from my bedroom. We ran there, and Phoebe had her eyes tightly closed. I quickly went to her side.

"Sweetheart? Now?" I said, taking her hand, and she nodded.

"It seems that your sons just heard their aunt say everything is ready, and they started to speed up the contractions," she joked with a wince, and I smiled at her.

"I think we should go get Noah. He wouldn't forgive himself for not being present when his brothers arrive," I suggested.

Noah was with Steven and Aida on their weekend visit.

Five hours later, we were in the hospital room with Noah on top of his mother, asking her if she was okay every time he heard her complaining of pain.

"Try to calm down, my child. Your mother already went through this when you were coming," my mother would tell him as she hugged him.

"Yes, Grandma, but I was just one baby. My mother will have two. I've seen that many things can happen and go wrong," he pointed out.

"Everything will be fine, Noah, relax."

The doctor entered the room and gave us news moments later.

"I think you won't be able to give birth naturally, Phoebe. One of the babies is not in the ideal position, and the last thing we want is to put any of them in danger, so it will be better to perform a c-section."

"Do whatever is necessary, Doctor. The only thing I want is to have my little ones in my arms," said my sweetheart.

The doctor nodded and left the room to prepare everything.

Phoebe squeezed my hand and smiled at me. "Everything will be fine," she assured me.

I took a deep breath, seeking in her lips a bit of peace amid this anxiety I had inside me.

As my father said, all the fear that harbored me dissipated the moment I heard my children's cries and had them in my arms. They were so small and reddish. Their hair was brown like mine, and although Phoebe and the family said they looked like me, I saw my sweetheart in them. The only thing that dominated were my grandmother's genes, as both had beautiful blue eyes like their grandmothers and aunt.

We decided to name them with names that have four letters at Noah's request, so Luca and Blas were received with all the happiness, emotion, and tenderness within our little family.

In the blink of an eye, two years of our lives passed, and nothing had changed, except that we had an almost pre-teen in the house and two little walkers who believed they were the owners of everything, and we were their servants.

At the World Cup, I had the honor of wearing my country's red jersey. My sweetheart had dedicated herself completely to our children, and although I encouraged her to practice what she likes so much, she told me that since she has the possibility, she wanted to give more attention to our children, something she couldn't do with Noah, who was entering a stage where he wanted to receive more attention.

The wedding day had finally arrived, and we had chosen the place where my parents met to give the long awaited, "I do." The wedding was organized by my mother at Phoebe's request, and she didn't regret it.

The place was in a high area of the French Riviera, where the path to the altar was like a mirror that reflected the blue of the sky, decorated with a huge variety of white flowers. It was a sublime and emotional moment when I saw my beautiful Phoebe in her cream colored dress walking to me hand in hand with Noah, and the most exciting thing was to hear that we were finally declared husband and wife.

My wife's body hadn't changed in my eyes, and the desire I felt for her had changed much less. On the contrary, whenever I had the opportunity, I found a way to end up between her legs, enjoying her and that beautiful body that made me fall in love.

"Do you like it?" she asked, stopping at the bathroom doorframe, her hair loose, wearing a beautiful blue transparent lace suit with floral embroidery that perfectly marked her nipples that I loved.

She turned, making my mouth fill with saliva and making it almost impossible to swallow. The blue thread was the only thing that could be seen at the back. My cock sprang to life seeing my now wife in that outfit that wouldn't be on her body for long and would end up in the trash because the idea was to remove it until she was unprotected and without barriers for my delight. I would make the days of our honeymoon fascinating and of quality.

"I still don't understand what you liked about me. We were people from completely different worlds, and now, seeing everything we've lived through, it's difficult for me to come to terms with the fact that we've been together for years," she admitted, standing in front of me.

"Now you're my wife, and I promise you that nothing and no one will separate us. You have no idea how long I've waited for you to come into my life, and although my profession makes me be surrounded by a lot of people, my heart, mind, and body are only yours. If they knew how much I'm fascinated by all this," I said, massaging her backside, "how hard it makes me to see all this bouncing against my pelvis."

And now laying her body on the bed, I positioned myself on top of her, rocking my hips so she could feel my hardness.

"I can't believe you fell in love with a woman like me... I'm not like the supermodels you used to date." She had made this comment before, and I remembered very well the answer I gave her at that time. It was the same one I gave her now.

"Your body is the most beautiful and delicious thing I've ever seen. A real body of the most real woman I've had the pleasure of knowing and who is now completely mine. The day I saw you arrive at Alan and Susy's party, in that pink dress holding Noah's hand, you don't know the intense way I fell in love. To the point that the only thing in my mind and heart was the way I was wishing for your love, for you to fall in love with me, and now, along with our children, you are everything to me."

"That's right, we are all for you," she said, caressing her belly.

I jumped off the bed immediately. "What?" I exclaimed, and she smiled.

"It seems that not abstaining when I had the respiratory infection almost two months ago brought us a new smurf," she said, and I couldn't help it; I launched myself on her to kiss her until we were both out of breath.

"Thank you… thank you for giving me the family I had dreamed of so much."

"Thank you for loving me and accepting me along with Noah. For staying by our side when you had no obligation to stay," she confessed, hugging my body tightly.

"Gladly and without hesitation, I would do it again, having the certainty that it would be the best decision I've made in my life," I assured her, then devoured her lips, and this time, I was willing to have less talk and more action.

I set out to show her with devotion how she had become the woman who gave meaning to my life and to the word love. Phoebe had taught me that love comes in different ways and in different packages. Mine came in a large package and in a two-for-one. Two different loves, but equally intense, that did nothing but multiply, making me the luckiest man in the world.

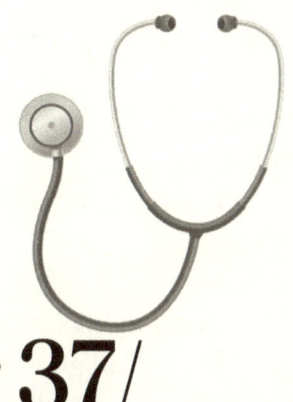

Chapter 37/ Epilogue

Phoebe

Seven years later.

"Mom, we're going to be late," I heard my oldest son say.

"Noah, relax, we still have two hours, and we're twenty three minutes away from the event. We're fine with time," Omar said, trying to calm Noah down.

It was a very important day; he would sign his first contract as a professional soccer player, and we couldn't be more proud and excited for him.

"Yes, Nono, it's not mom's fault that Leia soiled her diaper before we left," said my nine year old son Blas.

"We're ready now," I mentioned as I arrived in the living room.

"And is it necessary for everyone to be there?" Noah said, and Juan, my six year old, was the first to speak.

"Don't you want us with you, Noah?" he whined, making a pout and running to his room. Juan was the most emotional of my children; he and Noah had a special bond—the love for soccer.

"Juan!" Noah called, but then Luca, who was the most stubborn and rebellious of my sons, walked to his room.

He put his hands on his hips. "I don't want to go either now."

"Juan, Luca. Come here," Omar called them with that voice I loved, with a commanding tone.

Both appeared in front of us with their arms crossed, one with tears in his eyes and the other with a furrowed brow.

"We will all go to support Noah, because if we stay here, he won't know what it's like to see his family cheering for him, because we feel proud of his achievements; however, it's your decision, Noah," Omar said. "Do you want to be alone and without your family on such an important day?"

He shook his head, biting his lip. "No, I don't want to be alone. I'm sorry, I'm just very anxious and nervous."

Omar approached and put a hand on his shoulder.

"I was once where you are now. Of course, I was three years older than you, but the best memory I had of that day, apart from signing and being given a number along with the team jersey, was seeing my family in front of me cheering because I had achieved my dream. Don't forget who you are, okay?"

Omar always had the right words. He knew how to reprimand without the need for shouting or punishments. Omar was born to be the father of all my smurfs.

"Papa," babbled six month old Leia in my arms, holding her arms out.

Omar came to take the baby. "Now, let's go. Remember that we're going to a place where there will possibly be many people and..."

"We must stay together, not talk to strangers, and if something happens, go directly to Emilio, Mom, or Dad," all the children said in unison.

"Tell me why we call them smurfs? I think mini robots would suit them better," I commented with a laugh.

"I heard my name around here," said Emilio, our head of security.

"You arrived just in time to help us get everyone into the car," Omar said, and Emilio nodded.

The children climbed in the van with one of their nannies, while Omar and I would go in the other car with Noah and Leia.

"Well, what a beautiful woman we have here," expressed Emilio when I passed by his side, causing Omar to growl in displeasure.

"I don't like you talking to my wife like that, Emilio," he warned.

"I've always told her she's beautiful, and I'm very clear that she's yours. You know that for a long time I haven't been interested in skirts."

"That's why you're here. Now, stop looking at my woman and coordinate our departure."

"Yes, boss," he said, closing the door.

Since the attack on my sister in law Aitana and her son, Oliver, Omar tripled the security we already had.

We soon arrived at the imposing stadium. At the entrance, we were greeted by Steven with Aida and their two children —nine year old Mario and five year old Jazmín. Omar's parents were also there, along with Aitana and her imposing husband Ovidio, accompanied by their children.

We didn't waste time, and the ceremony began right on schedule. The emotion I felt seeing my son smile widely, fulfilling his dream, was something very overwhelming for me.

The memories of the moment I found out he was coming into this world, the difficult times we went through alone, him and I, before finding Omar, and all these ten years since Omar has been in our lives. They went like water slipping between my fingers.

Time passed very quickly, and everything had been worth it, as my son managed to fulfill his dream, not because of connections or privileges, but because of his effort and dedication.

"Is everything okay?" asked Steven, standing beside me.

"Yes, it's just seeing how time has passed and the turn my life took so many years ago is what brought us here, to this moment."

"Our son is fulfilling his dream."

I nodded. "That's right, our son has fulfilled his dream."

"He's not just yours; he's mine too," affirmed Omar as he approached.

"And mine too!" said Aida, playing with Leia and Jazmín. We were already celebrating this moment in our house; Noah had invited his closest friends to eat at our home.

"I belong to all of you. Don't fight over me," said the celebrated one, much calmer than how he was this morning. "Will you join me in a toast?"

We nodded and prepared our respective glasses.

Noah positioned himself in the center of the place, calling everyone's attention. "Good evening. If you're here, it's because you know the ups and downs of my life and my career to achieve what I have today. The truth is that many years ago—Mom could say exactly how many—I had a dream in which I had a large family. At that moment, I thought it would be because of the possibility of wanting to be part of Omar's enormous family, but it turned out to be a déjà vu.

"Well, this was the precise moment I saw so many years ago. My parents are with me, I have more siblings than I wished for and whom I love with all my heart. These opportunities came into my life, thanks to the effort and dedication that I learned from you, your advice, your time, and I want to take this space to thank you, my parents, Phoebe, Omar, Steven, and Aida for everything you did, do, and will do to support me.

"For the first eight years of my life, it was just my mother and I against the world, then came Aida, Omar along with all his family, Steven, and now I have six siblings, friends I can count on, and a millionaire contract to do what I like most. Play soccer. If at this moment I opened a dictionary of synonyms and antonyms, I could swear that for the word happiness as a synonym, they would find my name. Cheers."

"Cheers," we all said in unison.

I turned around and wiped the tears that were overflowing down my cheeks until I felt my son's embrace.

"Don't cry," he said, wiping my cheeks with his thumb.

"I cry because my little boy is no longer a boy, but a man. I cry because I feel proud of you, of the man you have become," I said through tears.

"I promise to make you feel even more proud," he swore, giving me a kiss on the cheek.

"Noah!" shouted the young girl who had Noah captivated with her beauty, Ariana. She would always see him as a friend; I hoped later on she didn't become his heartache.

He left to attend to her just as Omar appeared behind me.

"What are you thinking about?" my husband whispered in my ear.

"About you, our children and family, and how much I love you," I said, wrapping my arms around his neck.

"I love you too. More than you could imagine," he said, and I shook my head.

"I was also thinking about how fortunate life has been for me, especially since you've been by my side." I kissed his lips, and with that kiss, he reaffirmed that even with the passage of years, love was capable of expressing itself in the purest way, and that's what Omar's love taught me.

To love without doubt, without limits, without complexities, and that would be the same type of love that I would teach my children, one that breaks all kinds of schemes. Like the one I am living at this moment with my retired soccer player, and I would gladly live until the last days of my life.

Acknowledgments

First of all, gracias to God, without His guidance none of this would be possible.

To my beautiful peeps in my book club "Hablemos de Libros y más," you guys are the heartbeat behind my stories. Thank you for cheering me on, laughing with me, and sometimes crying with me through every twist and turn.

To my kids and husband, who hold me up even when I don't notice it. You're my roots, my reason, and my forever team.

To my editor, Ashley @enchantedauthorco, thank you for squeezing me into your crazy-tight schedule and still polishing this story with all the magic you always bring. You turned chaos into art, and I'll forever be grateful.

To my cover designer, Dani @Primm_Rose.design. Thank you for your patience and creativity, and for giving me the exact beautiful covers I dreamed of for this book. You make my words shine before readers even open the first page.

To my formatting specialist, Jess from @LotusEdiciones, thank you for giving my books that final touch of elegance with your amazing designs. Every detail you add makes my stories shine brighter on the page.

To my incredible art designers, @Anna.artt_ and @shy. illustrator, thank you for breathing life into my characters and turning imagination into visuals. Your talent makes my world come alive beyond the words.

To my gorgeous PAs, Alanna @iammichbooks and Brie @multimedia_with_brie—thank you, girls, for keeping me sane and organized. You two are the real MVPs.

To Ruby and her amazing team at @TalesandTeacupspr, thank you for helping this humble indie author find her ideal readers. You're making my dream audience a reality.

To my magnificent beta readers, Kariany, Patty, and Nahely. Thank you for always supporting me, for loving my books, and for never being afraid to give me those honest comments I need to grow.

To my ride-or-die group, Leidy, Clau, Cony, Pao, Candy, Suvy, and Lu. Thank you, ladies, for always being there for me. Your love and loyalty are my safe space.

Last but never least, this book is dedicated to my mom and my sister, two incredible women who life blessed with a second chance at happiness and love. This is also a hug for all the mamas, like Phoebe, who choose to fight for their kids, putting their own happiness aside just to make sure their children will be okay.

And to you, dear reader… I love you. Thank you for your support, your trust, and for letting me tell you love stories. Without you, there would be no magic in these pages.

About the author

Valery Archaga, born in Tegucigalpa, Honduras in 1993, is a romance and contemporary author who began her writing journey in 2021 with her debut digital novel Solamente Tú, the first installment in the Los Galeanos saga. She now lives in Charlotte, North Carolina with her husband, three children, a small Chihuahua named Chloe, along with her personal bodyguard, a Rottweiler named Monie. She has gone on to self-publish more than twenty books, including additional series such as Todo Ocurrió and Corazones en Caos.

Desiring Your Love marks her debut in the English-speaking community, expanding her storytelling to a broader audience.

Keep in Touch with Valery Archaga

Instagram: @ValeryArchagaWrite / @valeryArchaga (Her Spanish Profile)
Tiktok: @Valeryarchagawrites / @ValeryArchaga
Goodreads : Valery Archaga
Website: valeryarchagaauthor.com